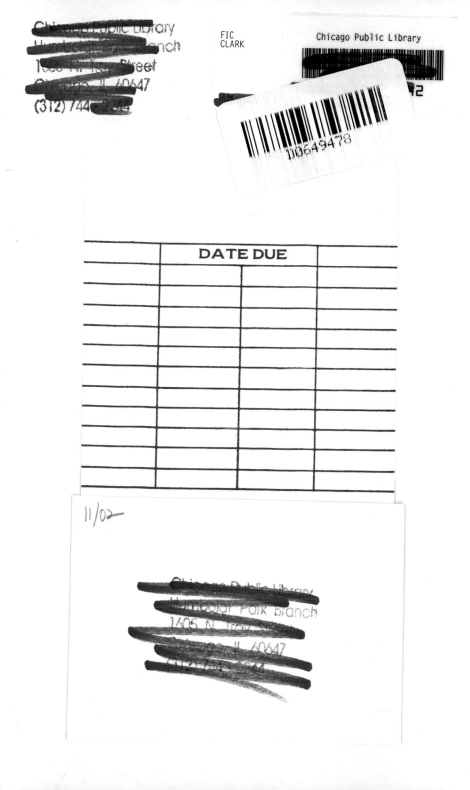

DATE DUE

11/02

JACK CLARK

THOMAS DUNNE BOOKS / St. Martin's Minotaur ⚑ New York

THOMAS DUNNE BOOKS.
An imprint of St. Martin's Press.

WESTERFIELD'S CHAIN. Copyright © 2002 by Jack Clark.
All rights reserved. Printed in the United States of
America. No part of this book may be used or
reproduced in any manner whatsoever without written
permission except in the case of brief quotations
embodied in critical articles or reviews. For information,
address St. Martin's Press, 175 Fifth Avenue,
New York, N.Y. 10010.

www.minotaurbooks.com

Book design by Michael Collica

ISBN 0-312-28960-X

First Edition: November 2002

10 9 8 7 6 5 4 3 2 1

For my mother,
who told me a million stories
and
for my father,
who gave me my first book

ACKNOWLEDGMENTS

Vince Clark and Nancy Watrous both made major contributions to this book. Many thanks to them and to Katina Alexander, Michele Barale, Randy Buescher, Mimi Devens, Kevin Dunn, Marilyn Fisker, Bob and Dori Foley, Ron Foreman, Ryan Gantes, Lisa B. Gertz, Steve Grossman, Francis Leroux, Sydney Lewis, Bob Meyer, Robin Rauch, Janet Roderick, Sarah Russe, and Mary Valentine. Several Chicago police officers—past and present—also helped out. Thanks to all.

ONE

THERE wasn't much to see on Madison Street. Thirty years of arson, neglect, and civil insurrection had taken their toll, and now the heart of the West Side was mostly rubble and weeds. Wildflowers sparkled in the afternoon sunshine.

There was an occasional pedestrian and, now and then, someone waiting at a bus stop. Everybody was black but me. Heads turned as I passed, and I got a feeble wave from a sad-looking whore sitting all alone on the good half of a fire-damaged sofa. I saluted, drove under a railroad viaduct, and continued west.

The address I was looking for was on one of the better blocks. Two buildings had survived. I pulled to the right, to a bed of gravel and dirt that covered a trench from an old construction project. Faded gold leaf said WESTERFIELD'S PHARMACY & SUNDRIES, and if you squinted a bit you could see that it had been a grand place way back when, when the West Side was affectionately known as the best side of town.

The entrance was surrounded by a high terra-cotta archway with an ornamental tree at the very top. Sturdy branches were holding a book aloft. The address was inscribed on the open pages, and glazed leaves floated down on either side of the archway, suspended in midflight. It must have been quite a sight, back when the terra-cotta was shiny white, long ago when Madison Street was so packed with commerce that it had no real trees to call its own.

Now it just looked sad, another once-beautiful building that would soon crumble and die.

The terra-cotta tiles were cracked and chipped and were as dark as burned mustard. The bricks needed tuck-pointing. The burglar gates were rusted and bent. The windows, covered with years of grime, were patched with rotting plywood and rusty bolts. The trim hadn't seen paint in a long, long time.

But it was still the best-looking place on the block.

Across the street, a ramshackle two-story structure looked near collapse. Upstairs, some dark city birds were flying in and out of holes where windows had once been. There'd been a fire up there long ago. The bricks were streaked with black soot. Sections of the roof were gone.

Downstairs, someone had added a porch right on top of the city sidewalk. It was a crude job, built with odd pieces of lumber— salvaged from the ruins, I presumed—and it extended clear to the curb. If I'd ridden my horse, this would have been the place to tie it. All that was missing was the watering troughs, the tumbleweeds, and a halfway-decent saloon.

There were two old codgers relaxing on the porch. They were surrounded by stacks of used tires. "Flats fixed," a crude hand-painted sign read. Beyond them, in the expanse of weeds that stretched to the next street, a half-dozen guys were keeping cool in the shade of two giant weed trees. They were reclining on beached automobile seats and homemade hammocks, drinking and smoking, waiting for anything or for nothing. By the time I opened the door of my Oldsmobile, every head was turned my way.

I climbed a crumbling curb and stopped on a fragmented sidewalk. A poster of Dr. Martin Luther King Jr. sat behind a drugstore window. The photo was obscured by dust, tattered, and faded. On the front door an ancient-looking sign read: GREEN CARDS WELCOME. Another said: YES, WE'RE OPEN.

A buzzer sounded as I opened the door. Hinges squeaked, something clicked, and someone moved deeper into the shadows.

I stopped in the doorway and waited while my eyes adjusted to the dim interior.

The bill of a hat shone softly. There was a badge on the hat, but it wasn't a policeman's. A security guard, I finally realized, in full uniform down to the gun on his hip. The click had probably been the sound of the holster being unbuckled, and now his hand was resting lightly on the butt of a large revolver. A pair of dark eyes studied me.

"The boss around?"

The guard lifted his hand from the gun, and a finger pointed across the store. A mocking smile flashed across his face; then the hand dropped back into place.

The guy behind the counter was thin and black, not quite thrity, I guessed. His eyeglasses were thick, with bulky black frames, and behind them his eyes seemed much too big for his face. A plastic tag pinned to the breast pocket of a white jacket said: "Jimmy Madison, Pharmacy Technician."

He stuck a yellow pen in his mouth and began to back up as I approached. I could read the fear in his eyes as they moved from me to the guard, then back again. What was he so afraid of, I wondered. I was just a mild-mannered private eye. "I'm looking for Eugene Westerfield," I said.

He continued backward, then bumped into an odd-looking wall. One section had recently been painted glossy white. But the paint didn't extend much beyond Jimmy himself. Somebody had slapped it on in a hurry, and there was no clear border between the new paint and the old, a dirty white that had faded almost to blue.

Jimmy hung there a long moment, his huge eyes jumping from the guard to me. He tried to say something, then seemed surprised to find the pen in his mouth. He wiped it on a sleeve, then baby-stepped back my way and dropped the pen in the fold of an open textbook. "Mr. West . . . He's not in today."

"When do you expect him?" I asked, but he didn't appear to understand. "Will he be here tomorrow?" I tried again.

"Maybe tomorrow." Jimmy nodded his head. "Tomorrow or maybe next week. Next week be . . . would be better."

"He sick?" I asked.

"Huh?"

"Mr. Westerfield," I said. "He's home sick?"

"No. No. No." He shook his head. "He's on his vacation."

"But you don't know when he's coming back?"

"No," he said, but then he seemed to change his mind. "Next week for sure."

"Where'd he go?"

"Huh?"

"On his vacation?" I asked. "Where'd he go?"

"Oh." He nodded his head, as if that were an answer.

"Tahiti?"

"Huh?"

We probably could have spent the afternoon going back and forth like that. And I might have eventually got some truthful answers and, if I had, it probably would have saved everybody a lot of time and trouble. It might have saved Jimmy much more than that. But I wasn't really interested in the whereabouts of Eugene Westerfield. And I wasn't there for the truth.

I was there because a minor traffic accident had blossomed into an off-duty traffic altercation. Off duty because a cop was involved. I was working for the cop's lawyer. We were trying to help the cop keep his job. The truth would probably just get in the way.

"I'm looking for a Chevy station wagon," I said. Something changed in Jimmy's eyes as I rattled off the license number, and he seemed to relax a bit. "It's registered to Eugene Westerfield."

"Out back." He pointed the way.

"Who drives it?"

"I do, usually."

"You wouldn't have been driving it last Tuesday?"

"I thought that might be . . ." He stuttered a bit, then gave up. "Are you from the police?" he asked clear as a bell.

I flashed my ID. "My name's Acropolis. I'm an investigator for the law firm of Siegel and McGovern. Why don't you tell me what happened that day?"

"Sure," he said. "Let me just—"

"Take your time," I said.

He looked up at the ceiling, then down at the floor. "See, I picked up this hitchhiker."

"Just out of the blue?"

"See, I know him. I know him from . . . from where I live. And then when I was trying to get on the highway this car came around and hit me."

"OK."

"And then this hitchhiker wouldn't let me stop. I wanted to stop, but the hitchhiker pulled a gun and told me to keep going."

"OK."

"And then he started shooting at the car and the car was shooting back."

"OK."

He shrugged. "And that's it."

"What's this hitchhiker's name?"

"Don't know."

"I thought you knew him."

"Well, I do," he said. "I know him to see him, but I don't know his right name. I only know what they call him."

"His street name. OK, what's that?"

He looked at the ceiling again. "Player Dog," he decided. "But that was from years ago when I used to know him. I don't know what they call him now."

"OK. Let's see if I've got this straight. You picked up this Player Dog and . . . Wait. Where'd you pick him up?"

He went back to his friend the ceiling. "At a bus stop."

"Where?"

"On . . . Ah . . . Forty-seventh Street."

"Good. What was the cross street?"

"Halsted," he said quickly.

"OK, you picked up this Player Dog at Forty-seventh and Halsted and you were giving him a ride. . . . Where were you giving him a ride to?"

"Just . . . He was just tired of waiting on the bus, so . . ."

"You were gonna take him home with you?"

"No. No. No. He was going north. Downtown. And I was going that way. So . . ."

"OK. You picked up this Player Dog and offered to give him a ride downtown, and when you were getting on the Dan Ryan Expressway you had an accident with a Toyota pickup truck. How's that so far?"

"Yeah. That's right."

"And then after the accident you wanted to stop, but Player Dog pulled out a gun and told you to keep driving?"

"Right."

"And then he started shooting at the pickup truck?"

"Right."

"And the driver of the pickup started shooting back?" He nodded. "But nobody got hit?"

"Just the car."

"Did you report this incident to the police?"

"No."

"Why not?"

"Ah . . . I don't know."

"Did Player Dog threaten you?"

"Yeah. He told me not to tell anybody."

"But did he threaten you?"

"Yeah. He said not to tell anybody or he'd shoot me."

"OK. Where'd you drop him off?"

"Downtown?"

"Can you be more specific?"

"State Street."

"Downtown on State Street?"

"Right."

"Would you be willing to sign a statement detailing what you've just told me?"

"Sure, I guess so."

The security guard held the door for me. I walked out to the Olds, opened the trunk and then my briefcase. A horn sounded as I pulled out a legal pad. *Toot. Toot.* A CTA bus was heading for the Loop. The driver pointed toward the tire shop. The old men on the porch waved back.

I carried the legal pad inside. Nobody said a word as I wrote up the statement. An insect was buzzing the front windows. It sounded like one of those enormous flies. The kind that lives on into January or February and then dies a fat old man on a frosty window ledge. Somewhere in back, a faucet was leaking.

It was a pack of lies, of course. But they were the right lies— at least from my side of the playing field. I tried to make them sound a bit more plausible. But if Jimmy changed his story later or fell apart at the Police Board hearing, that wouldn't necessarily be bad news. That would simply prove he couldn't be trusted. Which would leave Tracy Grace, the off-duty cop who'd be paying for my time, the most credible witness to the incident on Forty-seventh Street.

Jimmy's version of events was close to the one Tracy Grace had given police. The hitchhiker was the biggest inconsistency. Grace hadn't mentioned seeing any passengers in the station wagon. But the hitchhiker let Jimmy off the hook for the shooting. It helped in another way, too. I couldn't see the dimmest cop believing that Jimmy had taken a shot at anybody.

But the police probably wouldn't be getting to Jimmy anytime soon. When Grace had given them the Chevy's license number, he'd transposed a couple of digits. He'd remembered the right numbers later for his lawyer.

And Jimmy was the least of Grace's problems. A few minutes before Grace arrived at the police station, an old man in Canaryville had called 911 to report that a pickup truck had stopped just outside his garage. The driver got out with a gun in hand, shot out the passenger window of his own truck, then drove away. Raymond Purcell didn't transpose a single digit. The numbers he gave police matched perfectly with Grace's Toyota pickup. Purcell's description of the driver also matched Tracy Grace.

I finished writing, then read the statement back to Jimmy. "Wow, you're really good," he said, and he flashed the faintest of smiles.

"I'd like you to read it through again and then sign by the X."

While Jimmy was reading, I took a look around the store. The inside was as bad as the outside. Floor tiles were cracked and splintered. Exposed wires dangled from a hole in the ceiling where a fixture had once hung. The roof leaked. There were watermarks down one wall and a bucket half-full of murky water sitting in the middle of an aisle.

With the exception of that one spot behind Jimmy, the place hadn't seen fresh paint in years. There wasn't much on the shelves, and what there was, was covered with years of dust. There was a nearly empty rack of paperback books. The titles I recognized were long out-of-date. In back, a thin layer of dust covered the pharmacy counter.

The east half of the store was closed off with gray industrial fencing. A padlock dangled from the gate. Behind it were several cases of disposable syringes, a couple of vaporizers still in their cartons, and an open box of nylon stockings. Empty cartons had been tossed to the side. Beyond the cartons the entire back section of the room had been draped with heavy-duty plastic.

Jimmy held a ballpoint pen over the statement. "Is this really OK?" he asked, looking down at the paper.

"I don't follow you."

"I'd hate to get in trouble." He looked up, then dropped his eyes to the paper again.

"Why would you get in trouble?"

"The truth," he said flatly, and he looked right into my eyes.

"The truth," I repeated, then winked to let him know it was all just a game. "You'll be OK."

He glanced toward the door where the security guard stood looking out, then leaned forward. I thought he was going to say something he didn't want the guard to hear. I moved a half-step closer, but Jimmy never said a word. He dropped the pen to the paper and signed above the line I'd drawn.

I tore the single sheet from the pad, folded it, and slipped it into a breast pocket. "You got any chewing gum?" I asked.

Jimmy shook his head.

"Lifesavers?" I thought I should buy something. The statement had come too easily. Much too easily.

"Just pharmaceuticals."

"You the pharmacist?"

"I'm his assistant," Jimmy said. "He's at lunch." He gestured to the back, toward the dust-covered pharmacy counter.

I turned to go. A sliver of sunlight had found its way through the front window. Beyond the fence, something was glowing under the plastic wrap. "What's that?"

"Bunch a junk," the security guard said, and he pushed his hat back and smiled and I saw that he was just a big kid. Christ, was he old enough to carry a gun?

"That's the soda fountain," Jimmy said.

"Sodie fountain?" the guard said, as if he'd never heard of such a thing.

"I'll be damned," I said as it came into focus. It was an honest-to-god soda fountain with high-backed stools, a long counter, and a large mirror, which had caught that single ray of sun. Somebody had really gone to town with the plastic wrap.

"Mr. Westerfield, he's gonna open that up again when the neighborhood comes back," Jimmy said.

"Put me down for a malted," I said. I opened the door and went out to Madison Street.

The neighborhood was just as I had left it. Nobody would be ordering a chocolate phosphate anytime soon.

TWO

I WALKED through the weeds. A Chevy station wagon was sitting on a patch of oil-blackened gravel just outside the back door. The car had once been a respectable business gray, but rust had taken over. There were plenty of dents and scratches, the freshest in the left front corner. The bumper was crinkled, the quarter-panel crushed, a headlight broken. A fresh swath of red paint ran clear to the rear door.

I counted two bullet holes in the rear window and three in the tailgate, all on the driver's side. The only exit hole I found was just below the rearview mirror. No wonder Jimmy was shaky. It had probably sounded like the space shuttle cruising by.

"Dr. Z., I'm sorry," a woman spoke behind me. I turned. An old man was being pushed out the door of a flat one-story building just across a narrow brick alley. "St. Anthony's Medical Center," a sign read. An arrow pointed around the corner of the building: "Entrance Around Front."

"We have to get back to work," the woman said in an exasperated tone. I couldn't see her face, just a pair of dark hands jutting out of white sleeves. She gave the man one final push, then quickly closed the door.

He was somewhere near seventy, I guessed, tall and thin, and nearly bald. He was wearing a dark suit that hung much too loosely. He didn't look like he was used to being thrown out of places.

He tried the door, found it locked, then turned and started toward a parking lot that held half a dozen cars. He stopped and looked down at the weeds, like a man in the wilderness examining a sign he doesn't quite comprehend, then veered my way. He crossed the alley and angled away, following a path to the back door of the drugstore.

I scribbled a few notes, then walked to the Olds for my camera.

I was taking pictures of the station wagon when Dr. Z. came out. The security guard was right behind him. "He's not here. He's not here." The guard spoke slowly, as if he were talking to a child. "How many times do I have to tell you?"

The old man walked with his head down, a sad sack if there ever was one. He crossed the alley, opened the door to a beat-up Buick, started the car, and drove away. I scribbled the license number in my notebook and wrote "Doc Z." next to it.

"He just don't listen," the security guard said. I grunted and went back to taking pictures. "Here, take one of me," the guard said. I turned, then backed up to get the shot. He was posed against the side wall of the drugstore, standing at attention, his hat in hand, a serious expression on his face.

The afternoon sun tinted the bricks a soothing red. I pushed the button and the shutter opened and closed, trapping him there on Madison Street, on Westerfield's Pharmacy's very last day.

THREE

I GOT back in the Olds. The old guys at the tire shop swiveled in their seats as I passed. I went several blocks, then turned between a burned-out record store and a storefront church. I went down a block and headed back east.

There were scattered buildings here, two-flats and tiny brick houses. Some were in good repair, but others were sinking into ruin. I found a shady spot in front of a large, well-tended garden that sat all alone a half-block from the nearest house.

I focused my binoculars on the front door of Westerfield's, but there was nothing to see. The place looked like there hadn't been a customer since 1965, which made it a perfect fit for the neighborhood: a tire repair shop on a street with no cars, a drug store in a neighborhood with no people, a garden without a house.

I sat there and nothing happened. Nobody went in or out. The station wagon didn't move. The only sounds were the wind rustling through the garden, a few city birds singing their sad songs, and, far away, the steady whisper of the highway.

It had taken little more than a century for the West Side to go from boom to bust. Now it looked as desolate as the landscape of the moon. I sat watching the dust swirl. The dark side of the moon: another step backward for mankind.

I don't know what I was waiting for. Maybe for the pharmacist to return from lunch so he could get back to work at a counter covered with weeks of dust. Maybe I was just padding the bill. I picked up my phone, punched in the number of my favorite law firm and then Shelly Micholowski's extension.

"How'd you make out with that old man?" Shelly wanted to know.

"He wasn't home," I said. That had been my first stop. But Raymond Purcell, the old man who'd seen Tracy Grace take a shot at his own truck, wasn't to be found.

"So what's up?"

"I found the driver of that station wagon," I said.

"Good work."

"And I got a statement."

"Really? What'd he say?"

I read the statement.

"Hey," she said softly, "that's pretty good. I can't wait to see your expense sheet."

"Believe it or not, Shelly, there's nothing there. It's like he was waiting for me. But he is one terrible, terrible liar."

"I'm gonna pretend I didn't hear that."

"Pretend I never even called."

I hung up and went back to watching nothing. A CTA bus passed heading west toward Oak Park. The driver tooted the horn. A minute later a Loop-bound bus bounced by, a liquor distributor truck close behind. Nothing happened for a while; then my phone rang.

"Nick, it's Frank," Frank Stringfellow said. He ran a small agency out in suburban Oak Brook and he hated coming into the city. He was more comfortable in shopping malls, subdivisions, and industrial parks. "You busy?"

"I'm working something for Shelly. Nothing too pressing."

"Not another renegade cop?"

"That's about all she gets, Frank."

"I don't know how you do it," he said.

We'd had this conversation a thousand times. I didn't see any reason to have it again. "What've you got?"

"I was hoping you had time to run up to Rogers Park and do an address verification."

"Sounds like a job for the post office, Frank."

"All you gotta do is make sure the guy's still there. I'm gonna send Charlie and Vic up tonight. I'd really owe you one, Nick. This guy's been ducking me for months."

"I assume you mean over and above my hourly rate."

He laughed easily. "Your discounted rate, if that's OK."

"Shoot," I said, and I fired up my pen.

"Name of Leslie Crawford," Stringfellow said, and he gave me an address on Pratt.

"What's he been up to?"

"Just a nickel-dime shakedown."

"You want me to talk some sense into him?"

"No. No. No. I don't want him to know you're even there."

"You got a description?"

"Black male, six-one, one-seventy, light to medium complexion, short hair, snappy dresser. But don't spook him, Nick. Just tell me if his name's on the doorbell. That's all I really need."

"Check," I said. I hung up and put the car in gear.

A shiny red car came down Madison. It stopped suddenly, backed up, and stopped again, right in front of the drugstore.

Nobody got out of the car. Nothing moved. I put the Olds in park and brought the binoculars up. It was a shiny Honda coupe with out-of-state plates. It coasted forward, pulled over the buckled pavement and up the crumbling curb, and drove through the weeds to a spot a couple of car lengths from the station wagon.

The door opened and a woman got out and stood looking around the neighborhood. I brought the binoculars in close, but she spun around and showed me the back of her head, a few inches of light brown hair falling from under a blue baseball cap. I moved the glasses down. She was five-eight, I guessed, looking very fit in jeans and a sweatshirt. After a while she turned right into my glasses. She was just a kid, I saw, early twenties, pretty in a boyish sort of way. The sweatshirt was from the University of Wisconsin. The baseball cap had a Cubs emblem on the front. Her eyes were lost in the shadow under the bill.

She looked like a million other kids. They were all wearing college sweatshirts that year and baseball caps, and many of them had those trim, athletic builds that came from clean living and plenty of exercise. She would have looked right at home with the just-out-of-college crowd in Lincoln Park or jogging along the lakefront. But she looked light-years from Madison Street.

She waved at someone, the old men or the guys under the stink trees, a small friendly wave. I'm sure she had everyone's undivided attention. Then she took her cap off, flipped it into the Honda, and walked through the weeds to the station wagon.

She peered in through a side window. Time passed. I tried to remember what I'd seen in the wagon, but all I could recall was a couple of fast-food wrappers and several bullet holes. She finally straightened up, then walked around to Madison and into the store.

I punched in Stringfellow's phone number. "About that favor you're gonna owe me, any chance I can use it in advance?"

"Depends on the flavor."

"How about running an out-of-state plate?"

"Sure," he said.

"Wisconsin," I said, and I picked up the binoculars and read the numbers off the Honda.

"Probably take about an hour," Stringfellow said. "Where do I get you?"

"Try the car first; then leave a message at my office."

"I wish you'd get a cell phone, Nick. You're the only guy I know still uses a car phone."

"Let your fingers do the walking, Frank," I said as the phone went dead in my ear. Over on Madison Street nothing was happening again.

About ten minutes passed; then Jimmy and the girl walked out. They ambled to the Honda and the girl opened the door but didn't get in. She gestured toward the station wagon. Jimmy held up one finger and hurried back to the store.

The girl put her Cubs hat back on. The security guard came out, nodded at the girl, folded his arms, and waited to be relieved.

Jimmy returned with a large manila envelope. He pulled something out and the girl got very excited, moving around, laughing. I adjusted the binoculars, but Jimmy was in the way. He turned and reflected sunlight flashed. Was it a mirror? A piece of glass? By the time my eyes cleared, it was back in the envelope.

They hugged and then the girl slid behind the wheel. Jimmy waved. The Honda backed out and headed east.

I drove down to Madison Street and started after her.

Nobody had gone anywhere. The old men were still on the porch at the tire store, and the younger guys were taking it easy in the shade of the stink trees. Nobody would ever go anywhere.

I was almost even with the drugstore when a whistle came from under the trees. It was the kind that could stop every taxi in a three-block radius. Not that you'd have to worry about that happening out here. But it was more than enough to bring Jimmy back out. And there I was in my baby blue Oldsmobile. Nick Acropolis: the King of Surveillance.

I turned my head away and pushed down on the gas.

A block later, when I glanced back in the rearview mirror, Jimmy was still standing on the sidewalk looking my way.

FOUR

W E went east. The towers of the Loop were dead ahead, obscured by a faint Indian summer haze. You'd drive and drive and never get there. You'd stay in the ruins forever.

Beyond Western Avenue, the rubble gradually gave way to paved parking lots. Fancy concrete flower boxes graced the median. There was a new bank housed in a temporary trailer under a big sign that promised a real bank soon. I didn't see any customers and there weren't many prospects in the neighborhood. But there sure was plenty of parking.

A few blocks ahead, the dazzling new United Center looked like an enormous spaceship about to lift off. Beyond it, the old Chicago Stadium waited for the wrecking ball. Next to its replacement, the gray lady of Madison Street now looked small and cheerless.

I was relieved when the Honda turned north up Damen Avenue. Like much of the West Side, the stadium was no longer suitable for daytime viewing. I'd come back some night to pay my last respects. At night, the place wouldn't look quite so bad.

I followed the car north and soon left the West Side behind.

Twice, lights turned green and the Honda didn't move until horns blared. Cars sped around on the right.

A couple miles up, in the heart of Bucktown, the car turned down a narrow side street and slipped into a parking space. The girl got out, unlocked the side entrance of a narrow corner building, and disappeared inside.

The building was old, well over a hundred years, but it had probably never looked this good. The roof was peaked, covered with bright blue shingles, and spotted with gleaming modern skylights. The trim was freshly painted and there were new storms and screens.

There were apartments upstairs and a fancy-looking restaurant on the ground floor. "Gare du Nord," was written in red-neon script in the restaurant's center window, and under that a small printed sign said: "Open For Lunch."

I left the Olds in a bus stop and angled across the street. The restaurant looked closed, white tablecloths under slowly spinning ceiling fans.

The door the girl had gone through was locked. A window looked into a tiny hallway. There were mailboxes on the wall and junk mail and take-out menus scattered on the floor. Outside was a row of doorbells. I scribbled the names under them in my notebook, then headed across the street to a *Sun-Times* box. Back in the Olds, I flipped through the pages. I skipped the crime news. I almost always skipped the crime.

The last time I'd noticed, there'd been a Laundromat where the Gare du Nord was now. It had probably been gone for several years. But years before that a cop had been shot out front after a traffic stop. It's funny how certain places stay in your memory.

You could spot the neighborhood old-timers easily enough. Most looked slightly confused, as if they'd suddenly found themselves living in a foreign city. In the middle of the afternoon, they were almost all older women, Poles or other Eastern Europeans who'd worked hard all their lives and had the legs to prove it. If this was a normal November day, they'd be wearing babushkas. If it snowed, they'd be out with shovels, clearing their sidewalks from edge to edge. Most of them were widows, I guessed. Something in the way they walked—the way they lingered to look in a store window and the slender weightlessness of their bags—let you know that no one was waiting at home.

They wore simple, durable-looking dresses and carried string or canvas shopping bags even though most of their shops were gone. The delis that sold goods shipped direct from the old country, the bakeries using recipes that went back centuries, had been replaced by coffeehouses, nightclubs, and storefront theaters.

The newcomers all seemed to dress in degrees of black. They loved leather and boots, tattoos and rings. They were still dancing late at night while the old-timers were fast asleep, dreaming of their lost worlds.

My phone rang. "Nick. Frank," Stringfellow said. "You ready to write?"

"Shoot."

"Rebecca A. Westerfield." He spelled the last name, then gave me an address in Madison, Wisconsin.

"Thanks," I said. Oh, well. So much for my mystery girl. She'd been visiting the family store.

"You gonna get to that address verification soon?"

"Through rain, sleet, and snow, Frank." I cranked the starter and put the Olds in gear.

FIVE

ROGERS Park, north up the lake, was the last stop before the
suburbs. It was a neighborhood of huge apartment buildings.
The old white middle class had been moving out for years. They'd
been replaced by poor blacks and immigrants and a new middle
class of blacks, gays, and other regentrifiers who were busy con-
verting the apartments to condominiums, quickly pricing the poor
right back out. One thing had stayed constant: finding parking was
usually a problem.

So I took it as a good sign when I found a spot right in front of
the Lake Breeze Apartments. For once, it wasn't false advertising.
The beach was a half block down.

I strolled into the courtyard and up to a side entrance. Nothing
would stop me from my mission of verifying Leslie Crawford's
address. I stepped into a small vestibule. On one of the mailboxes
"L. Crawford" was printed in white on a strip of blue plastic tape.
Under the name was another piece of plastic: "2-N." Second floor,
north apartment.

Crawford's address was now verified. I'd earned my minimum
fee, thirty bucks plus mileage. I could call it a day and go on a
spending spree. But what the hell. I was a pro. I walked to the
entrance directly across the courtyard. I jimmied the inside lock,
then climbed two and a half flights to a window between the second and third floor. There were lights burning in the apartment

across the way, the one on the north side of the second floor. There were curtains in the window. I could see a corner of a rug, a floor lamp, and the arm of an easy chair or sofa.

In the other second-floor apartment, somebody was moving out. I stood there a couple of minutes, listening to the muted sound of assorted TVs, watching a crew of furniture movers at work. They were working much faster than any movers I'd ever hired.

I went back down the stairs and checked the apartment tags in the lobby, then across to Crawford's lobby. No doubt about it, someone had switched the tags for the second floor.

I walked around the side of the building, where a moving van was parked, then out to my car to dial Stringfellow's number.

"Your boy's on the move," I said when he answered.

"Dammit."

"He almost had me. He switched the tags in the lobby. They're loading a truck right now."

"Give me half an hour," he said. "You got your tracking unit?"

"It's in the shop, Frank." I didn't have the heart to tell him I didn't own one. Stringfellow had one so advanced he could call an 800 number and find the current location, speed, and direction of the vehicle he was shadowing.

"Nick, when it comes to technology, go the extra dollar."

"Frank, how can you lose a moving van?"

I walked down the block and sat on the cement wall of the turnaround and watched the waves roll in. An occasional gust of icy wind wafted from a mist moving slowly and steadily toward shore. A sailboat was heading for harbor. So long, Indian summer. I cupped my hands around a match and lit a cigarette.

Two cigarettes later, the truck nosed out of the driveway. On the side, an old-time furniture mover tipped his hat. "Cheerful, Careful, Dependable Service," the sign read. But next to the drawing the name of the moving company had been painted over.

Three guys in jeans and T-shirts helped guide the driver out to the street. "Come on. Come on. Whoa!" they shouted. It was a fairly wide street and the truck wasn't all that big, but the driver seemed to be having a hell of a time getting out of the driveway.

When he finally did, I started up the block, but the truck didn't move. I went back to the turnaround. A few minutes later, a guy in a gray sharkskin suit walked out. From Stringfellow's description I knew this was probably Leslie Crawford.

He walked to a shiny black Mercedes, opened the door, then turned and waved. I turned around, but there was nothing behind me but that cool white mist. The moving truck followed the Mercedes away. I hurried up the block to find four flat tires.

Stringfellow pulled up a few minutes after the service truck. "Jesus, Nick, you parked right in front. No wonder he made you."

"Frank, you see any other parking?"

"Dammit, I hate this filthy town."

He was a big man. He looked like he might have once played professional football, but I knew he hadn't. He hated to sweat, he'd once confessed. Not a hair was out of place. His suit was buttoned, his tie tight. His shoes were polished to a fine gloss.

He left his spotless Caddy double-parked. I slipped the lock in the lobby. The apartment door stood slightly ajar. Stringfellow pushed it with a foot.

Crawford had left in a hurry. An air conditioner was half out of a window. A Hide-A-Bed sat with the mattress tied in place and the cushions gone. There was garbage scattered around. Lots of take-out food containers. Pizza boxes, hamburger wrappers, Chinese rice containers, assorted skin magazines. Girls. Boys. Boys and girls together.

"How can people live like this?" Stringfellow asked. I made a note to call a maid service before I invited him for tea.

He walked with his head down, watching every step, steering clear of the garbage. His hands were tucked in his pockets. Big as he was, he managed to move from room to room without touching anything but the floor.

In the kitchen, I opened the refrigerator, then quickly closed it as the smell hit. There were eight coupons from a neighborhood pizza place stuck on a nail by the back door. Ten entitled you to one free pizza.

"He must have moved out of the hood." I held up the coupons for Stringfellow to see.

"I haven't had pizza since college."

"You went to college?"

"Yeah. While you were shaking down guys running red lights, I was reading sonnets."

"Speaking of shakedowns, what's Crawford running?"

"Oh, it's a long story," Stringfellow said. "My guy's a doc and Crawford got into his computer and pulled out a patient list."

"He broke into the office?"

"No. No. No. We're pretty sure he's some kind of hacker."

"Maybe he's into your computer. Might be how he knew you were coming?"

"Nick, I use the computer for billing and stuff like that."

"Your phone?"

"I got a guy comes once a month. It's always clean. Look, you worry about that truck you lost. I'll worry about my office."

Outside, the tow truck driver was still working on the Olds.

"Frank, about my tires."

"Nick, thirty cents a mile. You know that."

"Sure, Frank. Sure. You want to give it to me now? Maybe I can get a cup of coffee."

SIX

THE next morning was cool and windy, a typical gray November day. I picked up coffee on the way to my office, then spent some time paging through the Yellow Pages.

Every furniture mover in town seemed to know the story of Emanuel Jones, who'd died of carbon monoxide poisoning while working under a truck in his closed garage. Some thought he'd simply forgotten to hook up the exhaust tube that was found on the floor under the tailpipe. Others saw it as the work of some passing degenerate who'd pulled the tube out as a prank. Still others saw it as a crafty suicide.

Whatever the truth, the death had been the end of Manny's Moving and Storage. The company's equipment, including six trucks, had been auctioned off. I traced five of them easily enough, and they'd all been repainted. The last truck had ended up in the hands of some unknown "gypsy," one of the city's smaller movers, usually operating without a license or insurance. These companies didn't have Yellow Page listings. Most didn't even have offices.

But I was a pro, and the longer I worked, the quicker I'd recoup the money I'd spent on tire repairs.

I bounced all over the North Side, from one fly-by-night outfit to another. There'd been plenty of sightings, but nobody seemed to know who was operating the truck. I was about to give up when

I pulled next to a Hebard Storage truck at a light on Western Avenue.

"Hey, buddy!" I shouted to a guy waving a cigarette out the passenger window.

He held a quick consultation with the driver, then turned back my way. "Shitty Movers!" he shouted. "Only they spell it *C-i-t-y*. Lake and Morgan. Cheaper getting a trash compactor."

I waved and headed south to Lake Street and then turned east, under the elevated structure.

Just past Damen, there were several television news trucks. A group of people, mostly women and children, were marching back and forth with picket signs: THIS IS OUR HOME! WHERE IS THE REPLACEMENT HOUSING? "We're happy here!" they chanted. "We're happy here! We're happy here!" A passing elevated train drowned them out.

Behind the picketers, a wrecking crew was hard at work, demolishing a redbrick high-rise, part of the Henry Horner Homes. This wasn't the worst public housing project in town, but it was a long way from the best. There were about twenty buildings, high-rises and mid-rises, bleak, government-issue places of red brick and concrete. No grass or trees, just hard-packed dirt and cement.

I sped up when I got past the trucks, but then something slowed me down. I wasn't sure what. Something I'd seen.

I made a U-turn and headed back past the picketers. "We're happy here! We're happy here!" The wrecking ball paid no attention. It crashed into the building. Bricks fell. A guy with a droopy garden hose tried his best, but the thin stream of water did little to stop the clouds of dust from rising.

A block down, in the parking lot of another high-rise, a red Honda with Wisconsin plates was parked between a rusted Ford and a burned-out panel truck.

There were no TV cameras on this side of the demolition site and no protesters, just a handful of sidewalk superintendents. Cheers sounded each time the wrecking ball hit. It was an unusual sound in a place where there was usually so little to cheer about. But now part of their home was being torn down and this group apparently saw it as good news.

I'd spent years coming into places like this, and it had almost always been bad news. But now the city had decided to demolish the most crime-ridden buildings. I wondered if anyone really believed the guns and the drugs, the poverty and despair, would disappear with the buildings.

I took a quick walk around the Honda. Everything looked fine. The doors were locked, the windows closed. The car was clean. No bullet holes or blood, or signs of a struggle. The ignition appeared intact, no screwdrivers in the steering column, no loose wires under the dash.

"Hey, that's my car."

I turned and there was the girl from yesterday. She was coming from the nearest building, holding hands with two black boys who were dressed in identical school uniforms. Gray pants, white shirts, red ties. But why weren't they in school? The older boy carried a flashlight. He was about ten years old. They both looked scared. Maybe they'd already learned an important ghetto lesson: white men generally meant trouble.

"Detective Phillips," I said, and I flashed my PI license. "This your car?"

"Yes." She dragged the boys a few steps. "Is something wrong?"

I held out my hand. "Could I see some identification?"

She released the boys, took out a thin blue wallet and then a Wisconsin driver's license. I took my time reading the same name and address I'd got from Stringfellow yesterday afternoon.

"OK, Rebecca." I handed the license back. "Sorry to bother you. A lot of stolen cars end up down this way. We see out-of-state plates on a nice-looking ride we like to check it out."

"I understand," she said, sounding very earnest.

I should have quit right there. "Could I have a word in private?" I asked instead.

"Oh, sure." She turned to the boys. "Guys, thanks for walking me down." She pulled them into a big hug, one in each arm.

"Bye, Becky!" they called, and then ran back inside.

"I don't know what you're doing here," I started my little speech. "It's none of my business, really. But I want to warn you. You might come down here ninety-nine times and everything's fine. But the hundredth time, the odds are gonna catch up with you. Something bad is going to happen. I can practically guarantee it."

"My friend told me the same thing," she said. She gestured and I looked up and there was a woman watching us from a breezeway about eight floors up.

"Smart lady," I said.

"She really is."

"OK, Rebecca," I said. "I'll wait until you get out of here."

"It's Becky."

"OK, Becky. Have a nice day." I started for my car.

"Officer!" she called behind me.

It had been years since anyone had called me that.

"The reason I was here . . . ," she said, and she held out her hands like she was checking the weight of some invisible package. "My friend's son went out last night and he didn't come back. I was wondering if you could . . ."

"You'd have to call Missing Persons," I said. "I just handle stolen cars."

"She already called"—she was still holding the package—"and nobody really took her seriously. They said he wasn't gone long enough. I don't quite understand that, but I thought maybe if you said something. I just thought it might be that my friends are so poor and that they live here and that they're black." She was going about a mile a minute now, moving the package around, checking for the label, the return address, postage, whatever. "I'm not saying the police are racist or anything, but I think sometimes they might try harder if the person had more money or lived somewhere else or something." She ran out of steam, dropped her arms, and stood looking at me.

I opened my notebook. "What's your friend's name?"

"Jimmy," she said, and I thought instantly of the Jimmy from the Westerfield store. "Jimmy Madison," she said, confirming my guess. Jimmy Madison from Madison Street. Jimmy who'd been worried about telling a few white lies.

"Date of birth?"

"I'm not sure. I know he's twenty-five."

"When was he last seen?"

"Last night."

"Where?"

"Right here." She pointed toward the building. "He got a phone call and he told his mother he'd be right back. It's really not like him."

"OK." I closed the notebook. "I'll make a couple of phone calls. Maybe I can get some action."

"Thanks," she said. "Do you have a card or something?"

"Why don't you give me your number and I'll have someone from Missing Persons get in touch?"

She didn't say anything. She just stood there looking at me, and then her upper lip curled into this odd little smile. "You're not really from the police, are you?"

"I'm not?" I held her gaze.

She shook her head. "I don't think so. You never really showed me your identification. You pretended to, but you didn't. Your car looks too nice to be a police car, and don't police cars usually have spotlights? And where's your partner?" She looked around as if he might suddenly appear.

"You don't want to meet my partner."

She didn't say anything to that. We stood there staring at each other. Her eyes were a deep brown and, under other circumstances, I might have enjoyed staring into them. But not when she'd caught me like this.

"So who are you?" she broke the silence. "And why were you looking at my car?"

"Just doing my job, ma'am." I tried the old Joe Friday line.

"You were following me yesterday, too."

I couldn't help but smile. Maybe she should be the detective. "I was?"

She nodded her head. I held her gaze.

We stood there for a long while, nobody saying anything; then I slid my wallet out and let her read my private investigator license.

"Are you working for my father?" she asked. "Is he all right?"

"I can't tell you who I'm working for."

"Just tell me he's OK."

"I never met your father," I said. "That's the truth."

"So you don't know where he is?"

"No."

"Did my mother hire you?"

"I'm not going to play Twenty Questions." I turned and started for my car. She followed along. I cranked the engine, then lowered the window.

"Do you really have friends in the police department?"

"I'll make a couple of calls." I picked up the phone.

"Wait for me, OK? I have to talk to Mrs. Madison."

"Here, use my phone." I held it out.

She sprinted away. "Goddammit," I said, but I didn't go after her. I glanced upstairs. The woman on the breezeway was gone.

It was still early and the drug addicts would still be dreaming their drugged dreams. The dealers would be counting their money or getting their goods ready for later. And the decent folks would be at work or at school, or hiding in their apartments watching TV.

SEVEN

I PUNCHED in a number. "Violent Crimes," a familiar voice answered.

"Judy, it's Nick. How's tricks?"

"Hey, Nick." I could almost hear the smile. "When are you coming home?"

"Lovely, Judy," I said.

"I wish they'd change their minds."

"Fat chance," I said. "Is Casper around?"

"You're really out of the loop. He's at Area Four."

"Jesus, what'd he do to deserve that?"

"I don't think he minds, Nick. They made him a lieutenant."

"Wow," I said, and then I said it again. "This I want to hear."

"I better let him tell you. Bet you forgot the number."

She gave me the number, but I didn't dial it right away. I sat there with the phone in my hand. My old partner John Casper was now a lieutenant. Boy, oh, boy, I wasn't sure how I felt. We'd been a three-man homicide team, once upon a time, John Casper, Andy Kelly, and myself. Now Casper was the only one left on the force. And he'd been promoted twice. I didn't know whether to laugh or cry. I dialed the number instead.

A few moments later he was on the line. "Well, well, well, my long-lost partner." There was a snide chuckle in his voice. "Where you been hiding, Nick?"

"Here and there, John," I said. "Mostly there. So tell me, how the hell did you pull this lieutenant thing?"

"Hayes resigned. They needed someone to take his place."

"Hayes resigned?"

"Don't you ever read the papers?"

"Just the comics."

"I got a letter from Andy the other day," Casper said.

"Why'd Hayes resign?"

"The Nelson case. That ring any bells? Catherine Nelson."

"The stewardess?"

"That's the one."

"I thought that was all locked up."

"That's exactly the problem. Turns out the guy Hayes got a confession from was locked up at the time of the murder."

"So they made him resign?"

"Couple other things, too."

"Like what?"

"Other confessions that didn't hold. DNA-schmee-NA. You know how it goes."

"Well, congratulations."

"Andy was asking about you. He said you don't write."

There was nothing to say to that.

"The poor fuck's locked up, Nick. The least you could do is write him a letter now and then."

I let another silence stretch out.

"Look, maybe you've got a right to be pissed. But he was your partner; don't forget that."

"John, not a day goes by I don't remember. That's why I'm out here looking in."

"One of the things I admire about Andy, he's not sitting around feeling sorry for himself."

"He robbed a bank, John. He's supposed to be in prison. I didn't rob any bank."

"Nick, you gotta play whatever song comes up on the jukebox."

"You're breaking my fucking heart," I said.

"Who's that, Hank Williams?"

Neither one of us said anything for a while. "You know anybody at Missing Persons?" I finally remembered why I'd called.

"Is this more of your sleaze work?"

"John, they bring you up on charges, I know the first call you're gonna make." He'd call Shelly's law firm, just like I had.

"Yeah?" He sounded like he didn't believe it. He let some time pass. "Who's missing?"

"Name of James Madison," I said. "Goes by Jimmy."

"You got a date of birth, address, anything?"

"He lives in the Horner Homes," I said. "He's twenty-five. That's all I know."

"This isn't the kid from that drugstore?"

"How's that?"

"Westerfield's drugstore on Madison Street," he said. "You're not working something out this way, are you?"

"Pretend I asked you that first," I said softly.

There was a long silence and then he actually went for it. "Sure, what the hell." He laughed. "I'm a public servant. I've got nothing to hide. That's the new department policy, by the way. Irving Kaplan. That ring any bells?"

"Irving Kaplan?"

"He used to work at Westerfield's."

"He quit?"

"Yeah, he quit all right. When somebody walked in with a twenty-two and emptied it into him."

"When's this?"

"Going on three weeks."

"You clear it yet?"

He snorted. "Guy walks in, asks for Kaplan. When Irv comes out, he opens his briefcase and fires right through the lid. Six shots and every one's a winner. Kaplan was dead before he hit the floor. The guy drops the gun back in the briefcase and walks out."

"You thinking mob?" I could see that freshly painted drugstore wall and the fear in Jimmy's eyes as I'd approached. He probably would have fainted if I'd brought my briefcase along.

"You ever hear of the outfit using black hit men?"

"I thought that was the new trend."

"Why we haven't ruled it out. That and the fact that we've got nothing else."

"No motive?"

"You want a lot for thirty-five cents," he said, but then he went on. "Only thing we've been able to come up with is gambling debts. Irv liked the ponies."

"Brings you right back to the mob," I said. "And don't they usually break your legs first?"

"I didn't say that's what happened. I said it's all we have. Far as we can tell, Irv didn't owe anybody. We're grasping at straws, Nick. The man's got no enemies. Nothing. John Q. Pharmacist. Super straight arrow. Wife's devoted to him. He wasn't a kink. Not even a whisper. He came right home after work and took his wife out on picnics. It's sickening."

"Somebody hired a pro," I said.

"Would a pro really shoot through the briefcase? What's the point of that?"

"John, if he was six for six, I don't think you get to argue. How about the business?"

"Yeah, there's something about that drugstore definitely gets the old curiosity going. Remember Diane Keating?"

"Sure," I said. She'd been strangled by an old boyfriend. Going through her apartment after the murder, we'd found welfare check stubs in twenty-two different names. She'd invented entire families. All together, she'd been raking in about nine thousand dollars a month, most of which she blew on recreational drugs. The press dubbed her the Welfare Queen.

"It's the same old song," Casper said. "You know what Kaplan was doing before he died? He was filling out prescriptions."

"Didn't you say he was a pharmacist?"

"You're missing my point. He wasn't filling prescriptions, which is what pharmacists do. He was filling them out, which is what doctors do."

"He was forging their names?"

"He just filled the body of the script. I don't know who signed 'em. There must have been two dozen pads all ready for the doc's signature."

"He's prescribing without a license?"

"That I don't know. But I know there's no cash going through that store. My guys were in and out for days and they didn't see one single customer. Nada."

"So who are all the prescriptions for?"

"Oh, I don't know. Maybe some of Diane Keating's kids, assorted other ghosts."

"I'm still missing something," I said.

"It's all paper, Nick. Little bits of paper that you take straight to the bank."

"So follow the paper."

"Only trouble is, Kaplan had nothing to do with it. He's semi-retired. Used to own his own store. He was just working part-time for walking-around money. It all checks out."

"What about witnesses?"

"Just Madison and Westerfield. And now you tell me Madison's missing. You think there's some connection with the Kaplan hit?"

"I just got on this two minutes ago," I said. "Any chance I get a look at the file?"

"There's really nothing to see, Nick. That's the problem."

"Hell, it'd give me some background anyway. Make a copy and I'll stop by the house and pick it up."

"Christ, I start letting civilians go through our files, I really will be talking to Shelly."

"That's how you think of me, John, just another civilian?"

"Didn't they tell you when they took your badge?"

"Go fuck yourself," I said, and it came out a bit stronger than I'd intended. I listened to the pops and fizzes on the line.

"So what're you working anyway?" he asked after a while.

"Look, do me one favor. Call somebody over at Missing Persons and see if you can light a fire under this Madison thing."

"Why do I get the feeling you think I owe you something?"

"He could have robbed your bank," I said.

He chuckled. "One of the differences between us, Nick, I do all my banking by mail. I hate waiting in line. And I never leave home without my gun. I would have shot the son of a bitch, and don't think he doesn't know it."

"You gonna call Missing Persons?"

"I'll tell 'em he's a witness to a homicide. That might get some action. If I could spare the manpower, I'd send some of my own guys out. But we're swamped. Every shyster in town's trying to get one of Hayes's cases tossed. We've been going back through everything he touched. You have any idea what a pain it is, trying to find witnesses years after the fact?"

"Whatever you can do, John."

"You really should stop by the house some night."

"Maybe later in the week."

"You know it's been three years."

"Come on," I said. "It hasn't been that long."

"Longer," he said. "It was three years on the Fourth of July."

"Shit, John," I copped a plea, "you know how it goes."

"The kids still ask about you. You know kids, never forget anything. I keep wanting to tell 'em you're just another asshole. But then I decide I should protect 'em from the truth as long as possible."

"Tell 'em I said hi."

"Asshole," he said, and the line went dead.

I sat there holding the phone. After a while I dialed Shelly's number. "This Westerfield thing is sort of heating up."

"What Westerfield thing?"

"The kid who was driving that station wagon disappeared last night. Turns out there was a murder in that store a few weeks back. Looks like a contract hit. I thought you might want me to dig around. See what turns up."

"Nick, I know you miss working Homicide and everything, but what's any of this have to do with my client?"

"Well . . . ," I started, and then I realized I had no answer.

"Did you talk to that old man yet?"

"What old man?"

"The one who started this whole mess, Nick. Remember him?"

"Oh, yeah." I remembered Raymond Purcell, the old man who made the 911 call about Tracy Grace shooting his own truck.

"We need him, too. Oh, by the way, Tracy Grace said thanks for the good work on that driver."

"Hey, where is he, anyway?"

"The POW camp," she said. This was the Records Division down at police headquarters. It was used as a holding area for cops on their way out. A place where they wouldn't be seen or heard by the public. I'd spent some time there myself, waiting while the Police Board sharpened the ax.

"Really," I said. "Look, tell him I might call, OK?"

"About what?"

"Oh, I might want him to pull a couple of files."

"Nick, isn't he in enough trouble?"

"Hell, he's already got a good lawyer," I said.

The phone went dead in my ear.

EIGHT

THE same two boys walked Becky down. They went through another three-way hug; then Becky handed me two photographs. "I thought these might help."

The first was a graduation shot, Jimmy in a gold cap and gown, holding a very serious pose. In the other, he's standing in front of a window, the Loop off in the distance.

"That's from a few months ago," Becky said. "The other's his high school graduation."

I filed the photos on the dashboard. "I'll pass 'em on."

"Are you really going to talk to someone or are you just—"

"Already did," I said. "They should be out before long."

"You could look yourself. If you're not doing anything."

"I'm kind of in the middle of something."

"We could both look," she said.

"One big difference between me and the police is they're a nonprofit organization."

"I have money," she said. "How much do you charge?"

"Standard rate is fifty an hour plus expenses."

"Fifty dollars?" She sounded shocked. She should price some of the big boys, if she thought that was high. "Do you give a student discount?"

"Depends."

"I could pay you to find my father," she said.

"He's missing, too?"

"I'm not sure."

"Come on. He either is or he isn't."

"You're really not working for him?"

I shook my head.

"Oh, I wish you were." She sounded about seven years old.

"When did you see him last?"

"Labor Day," she said. "Before I drove up to school."

"And then what?"

"Then he didn't call on my birthday. He never forgets. And when I called home my mother said he'd decided to take a vacation."

"What else?"

"My mother's acting strange."

"How so?"

"I can't explain it."

"What does she say?"

She shrugged. "My father's on vacation."

"Where?"

"She's not sure. He just wanted to get away."

"You think she's lying?"

She nodded and bit her lower lip.

"Why would your mother lie to you?"

"Why would my father go away without calling to say good-bye?"

"OK. Let's assume she's lying, what's she covering up?"

"I don't know."

"Maybe she hit him on the head and buried him in the basement."

"His office," she said.

"She buried him in his office?"

"No." She shook her head. "My father's not dead. I thought of that and . . . I can't explain it, but I know he's not dead."

"What's this about his office?"

"It's locked, and it's never locked."

"This is at home?"

She nodded. "And when I asked my mother about it she lied and said she didn't have a key. But then the other night I couldn't sleep and the light was on in there. I knocked and my mother wouldn't open the door. She told me to go back to bed. And then in the morning she wouldn't talk about it."

A squad car came down the street. The car slowed and two cops looked our way, then continued on.

"So why are you following me?" Becky asked, and she crossed her arms and waited for an answer.

I blew some smoke her way. It was easier than telling her the truth. She'd seemed a little too interested in that station wagon. But mainly I'd followed along just out of curiosity. She'd looked so out of place on Madison Street.

Becky fanned the smoke away. "My dad smokes a pipe," she said. She stood with her arms crossed, tapping the toe of one shoe on the street, holding her tough-girl pose. Time passed. The same squad car came down the street again. The car slowed and the cops looked our way, but, once again, they didn't stop.

"They're not doing anything," Becky said.

"Missing Persons is plainclothes," I let her know.

"Why do they keep driving in circles? They could be looking for Jimmy."

"It's OK to talk like that to me. But don't do it to them."

"I'm not afraid of the police," she said.

"You should be," I said. Every Police Board case I worked left me more fearful. Some of these guys made my old partner Andy Kelly look sane.

The squad car came down the block again. I could tell by the way it was moving that this time they planned to stop. "Let me do the talking," I said as I got out of the car.

The guy in the passenger seat stuck his arm out the window and pointed a finger right at me. "You're Nick Acropolis," he said. He was a white guy, my age or a little older. He had that beat-man sprawl from too many years of sitting on his ass, day after day after day, from too many discount meals at corner Greek joints and too much after-hours booze. In other words, he looked like half the force. His name tag said "Thompson," but that didn't ring any more bells than his face.

"I know I know you," I said. "But I can't quite—"

"No, no." He smiled. "We ran your plates. A couple honkies hanging out by the projects. Soon as I saw your name, I knew who you were. I went to grade school with Andy Kelly. I was telling my partner here what happened. You got royally fucked."

"The way it goes," I said.

The partner leaned over. He was a skinny white guy, young, an obvious rookie. "That really happened?" he asked.

I nodded my head.

"Unbelievable," he said, and he shook his head.

"Andy was a nutcase all the way back in kindergarten," Thompson let us know.

"He ought to be out in about two years," I said.

"I had enough of him in grade school," Thompson said. "Well, see you around. Just wanted to say hi." The car started away.

"Officer," Becky said behind me. The car stopped.

I spun around. "I told you, let me do the talking."

"I want to ask them about Jimmy."

"What's up?" Thompson asked.

"I'm working a missing persons case," I said. "Name of Jimmy Madison. Let me show you a picture." I reached into my car and then handed him the recent photo. "This is from a couple of months ago," I said.

Thompson glanced at the picture, then held it out for his partner to see. The partner shook his head. Thompson handed it back with a shrug. "How long's he been gone?"

"Just since last night," I said. "He lives right there. He said he was going out for a couple of minutes and never came back."

"They're all gonna be missing before long," Thompson said.

"How's that?" I asked.

He pointed toward the demolition site. "This is just the beginning. They're gonna blow everything sky-high and build town houses for stockbrokers and lawyers."

"Come on," I said.

"Suburbanites." He said the word slowly, as if it were some new breed of cockroach. "They all want to live near the Loop."

"That's what my dad says, too," Becky let us know.

"See." Thompson smiled. "I've been buying land for years."

"Out here?" I asked.

He nodded. "And, let me tell you, it ain't cheap. Used to be you could pick it up for a song. Not anymore. The word's out. The West Side will rise again."

I held out my business card. "You happen to see that kid floating around, give me a call."

He looked at the card but didn't take it. "A private eye." He shook his head. "Too bad. I heard you were one hell of a copper."

"I don't need anybody to talk for me," Becky said as the squad car pulled away.

"You'd be wasting your time with those clowns," I said. "Christ, twenty years on the job and he's still working a beat car. About the only thing he's interested in is what's for dinner."

"It's nice to know you really were a cop," she said. "Who's Andy Kelly?"

"My old partner."

"He's in prison, right?"

"You don't miss much, do you?"

"You said he'd be out in two years. What'd he do?"

"That's with time off for good behavior," I said. "Knowing Andy, he might stretch it out a bit."

"So why's he in jail?"

"He robbed a bank."

"Really?"

I nodded. "While I was waiting in line."

"You're kidding, right?"

"Why would I kid about something like that?"

"If I hire you will you tell me the truth?"

"Are you hiring me?"

"Depends what kind of discount you give me," she said.

"What can you afford?"

"Not much."

"I'll tell you what," I said. "I'll give you my all-time lowest rate, a flat hundred a day. How's that sound?"

She smiled. "I could probably manage a couple of days," she said. But then she eyed me suspiciously. "And in return for this generous discount?"

"Well, there is a catch," I said. "But not what you're thinking. Actually two catches."

"Yeah?"

"If another job comes up, I'll probably have to give it priority. That sound fair?"

"What's the other catch?"

"You buy lunch."

"Deal," she said, and she reached out and we shook. She had a nice, solid grip.

"Let me get you to sign something," I said. I walked around and popped the trunk and opened my briefcase and pulled out a standard form and started filling in the blanks. The form explained that Rebecca Westerfield was hiring me for help in investigating a confidential matter.

She read it through then signed by the X.

I felt like whistling. The sky was gray, the projects dreary. But it was shaping up to be a beautiful day.

I hadn't been this close to a homicide investigation in years. I could almost smell the blood.

NINE

WE had lunch in Greektown—Becky's choice—and I had to explain, not for the first time, that I didn't have an ounce of Greek blood. "When he was young, my father was a sailor. He made one trip to Athens. When he came home he changed his name."

"I was there once," Becky said. "I can almost understand."

"Well, fill me in." It was the family mystery.

"Don't tell me you have that name and you've never even been to Greece?" I nodded. "Oh, you just have to go," she said. "I can't explain it. You go, you'll see."

"What did Jimmy give you yesterday?"

"I don't know what you mean."

"Yesterday. He gave you something in a manila envelope."

"Oh, that." She smiled. "Where were you hiding?"

"What was in the envelope?"

"Don't go away," she said. She got up, walked outside, and returned a minute later.

The photograph was from a lost world. The gold leaf was shining in the sunlight. The terra-cotta was a glowing, creamy white. Even the sidewalk sparkled.

Three people were holding hands in front of the Westerfield drugstore, a man in medical whites and two kids. The man stood in the middle, a stocky, healthy-looking guy, with a prominent nose, thick, bushy eyebrows, and a look of parental amusement on his face. The kids looked to be about eight or nine. The boy was looking straight at the camera, his free hand resting on the seat of a big red bicycle, a serious expression on his face. There was a huge basket on the front of the bike. "Westerfield's" was written in old-fashioned script on a metal plate inside the frame.

"My dad and me and Jimmy," Becky said softly. In the photograph, she appeared to be taking a bow, as if she'd just finished a dance. "It makes you want to cry, doesn't it?"

It was that kind of picture. Like one taken just before a war.

"Jimmy used to live right across the street." Becky pointed. For the first time I noticed the reflection in the drugstore window, like a ghost in a mirror.

In the reflection, you could see the buildings that had once stood across from the drugstore. I could make out part of a theater marquee and a row of stores. "The Crown Theater," I remembered.

"Jimmy used to live above the shoe store." Becky pointed to a spot just out of the picture. "It was so sad yesterday to see it all gone."

"It's been gone for years," I said.

"My dad never let me come back after '78."

"The anniversary riot," I said. It began ten years and a day after the 1968 riot. The two riots had destroyed huge sections of Madison Street. Somehow Westerfield's had survived both.

"I knew Jimmy the instant I saw him," Becky said.

"He's been working at the store all these years?"

She nodded. "My father's paying his way through school. We used to sit at the soda fountain and talk about growing up and being doctors and now it's so close. He wouldn't just go away."

"Did you ask Jimmy about your father?"

"He didn't know anything. Then right when I was leaving he said there was something he wanted to tell me, but he had to talk to his mother first."

"What'd he say, exactly?"

"Just what I said."

"Try to remember the exact words."

She didn't say anything for a few moments. "He said something happened. That's what he said: something happened."

"Something happened?"

"Yes. Something happened and that's why my father went away. But I shouldn't worry. My father was OK. He just needed rest. He'd be back soon and everything would be just like it used to be."

"Your father's OK?"

"That's what he said."

"Something happened, but he didn't say what?"

"He had to talk to his mother first."

"Did you ask her about it?"

She nodded. "He never said anything."

"What do you know about your father's business?"

She shrugged. "He owns a drugstore."

"Who works for him besides Jimmy?"

"I don't really know," she said.

"How about that security guard? Is he always there?"

"I don't know."

"How about Irving Kaplan?" Becky shook her head. "You never heard of him? Irv?"

"I'm sorry," she said.

"Who's minding the store with Jimmy gone?"

"It's closed," she said.

"Nobody's there at all?"

She shook her head again.

"You don't know anybody besides Jimmy worked for your father?"

"There's Mr. Rogers," she said.

"Who's he?"

"I'm not sure. It's funny, he'd call and my mother would put her hand over the phone and say, 'The *shvartze*.' Then my dad would get on and say, 'Hey, partner, what's happening?' It was always so weird. My parents don't talk like that. But that's what they said when Mr. Rogers called. 'The *shvartze*' and 'What's happening?' "

"Mr. Rogers?"

"Nathan Rogers," she said. "I don't know if he's a real partner, but that's what my dad always called him."

"Do you know where to find him?"

She shook her head. "I'm not much help, am I?"

"You're doing fine," I said. "What's a good time to go up to your house?"

"My folks' house in Wilmette?"

I nodded. "Sometime when your mother's not home, so we can take a look at your father's office."

"She sees her shrink at two."

"A psychiatrist, is that something new?"

"Oh, god, no. She's been going as long as I can remember. Every Tuesday at two."

TEN

THE Westerfield house was a big blue place surrounded by tall trees. It was on the right side of the tracks, a few blocks off the lake. A wide, bowed porch wrapped around the side. Matching porch swings, on either side of the front door, swayed in the breeze.

Ten to twelve rooms, I guessed, two stories and an attic where you could while away rainy afternoons rummaging through old steamer trunks and reading back issues of long-defunct magazines—saved by some previous owner—as the rain drummed lazily over your head.

I slumped low in the passenger seat as Becky pulled between neatly trimmed hedges. She stopped in front of a three-car garage, got out, peeked in a garage window, then waved for me.

She unlocked a side door and we walked into a hallway and up a short flight of steps to the kitchen. It was right out of *House and Gardens,* white, light and airy, and spotlessly unused. There was a glassed-in breakfast nook that probably had every squirrel in the neighborhood begging for leftovers.

We went the other way, past a large formal dining room where a crystal chandelier hung from a beamed ceiling. There was a thick Oriental rug on the floor and enough dark wood for a funeral home. The table was cluttered with mail and newspapers, coffee cups and saucers. The curtains were pulled tight.

Becky led me up a flight of stairs and down a carpeted hallway. She tried the shiny brass handle and I did the same, but it refused to turn. I knelt down, handed Becky my penlight, then went to work with my set of miniature tools.

It took me about ten minutes. "Wow!" Becky said when I opened the door.

"A pro would have been in a half hour ago." My bones creaked as I stood up.

Becky flicked on recessed lights. There was more dark wood, a double pedestal desk with brass fittings, a credenza, a globe in a wooden stand, a huge dictionary on top of an old pulpit, a two-drawer file cabinet, and a couple of glass-door bookcases crammed with hardcovers and paperbacks. There was wood paneling on the walls and wooden shades on the windows. On the floor, a red bird glided along a brilliant blue Oriental sky, searching for a tree or a telephone wire or the smallest sliver of land, but there was nowhere to light, just that endless sky.

Becky took a deep breath. "I love this room," she said, and she stood there taking it in. After a while, she crossed to a wall of framed photographs and awards. "My dad," she said proudly.

The photographs were a chronicle of male pattern baldness. His hair got grayer and grayer as the years went on, then began to disappear completely. But Eugene Westerfield didn't seem to mind. His face usually sported a cheerful grin.

Most of the photographs were standard family shots. But in several Westerfield appeared to be accepting awards. In one he was standing on a stage, holding an award while shaking the hand of a dashiki-clad minister.

"What's that about?" I asked.

"I'm sure it's up here somewhere." She gestured toward the other frames. "He's always getting something."

"For what?"

"Different things," she said. "But I guess it's all because he stayed in that neighborhood when nobody else would."

"I was wondering about that," I said.

The biggest frame caught my eye. Well-dressed pedestrians strolled past Westerfield's on the way to neighboring stores. But something was missing. "Wait a minute," I said. "Where's the movie theater? What year's this?"

"That's the future according to my dad."

"Dream on," I said.

I tried the desk drawers and then knelt down and got to work with my picks again. Becky flipped through a desktop Rolodex.

"Becky!" someone called from far away. "Becky, where are you?"

"Oh, shit," Becky said. "Mom, I'll be right down!" she shouted.

"Becky, what are you doing home?"

"Where do I hide?" I asked.

"Across the hall," Becky said without panic. "My room."

We both started out of the office. I flicked the lights off, but then Becky turned them right back on. "Wait," she said, and she ran back to the desk and pulled a card from the Rolodex.

"Come on," I whispered. I could hear the mother coming up the stairs. I turned the lights off as Becky came out, then closed the door behind her.

"Becky!" Her mother was almost at the top.

Becky opened a door directly across the hall. "The closet," she whispered. She opened another door and I went in. The door closed behind me and I was in the dark, surrounded by clothes and the faint, delicate scent of perfume.

"Becky, you're supposed to be back at school."

"I decided to stay down for a while," Becky said.

"Stay where?" She was in the room now.

"With a friend."

"Becky, I don't understand why you'd risk everything you've worked so hard for."

"Why is the store closed?"

"Becky, you have no business down there."

"But why is it closed? Could you just tell me that, Mother? Why is the store closed?"

"Becky, I want you to stay away from that store."

"If you would tell me where Dad is, I wouldn't have to—"

"Becky, would you please trust me?"

"But all you do is lie!"

I could feel the slap from my spot deep in the closet, and the next thing I knew the door was open and Becky was pulling clothes off hangers. The side of her face was red.

I pushed myself deeper into the closet. Becky turned and looked my way and, I think, for a moment she was actually shocked to find me there.

"Becky, what are you doing?" her mother asked, and she stepped into view.

I only got a fleeting glimpse, but that was enough to see the troubled look deep in those dark eyes. She wore the shell-shocked expression of someone limping away from a head-on crash. She was tall like her daughter but she was dark and lean, with raven black hair and a chiseled face sculpted in dark Mediterranean skin. She looked much too young to be married to the dumpy bald guy in the photographs across the hall.

"Nothing," Becky said, and she dropped the armload of clothes to the floor and closed the door. "Just looking for a dress."

"I wish you would wear a dress more often."

"I know, Mother. I know. And you wish I'd go back to school, too. And you want me to stay away from the store and not ask questions about Dad."

"Oh, Becky, your entire future—"

"I can't believe you hit me," Becky said.

"I'm sorry, Becky. I'm truly sorry. It's been very hard lately. Please forgive me."

"What happened to your shrink?"

"I went. I went all that way and I parked the car, but I couldn't get out. I don't know what's wrong with me."

"Isn't that when you're supposed to go, when you're not feeling good?"

"Oh, to be so smart, and to be young and beautiful, too. And you're going to be a doctor. I still can't really believe it. Oh, your father would be so proud."

"But where is he, Mom? Where is he?"

"I must have known you'd be here. Guess what I bought? I'll give you one hint." She began to sing, "There's a little shop in Northbrook Court." The song was followed by a high-pitched giggle, which sounded as counterfeit as Muzak. "Come on, I'll race you!" she called, and her voice got farther away. "We can split it."

Becky opened the closet door. She shook her head. "That's not my real mother," she said, and she handed me her car keys.

ELEVEN

I WONDER why your mother skipped her psychiatrist?" I asked on the way back to the city.

"Sure nuts enough, huh?"

But it wasn't just her mental instability that troubled me. "Your father would be so proud," she'd said. Maybe she really had buried him in the basement. It wouldn't be something to tell your psychiatrist, or your daughter.

We switched cars in Greektown, then got back on the highway and continued south in my Olds. "Tell me about this Rogers," I said.

"I only met him once. He came to the house. I remember he smelled of smoke. My father smelled that way for weeks."

"Smoke?"

"From the riots."

Suddenly it came back. The distinctive bouquet of the West Side. For years, you'd smell it every time it rained, the heavy aroma of charred wood. Eventually the ruins had been carted away or simply disintegrated. But the smell lingered like a bad dream.

"You couldn't have been more than a baby," I said.

"I was about eight," she said. "I remember being fascinated by Mr. Rogers. I'd known black people before, but he was different and my father seemed to act different around him."

"You just knew the cook and maid," I said.

"Not true," she said. "I was at the store every Saturday."

"Was Rogers around before the riots?"

"I don't remember him."

"How was your father different with Rogers?"

"I think he treated him with more respect."

"Respect or fear?"

She thought about it for a while. "I can't quite picture my father being afraid."

I took the Sixty-third Street exit and headed east. The Jackson Park elevated structure covered the street from curb to curb. It blocked most of the sunlight, and the stars and the moon, and anything that passed for hope. Yellow lights cast a strange tint even in the middle of the afternoon.

"This is creepy," Becky said.

In an hour, we'd gone from one of the wealthiest neighborhoods in the country to one of the poorest. Becky's father had been making a similar trip for years.

"Where's that card?" I asked, and Becky handed me the card from her father's Rolodex. There were two addresses for Nathan Rogers. "Prospect Drugs" was written in parentheses after the second.

The store was beyond Cottage Grove, in a narrow building with the windows bricked up solid. A security guard was stationed in the doorway. "Right there," I said, and I pointed. "You sure you want to do this?"

"That's why we came, isn't it?"

I turned down a side street. A large group was hanging out in front of an abandoned apartment building. Somebody shouted as we passed, and a kid who couldn't have been more than eight took aim and a stone bounced off the hood of my car.

"Goddammit," I said. But I didn't stop. It was a small ghetto tax. I was thankful he'd missed the windshield.

"I can't decide which looks worse," Becky said when we were back in the darkness under the el, "this or Madison Street."

I pulled to the curb. The security guard had deserted his post. "I'll come with you," I said.

"I told you before, I don't need anybody to talk for me." She opened the door. "Besides, he's an old family friend."

A few minutes later, a skinny guy in a powder blue jogging suit crossed the street and entered the store. He had the unmistakable itch of a junkie.

A couple stopped out front. They were dressed for a night out. The woman opened her purse, pulled out several prescription vials, and handed them to the man. He went into the drugstore. The woman crossed the street, to a record/CD store.

A small yellow school bus double-parked just beyond my car. The door opened and a dozen women filed off straight into the drugstore. The driver came down the steps, a husky black guy. He gave me a small friendly nod, then sat smoking on the bottom step.

A few minutes passed. The bus driver flicked his cigarette. It bounced off one of the support girders of the el and nose-dived to the ground. The junkie came out with a prescription bag in hand.

The security guard reappeared. He nodded at the bus driver. The driver nodded back. The guard leaned against the burglar gates and took an easy look around the neighborhood. When his eyes reached my car they came to a sudden stop. He moved into the recess of the doorway, then slipped into the store.

The well-dressed guy came out with a small slip of paper in hand. He crossed to the store where his lady had gone.

A pair of junkies turned into the drugstore.

The women from the bus began to trickle out. Some headed across the street to the record/CD store; others went straight to the bus. The ones who got on the bus carried prescription bags. Most of those who crossed the street carried slips of paper.

A guy in a white pharmacy coat came out, carrying an open box filled with prescription bags. He angled kitty-corner across Sixty-third, into the front door of a storefront medical center.

A tall guy in a dark pinstripe suit came out and headed straight for my car. The security guard trailed behind. I met them halfway.

"Hi. I'm Nate Rogers." He flashed a perfect set of shiny white teeth and reached out a hand. Several rings glittered brightly. "Becky'll be right out. I thought I'd say hello."

I told him my name and shook the outstretched hand.

"Becky tells me you're a private detective."

I nodded.

"Well, I hesitate to tell you how to run your business, but I think you're wasting the young lady's time and money here. Eugene Westerfield is on vacation. I talked to him the day he left. Now I'll tell you the same thing I told Becky. Gene's very proud of her, and he would love nothing more than to be able to call her Doctor one day. But that's not going to happen if she doesn't get back to school. Her father will return before long."

"That's good to hear," I said. "You have any idea when Jimmy Madison might come back?"

He shook his head, then went on in that same stilted way, like a minister who'd never met the dearly departed addressing the bereaved. "I didn't want to alarm Becky, but the sad truth is, disaster often strikes in the projects. I'm glad to see they're finally tearing them down. It's long overdue."

"You don't think there might be some connection between what happened to Irv Kaplan and Jimmy disappearing?"

"I'm perplexed by what happened to Irv. He seemed like such an inconsequential man. I know it's not considered polite to speak ill of the dead, but the few times I saw him he looked like a man who'd long given up on life, who was just passing his final days. Yet, for some unexplained reason, somebody wanted him dead. Now I didn't mention this to Becky, but he's the reason for her father's vacation. Gene was very upset by the murder."

"Do you think it might be tied to your business?"

"My business?" He sounded shocked. "Irv had no connection with my business whatsoever."

"I thought you and Westerfield were partners."

"Oh, no, no, no. Gene and I go back years. But partners, no. I worked for Gene. There weren't many jobs available on the West Side when I was coming up, and I'm forever grateful to Gene for taking me on. He certainly gave me my start, no question about that. But this is my store, one hundred percent. And up on Madison Street, well, that's Gene's store."

"You don't have any way to get in touch with him?"

He shook his head.

"Can you get him a message?"

He shrugged. "Only if he decides to contact me."

"Well, if he does, ask him to call his daughter, would you?"

"I have no reason to think I'll hear from him. But if I do, I'll pass that on."

"Thanks," I said. "You seem to do pretty good here."

"It's a constant battle, competing with the big chains, but we try. We have our little niche and—oh, here's Becky now. I hope I cleared up some of your concerns."

"Sure," I said. "Thanks."

He opened his arms wide as Becky approached. She seemed to hesitate, then slipped into his embrace. "The lovely Dr. Westerfield," he said.

Rogers motioned to the security guard, then followed him back to the store.

"How'd it go?" I asked as Becky slid into the passenger seat.

"OK," she said without enthusiasm.

"What'd he say?"

"My father's on vacation."

"How about Jimmy?"

"No idea," she said. "He doesn't know anything about my dad's store. They're not partners, just business associates. But everybody inside seemed to know my dad."

The driver backed the bus out of the way. I waved, then pulled out and headed west. An elevated train rumbled overhead.

"I don't trust him," Becky said.

"He tell you anything else?"

"He said he thinks my dad went to Venice."

"Italy?"

"That's his best guess."

"Anything else?"

"I should go back to school. My dad will be home before long."

I turned down the first side street, made a U-turn, and pulled into a parking space. "What are we doing?" Becky asked.

"I'm kind of curious where this bus goes."

A few seconds later a junkie turned the corner. He pulled a prescription vial out of a bag, popped the top, and poured pills straight into his mouth.

"Welcome to Mr. Rogers' neighborhood," I said.

"My father would never let anything like that go on," Becky said softly.

"Well, Rogers told you they're not partners."

"I know," she said. "I hope it's the truth. I just can't imagine my dad having anything to do with him. He's creepy."

"How?"

"I can't explain it. Something about the way he talks, excessively sincere or something."

"He didn't say anything about Irv Kaplan?"

"Who's Irv Kaplan? That's twice you've mentioned his name."

"He's a pharmacist worked for your father," I said. "A few weeks ago somebody walked into the store and shot him."

"What?" It was almost a shout. She didn't say anything for a long while. "Dead?" she asked softly.

"Dead."

"Was my dad there?"

"Yeah, that's the funny thing. Your father and Jimmy were the only witnesses and now they've both disappeared."

"Maybe that's what Jimmy was going to tell me," Becky said.

"Run that by again."

"Jimmy said something happened and that's why my dad went away. Was my father right there?"

"He was in the store. I know that much."

"He hates the sight of blood," she said softly. "That's why he never became a doctor."

A minute later, the school bus cruised by and I pulled out and followed along. We went west and then turned north.

"They look like they go on forever," Becky said a few blocks later as we passed one public housing high-rise after another. This was supposedly the largest concentration of public housing in the country. One bleak building after another. Mile after mile.

"God, it's depressing," she said.

The bus pulled into a lot between two of the buildings and the women filed off. Some of them carried prescription bags; others carried bags from the CD/record store.

"Looks like Mr. Rogers has his own delivery service. Brings 'em straight from the projects." I turned back east.

"Where are we going now?" Becky asked.

"Let's go see where Rogers lives."

"What else aren't you telling me?"

"I don't follow you," I said.

"Why didn't you tell me about Irv Kaplan before?"

"I just found out this morning."

"So what were you doing at my father's store yesterday?"

"Nothing to do with Irv Kaplan."

"Who hired you to follow me?"

"That's a long story," I said.

"See, I don't know who to trust," she said. "I can't trust my mother. I know I don't trust Mr. Rogers. I'd like to be able to trust you, but you won't even tell me why you were following me."

"I can't sell out my clients just because you ask."

"But I'm your client, too."

"Look—"

"If you don't trust me, why should I trust you?"

"How would you feel if—"

"Oh, blah, blah, blah," she said, and she turned and looked out the window.

TWELVE

A T Forty-seventh and Drexel, I pointed toward the Sutherland Hotel. "Ahmad Jamal recorded there, place called the Pershing Lounge. There's a great cut on the album, 'Poinciana.' You've probably heard it." I tried my best to scat the ending. But if Becky recognized it, she wasn't letting on.

A few blocks later we turned south. Becky leaned forward. "Is this still the city?"

"Yeah. Welcome to Kenwood."

There were only two or three houses on a block. But it wasn't because others were missing. These were old mansions, set well back from the street. The Westerfield house would barely make the grade. "Remember the Leopold and Loeb case?" I asked.

"Two rich kids who decided to commit the perfect crime," I went on after a while. "A long time ago," I answered a question she hadn't asked. "Clarence Darrow saved them from the gallows."

I slowed down just past Forty-ninth Street. "Right there." It was an old stone house behind a big iron gate. It would have looked right at home in some ritzy section of London. There was a long driveway, bordered by well-trimmed hedges. The gate would be easy to get over, but that wouldn't get you anywhere. Floodlights were mounted on tall poles. Cameras pointed down from the roof.

"That's what one of my old partners would call a three-lawyer house," I said, quoting Casper. "That's how many you'd have to go through before you get to the owner, who respectfully refuses to answer on advise of counsel."

We drove around for a while. I always got a kick out of Kenwood. It was that Chicago rarity, a truly integrated neighborhood. All you needed was money. "Muhammad Ali." I pointed toward a huge place on Woodlawn Avenue.

"You're quite the tour guide," Becky said with a bit of a mocking tone.

"And you're like every woman I've ever known."

"Oh, really?" The tone was now British.

"Yeah, really." If they didn't get their way, they'd figure some way to drive you crazy.

I went back to Forty-seventh Street, then turned west. "OK," I said. "All right. You win." But that was as far as I was going with that particular song. "There was a traffic accident last week." I pointed straight ahead. "Jimmy was driving the station wagon. Somebody got a little excited and shots were exchanged. That's why I was on Madison Street when you showed up. And you seemed to have some interest in that station wagon."

"That's the car I got my driver's license in," she said. "I couldn't believe how bad it looked."

"It's seen better days," I agreed.

"What if I'd gone back to Wisconsin? Would you have followed me to Madison?"

"Never know," I said. "I might have."

"So, like a fool, I hired you."

"Yeah, it all worked out."

I stopped at the light just before the Dan Ryan Expressway. "I think my guy was coming this way and then, according to him, Jimmy ran the light and clipped his right rear."

"I still don't understand who you're working for."

"The lawyer who represents the other driver."

"You're on his side?"

"I'm not on anybody's side. It's just a game. He's a cop. The city's decided this is a good excuse to throw him off the force. We're trying to keep him on."

"But they should throw him off."

"That depends on the circumstances, doesn't it?"

"You're playing with words. You know and I know Jimmy didn't shoot at anybody."

"No. According to Jimmy he picked up a hitchhiker and the hitchhiker was the one with the gun."

"Do you realize how ridiculous that sounds?"

"I didn't say it was true. I said it was what Jimmy told me."

"Jimmy's no liar, Nick."

"You can't have it both ways, kid. Either he's a liar or that's the truth."

"He's not a liar," she said softly. "And I'm not a kid."

I glanced in the rearview mirror. "Here's our bus again." When the light changed, I pulled to the right, then followed along behind. "Let's see where he goes."

"I have to figure out what to do," Becky said as we went under a long viaduct. "Maybe I should go back to school."

"Best-case scenario: your dad's gonna show up, no matter what you do."

"And the worst case?"

"We already talked about that," I said. "He could be dead."

"He's not dead."

"Something else you might want to consider," I said. "Sometimes you're better off not getting answers."

"Why?"

"Maybe your father's business isn't exactly on the up-and-up."

"That just shows you don't know my dad."

"Becky, I saw three junkies go into that store. Plus the guy who pulled the stunt with the pills."

"That's not my dad's store. Did you see any junkies there?"

"No. But that's kind of funny, too. I didn't see anybody. I was there for almost an hour and you were the only one who went in or out. I can't figure out how that store survives. But your father seems to be doing pretty good. I mean, he's got that big house in Wilmette."

"You haven't met my dad, so I'm not mad. You just don't know the kind of person he is. The reason he's on Madison Street is because those people need him."

"What people?"

The bus stopped in front of a corner drugstore. I looked back in the rearview as another group of women came down the steps.

"Well, well, well," I said. "Looks like this guy drives around all day delivering women to drugstores."

I went east to the Dan Ryan. Nobody said a word all the way back to Greektown.

THIRTEEN

TWENTY-FOUR hours hadn't done anything for Madison Street. Westerfield's dream was exactly that. It was easier to imagine colonies on the moon.

The burglar gates were padlocked shut. A sign on the door said, "Sorry We're Closed." I crossed to the tire shop.

The two guys on the porch looked so much alike they had to be brothers. They had the same wiry build. Their hair was turning gray in all the same places. They were sixty or seventy or somewhere in between. They were wearing Sinclair Oil coveralls with their names stitched above patches of Dino the friendly dinosaur. I hadn't seen the little guy in twenty years. One was Clyde, the other Jesse.

"So how's the tire business?" I asked as I approached.

They broke into broad smiles. "It be rolling right along."

"Any idea why the drugstore's closed?"

"That what everybody wants to know," Clyde said.

"Everybody?" I asked, and I glanced across the street. The place looked like it had been closed for fifty years.

"Been a parade all day," Jesse said.

"First Thomas be here, bright and early," Clyde said.

"Thomas?" I asked.

"Then Willie be by," Jesse said.

"Willie?"

"Wet Willie. Yeah, he be here."

"Police be by."

"The police were here?" I asked. "Detectives?"

"Sure were," Jesse said.

"Mr. Gene's girl," Clyde let me know.

"That's right, little Miss Becky," Jesse said. "Nice child."

"What'd the police want?"

"Same as everybody else," Clyde said. " 'Why's the store closed?' 'Where's Jimmy?' 'Where's Mr. Gene?' 'What happened to Irv?' "

"What do you know about Irv?"

"They carried him out," Clyde said.

"Sure did," Jesse agreed.

"You were here?" I asked.

"That we were."

"Did you see the guy with the briefcase?"

"That we did."

"Would you recognize him if you saw him again?"

"Recognized him all right the other day," Jesse said.

"Wasn't him," Clyde said.

"Sure was."

"Different hair," Clyde said.

"He came back?"

"Sure did," Jesse said.

"You sure it was him?"

"Sure am," Jesse said.

"Different hair," Clyde said again.

"What was different about it?" I asked.

"Man who done shot Irv had red hair," Clyde said.

"Same man," Jesse said.

"Maybe he dyed his hair," I suggested.

"Wig," Jesse said.

"Did you call the police?"

"No phone," Clyde said.

"He went into the drugstore again?"

"Saint Anthony's," Jesse said.

"What day was this?"

"Day before yesterday," Jesse said but then changed his mind. "No. Day before day before yesterday."

"Saturday?"

"Day before day before yesterday."

"What time of day?"

They hemmed and hawed, but neither could remember.

"Morning or afternoon?" I asked.

"Afternoon," Clyde decided.

"How many years you guys been here?"

"Since the burnings," Clyde said.

"We come for the bricks," Jesse added.

"The bricks?"

"Used to do bricks," Clyde said.

"So where is Mr. Gene?" I asked.

"Don't rightly know," Clyde said.

"How long's he been gone?"

"Been a while, now," Clyde said.

"Couple weeks," Jesse said. " 'Bout."

"He be back," Clyde said.

"Oh, sure," Jesse agreed. "You got a card?"

"A card?"

"Got a pile." Jesse held up a short stack of business cards.

"You mind if I look?"

There weren't any cops, unless you happened to count Special Agent Steve Johnson of the FBI. There was a card for Michael Brewer, an investigator with the Illinois Department of Public Aid, and one for John Olmstead, a *Tribune* reporter. "Who's this?" I held up a card for a private detective, but neither brother bothered to look.

"What's it say?" Jesse asked.

" 'William Harris,' " I read the name off the card.

"Wet Willie," Clyde said.

"What'd he want?" I asked.

"Looking for Jimmy," Clyde said.

I wrote names and phone numbers in my notebook.

"Where's yours?" Clyde asked when I handed the cards back.

I dug through my wallet and found a card with Frank String-fellow's name on it. Jesse added it to the collection.

FOURTEEN

I WALKED across the street and through the weeds—past the patch of gravel where the Chevy wagon had been parked—and then around to the front entrance of St. Anthony's Medical Center. The lobby was crammed with kids playing pinball and video machines. More kids were running in and out begging their mothers for quarters.

I went through a second doorway. Straight ahead was a reception desk. TAKE A NUMBER AND SIT DOWN, a sign commanded.

It was mostly women and children waiting. There were two pregnant girls, sitting side by side. Neither looked much past sixteen. Another girl, about the same age, sat with two small children in her lap. One kid was coughing; the other had snot running down his face. There was a bum asleep with his number clutched in his hand. Two junkies were whispering in a corner.

There were several NO SMOKING signs, but nobody seemed to be paying any attention. One woman sat smoking and coughing into a bloody handkerchief. Next to her an old man shared the same coffee-can ashtray. The side of his face was swollen.

Behind the desk, a woman in medical whites was waiting while an older woman searched through a large purse.

"You know I've been here before," the older woman said softly.

"I'm sorry, we can't do anything without a card," the woman behind the desk said. I recognized her voice. She'd been the one pushing Dr. Z. out the back door. A name tag read: "M. Hennessy, R.N."

The woman began emptying the purse onto the counter. "I know it's in here somewhere," she said. "I remember I . . ." She stopped, reached up and unzipped a jacket pocket and pulled out a small brown card and handed it to Nurse Hennessy.

Hennessy placed the card facedown in a photocopy machine. The machine spit out about ten copies. She placed one on a clipboard with a printed form, then handed the aid card back to the woman. "Have a seat. The doctor will call you."

Hennessy filled out a few boxes on the top of the form, then dropped the clipboard into a box where several others waited. She looked my way.

"I'm trying to find out why the drugstore's closed." I pointed in the general direction of Madison Street. "Westerfield's."

"Hold on." She dropped the rest of the photocopies into a box marked: "Extras," then grabbed a clipboard. "Dr. Lutton!" she called.

An old man stepped behind the counter. He must have been pushing eighty. His hair was as white as snow, his face a wispy chalk marked with slender blue lines. He was wearing a white lab coat, spotted with blood. A stethoscope hung around his neck. A fat, smoldering cigar jutted out of a corner of his mouth.

"This gentleman has some questions," the nurse said as she handed him the clipboard.

"Who you?" he croaked with the cigar still in his mouth.

"I'm trying to find someone over at Westerfield's."

"Madison Street," he said.

"It's all locked up," I explained.

He took the cigar out of his mouth and gave me a big brown smile. "Yeah. Gene ran away with his tail between his legs." He looked down at the clipboard. "Mulvey!" he shouted. The old man with the swollen face got up from the bench and staggered forward.

"Why's the drugstore closed?"

"Better ask Gene Westerfield," Dr. Lutton said.

"You have any idea where I might find him?"

"That's the sixty-four-thousand-dollar question," he said.

"How about Irv Kaplan? Anything you can tell me about that?"

"Irv," he said softly, and he shook his head. "Irv's dead. Look, buddy, I got patients backed up. Come by some other time." He looked down at the clipboard. "Mulvey!" he shouted again.

"Right here," the old man mumbled. He could barely open his mouth. And compared to Dr. Lutton he wasn't old at all.

"You're drunk," Lutton said. I could smell the whiskey.

"Think I'd come in here sober?"

"Come on," Lutton said. He grabbed Mulvey's shoulder and pulled him toward the back.

Nurse Hennessy was watching me with steady gray eyes. "Anything you can tell me about Irv Kaplan?" I asked.

"Talk to Dr. Lutton."

"How about Dr. Z.?" I asked. "Is he in today?"

"Dr. Z. is no longer associated here."

I headed back toward the penny arcade. Just to the right of the door was a small alcove. A man was standing behind a counter watching me. He was wearing a jacket with "Security" printed across the chest and he was, by far, the healthiest-looking specimen in the room. A brass name tag and a silver star were pinned to his blue shirt. I nodded my head and angled his way. He pointed toward the front door, then followed me outside.

"Nothing like fresh air," he said as I lit a cigarette. His name tag said: "Dolan." "You still Homicide?"

I shook my head, then flashed my license.

"You don't remember me, do you?"

"Sorry," I said.

"No reason you would, really. Me and my partner were the ones who found that little boy in the Columbus Park lagoon."

"Oh, yeah," I said. "What was his name, Matthew something?"

"Wallace," Dolan remembered. "Matthew Wallace."

"That's it," I remembered. Matthew Wallace wasn't quite two years old when he'd disappeared from a backyard barbecue. He'd ended up facedown in the lagoon, a half-mile from home. There were no signs of violence or abuse. Nothing. Not one single witness. Could he have walked a half-mile in broad daylight? Or had someone picked him up and thrown him in? The only answer we ever came up with was the one the medical examiner supplied: death by drowning.

"I still wonder how he got there," Dolan said.

"One more mystery," I agreed. "Like Irv Kaplan."

"Who?"

"The pharmacist that got hit at Westerfield's." I pointed that way. "I thought you'd know all about it."

"Really. Right there. A hit?" He seemed genuinely surprised. "This is my first day here. I'm just filling in for a buddy."

"Was he here Saturday?"

"Either him or one of the other guys," Dolan said; then he hesitated. "Look, if you're not on the job, I don't know if I should really be talking to you."

"Most of what I do is Police Board work," I said. "And, believe me, I don't work for the board."

He smiled. "I might need your services someday."

"Let's hope not."

"So this hit is a Police Board case?"

"It's a little peripheral. Probably nothing at all. But I'd sure like to talk to your friend."

He hesitated, and I knew what he was thinking. Cops hated giving other cops' names away. "Gabriel," he said after a while. "Jack Gabriel. But he might not have been here. There's five, six guys rotate through. But Jack'll be able to tell you. I know he's on tomorrow. The afternoon watch at Fifteen."

"Thanks. What is this, anyway, straight security?"

He shrugged. "Just try and keep order, I guess. But hell, you saw, women and kids. It's funny. These guys have been bragging for years. Telling me it's the best off-duty job in the department. And hey, the pay's great. But I don't think I'll be coming back."

"Why not?"

"It's too depressing. I mean, everybody's sick, right?"

I shrugged. "It's a medical center."

"Let me ask you something: if your kid was sick would you bring him here?"

I didn't have to think long before shaking my head.

"These people must be blind," he said. "There's a doc in there, must be a hundred years old. Oh, well, I better get back, case anybody loses a quarter in a pinball machine."

"See you around," I said. "Thanks."

He opened the front door. "I wish I'd taken my vitamins this morning," he said, and went back inside.

FIFTEEN

Back in the Olds, I looked at that list of names I'd gotten from the business cards, then picked up the phone. I caught Mike Brewer, the Public Aid investigator, as he was walking out the door. He agreed to meet for a quick drink.

Before long, I was gliding along on that ribbon of fresh concrete through the old Skid Row. There wasn't a wino or a flophouse in sight. Every other corner sported new construction. There were loft conversions, sports bars, and restaurants with detailed wine lists that didn't include a single bottle of muscatel.

The police dispatch center was another addition to Madison Street. It was a large, glossy-looking place. Somewhere inside was the tape of a 911 call reporting the shooting of a pickup truck. I hadn't heard the tape, but I'd read a summary. I'd also knocked on Raymond Purcell's door in Canaryville, and it would be wise to try again soon. Shelly and her law firm were my number-one client. They weren't exciting, but they paid the bills.

Mike Brewer was leaning against the bar at Berghoff's, a Loop restaurant with the city's oldest liquor license. He was between one group in pinstripes and another in slacks and tourist T-shirts. They were all giving him plenty of room, as if whatever he had might be contagious. He was a slight guy with a bad complexion and crooked teeth. His eyeglasses were held together with tape.

His sports coat was ragged, his shoes down at the heels.

"You guys never lose that look," he said as we shook hands. On the phone, I'd told him I'd once been a cop.

"Bourbon rocks!" I called to a passing bartender, an old-timer in a black jacket and a long white apron. "Guy hasn't aged a day in ten years," I said as I dropped a twenty on the bar.

"I don't come much anymore," Brewer said. "I liked it better when it was just a joint."

"Cheers," I said when we both had drinks.

Brewer lifted his glass. "You notice how anything good they don't tear down becomes a tourist attraction instead?"

"Don't get me started."

"Yeah," he said. "The whole city's gonna end up an amusement park for suburbanites. Daleyland. But you're right. Let's not get started or they'll have to roll us out of here. So what's your interest in Gene Westerfield?"

"You actually know him?"

"Christ, I've been trying to build a case on him for years."

"Clean Gene?"

"That's his story," Brewer said. "And you gotta give him credit. He's been getting away with it forever. The man's not stupid. He's got so many games and he keeps switching them around. He knows we look for patterns so he keeps changing. By the time we figure out one he's on to another. But he's greedy and that's why we'll get him. That and a new computer program we're about to put in. A guy who's not stupid or greedy we never catch."

"Give me an example."

He smiled. "Let's remember: this is an exchange. Tell me something I don't know. Like what're you working on?"

"A missing persons case."

"Who's missing?"

"Jimmy Madison."

"Gene's good luck charm?"

"How's that?"

"His one good deed. Every time I talk to him he makes it a point to tell me how he's sending this poor ghetto kid through medical school. He'd rather talk about that than answer my questions about his business."

"Like for instance?"

"I'll give you my favorite. Cotton balls."

"Cotton balls?"

"Yeah. Until we stopped him a few years back, everybody got cotton balls. Didn't matter what ailed them, they got cotton balls, too. They prescribed so many cotton balls they had a stamp made up so they wouldn't have to write it out every time."

"How'd you stop 'em?"

"This is classic. Instead of going after Westerfield, we told the entire state we won't pay for cotton balls or alcohol swabs anymore. So now if you're a diabetic and you need swabs, tough luck, you're on your own."

"How much can you make on cotton balls?" I asked.

"Hardly anything, if you're legit. But what if you don't actually dispense the cotton balls? Now you're getting a couple of dollars a pop and your only cost is ink for the stamp pad. And because it's such a low-cost item, it was way under our radar. But he was charging us for hundreds of boxes a week. Do the math. Multiply it by fifty-two, then multiply that by the years he got away with it. It's probably how he paid for his Mercedes."

I took a sip of bourbon.

"And where does he find these doctors?" Brewer went on. "He must have an ad somewhere. 'Desperate MDs needed. Junkies, alcoholics, please apply, as long as you're licensed.' He actually had a suspected war criminal working for him. I'm not kidding. Some Austrian. Westerfield didn't care.

"He had one clown used to be on staff at Near North. One day he's doing a cesarean and he cuts the mother's femoral artery. By the time he lets the nurse call for help, the woman's bled to death. Young woman. Three kids, including the baby. The hospital revokes his operating privileges, but he's still got his license and he ends up working for Gene."

"I don't get what Westerfield needs doctors for."

"You happen to notice that medical center behind the store?"

"Westerfield owns it?"

"See, if I could prove that I might get some help from the U.S. Attorney's office."

"How does he hide ownership?"

"Easiest thing in the world. There's nothing more desperate than a doctor without money. They didn't go to medical school to be poor. You give him enough, he'll sign his name anywhere you want."

"Who's Dr. Z.?" I asked.

"Dr. John Zailradenik. What do you know about him?"

"Somebody threw him out the door of the medical center. He went over to the drugstore and they threw him out of there, too."

"Maybe he started to think he really did own the place. But don't worry. Gene'll find some new patsy."

"How about Dr. Lutton?"

He shook his head. "Nobody I know."

"So what we're talking about is welfare fraud?"

"It's a fine line between fraud and abuse and Gene plays both sides. Fraud, you don't perform the services at all. Abuse, you perform them or pretend to, but they aren't really necessary. Nobody who goes in that medical center sees only one doctor. At least not on paper. And every doctor they bill as a separate charge. And whether you come out with a prescription or not, the state of Illinois is charged for one. Usually at least three or four. Sometimes seven and eight. Everybody. And guess where these scripts are filled? That's right. Not Walgreen's, baby. No way.

"And who are we to question a doctor's diagnosis? And frequently the patients won't cooperate. A lot of marginal people have Public Aid cards. Prostitutes, crack heads, you name it. And sometimes they're in on it. They fake the symptoms for whatever drugs they want and then sell 'em to a crooked pharmacy or on the street. We found one place, you give 'em your card, they give you credit at a liquor store. They were charging the state hundreds of dollars for drugs and their only cost was a bottle of booze. And they don't even have to buy the booze for the renewal. They can run that through without the patient."

"You could do it with anything," I said. "I mean, it wouldn't have to be booze. It could be CDs or something like that."

"Sure," he agreed. "Years ago one place was giving out cigarettes."

"How about controlled substances?"

He shook his head. "They're too easy to track, too much paperwork. Gene's operation pushes a lot of expensive brand names. Prilosec for ulcers. Seldane for allergies. Prozac for depression. Propulsid for heartburn. None of 'em come cheap, believe me. Now a lot of places charge us for the brand name and dispense the generic, or they'll find some cut-rate generic that we're paying top dollar for and push the hell out of it. That's almost standard operating procedure now. But Gene, I'll bet he's not dispensing anything at least fifty percent of the time. Just paper. And it's not just drugs. There's all the over-the-counter stuff we pay for, too. Laxatives, throat lozenges, rubbing alcohol, ice bags, heating pads, vaporizers. You prescribe one or two for every patient, it adds up. Especially if you don't actually dispense them."

"Like the cotton balls."

"Exactly. But a vaporizer's a hell of a lot more expensive. It's almost a perfect crime. Abuse the poor. You can't go wrong. Here." He dropped a ten on the bar. "It must be my round."

I waved the bartender over. "Sprinkle the infield," I said, and I pushed my own money out front. "If you know all this, how come he's not in jail?"

"Oh, boy, where do I start? Part of the problem is we assume these practitioners are honest. All we require is the numbers off the Public Aid card and the patient's date of birth, and that's on the card, too. We don't ask the patients to sign anything. It's pretty much an honor system."

"Really?"

"The story I heard is that years ago somebody decided that by making them sign we were treating Public Aid patients like second-class citizens. Now they're virtually the only ones who don't sign. Most insurance companies, most third-party payers demand a signature."

"So once you've got the patient's aid card you can put those numbers on as many scripts as you want. And you can make a copy of the card and send it through a few weeks later as a follow-up visit and a renewal. And, since we don't send copies of the vouchers to the patients, they can't say, 'Hey, I never got those drugs' or 'those tests. I never saw that doctor. I never had any follow-up visit.'

"The patient doesn't know he's been cheated or used, however you want to put it. We go out when the paperwork finally clears and say, 'Did you get your medicine? Did you get your throat lozenges?' Well, even if they say no, even if they're sure they didn't, how can you prove it? The prescription's run its course. And who are we going to believe? A doctor? A pharmacist with a big house on the North Shore? Or some welfare recipient from the projects? Who's a jury going to believe? For that matter, who would you believe?"

He took a sip of his drink. "Gene's a slippery guy and, to be honest, my office doesn't like getting wet. Psychiatrists. That's their current flavor. Why? Because they're easy. They charge by the hour and there's only so many hours in the day. So when we spot a guy billing for twenty-six hours it's open-and-shut. We don't have to investigate.

"And if it was just Westerfield, it'd be easier. But it's not. This is a massive statewide problem. Anywhere poor people live, somebody's making money. I'm not entirely convinced that there isn't one enormous syndicate that controls the entire city."

"You ever hear of Prospect Drugs?" I asked.

"On Sixty-third Street?"

I nodded.

"What's this got to do with Westerfield?"

"Nothing as far as I know."

"So what's your interest?"

"Just curious," I said.

"You know, for an ex-cop you're not much of a liar."

"So they're doing the same things as Westerfield?"

"They've got wrinkles down there that Gene hasn't even dreamed of yet. But that's all I can tell you unless you give me more."

"When I know more," I said.

We sipped our drinks. On our right the pinstripes were talking about the best type of all-terrain vehicle to buy. "So they can drive around the jungles of the North Shore and Lincoln Park," I said. But Brewer wasn't paying attention.

"A couple years back I had the bright idea that the way to investigate a guy like Westerfield was to send undercover agents in posing as patients," he said. "It takes me a year to convince the bosses. They finally decide they'll give me one agent. Then it takes me months to put it together, get through all the red tape and get her an aid card. Now this is one tough girl, born and raised in the projects, managed to get herself through college and then a master's. Her very first day, I send her into this medical center on Roosevelt Road, and she's in there an hour and she had to leave. She said it was the dirtiest place she'd ever been in her life. Half the docs don't speak English; the rest look like refugees from horror films. Everybody's sick, coughing, throwing up, and she was terrified that she would get sick, too. So that's it, more than a year of work down the drain. But you know what? I don't blame her. You look at some of these doctors, I wouldn't let them stick a needle in me, either."

"Any idea what the FBI was doing at Westerfield's?"

"When was this?"

"Earlier today."

"Christ, I hate those sons-of-bitches. They never let you in on anything."

"Everybody hates 'em," I said. "There was a *Tribune* reporter down there, too. Olmstead. Know anything about him?"

"John? He's the guy discovered Westerfield."

"How's that?"

"He went down to Springfield and went through the Public Aid vouchers by hand. Took him damn near a month."

"Will he talk to me?"

"I'll give him a call."

"What's the chances you can get me a list of the patients that had prescriptions filled at Westerfield's on October twenty-first?"

"What's so special about October twenty-first?"

"The day Irv Kaplan got murdered."

"You think that had something to do with Public Aid?"

"I was thinking if there were people filling prescriptions in the store maybe they saw something."

"I might be able to come up with some names."

"How about a list of the people in the store yesterday?"

"No way," he said. But then he thought about it. "Well, maybe," he said. "See, here's the funny thing. Usually it takes forever to get your money out of Public Aid. That's why a lot of the legit stores don't even bother. If you're an honest practitioner and you're in Medicaid, you're being screwed. Sometimes I think we force people to cheat. But certain people get paid."

"The crooks," I guessed.

"You know what factoring is?"

I shook my head.

"Sort of like a collection agency," he said. "They buy your accounts at a discount and pay you immediately. The difference is, a collection agency is buying bad debts."

"Why sell good debts?"

"You get your money right away. A lot of legitimate providers have gone bankrupt waiting for the state of Illinois to cut a check. So they'll sell the accounts at a discount, say ten, twenty percent. But they get their percentage that same day instead of having to wait months for Springfield."

"Twenty percent," I said. "That's a lot of money."

"But what if the factoror doesn't wait two months? What if his bills go to the head of the line down in Springfield?"

"Drop a few dollars here and there."

"The right connections, you don't need money."

"Who's that?"

"Just rumors," he said softly, and he looked into his glass. "Nothing I can pin down. But the math is fascinating. Say all you had in the world was eight thousand dollars. And you used it to buy ten grand worth of accounts."

"OK."

"And a couple of days later we cut you a check for ten grand."

"So you just made two grand."

"A twenty-five percent return in a couple of days. Then you take the ten grand, now you can buy twelve thousand, five hundred dollars' worth of accounts. And when that money comes in you can buy almost sixteen grand worth of accounts. So you've almost doubled your money in three transactions. And it might only take you a couple of weeks. So maybe in a couple of days those vouchers from yesterday will turn up in Springfield. Here's the funny thing: Westerfield just started factoring his account. He never did it before."

"He must need money," I said.

"I heard he's on vacation," Brewer said.

"Venice supposedly."

"Oh, boy, I'm in the wrong line of work." He took a sip of his drink and got a strange faraway look in his eyes. I thought he might be floating down a canal on a perfect moonlit evening, a beautiful woman at his side. A moment later, the gondola sank and Brewer was back at the bar.

"Sometimes I wonder why I bother," he said. "I'm not too old to change careers. Make some money. It'd be nice to take the wife out on the town every so often." He held up his glass. "This is a big treat. Good liquor. A nice room. Thanks. I shouldn't be letting you buy all the drinks, but thanks."

"Cheers." I held up my own glass.

"You know what the worst thing is? Say everything goes right and we build a nice, tight case and get Gene convicted. You know how much time he'll do? My bet, six months tops. And if he's lucky he'll walk with a fine and probation. But he'll still have that big house and his daughter'll still end up being a doctor so she can take care of him in his old age. And you know if I asked these guys here"—he gestured toward the pinstripes—"if I laid out the whole case for 'em and asked them who they respect more, me or Westerfield, ninety-nine percent of 'em, if they're honest, would vote for Gene. The only thing matters is who's got the cash."

I waved for the bartender, but Brewer stopped me. "Time to go home to the wife and kids."

"Thanks for your help," I said. "If I don't hear from you, I'll call."

"And I'll be looking forward to hearing all about Prospect Drugs."

"Sure."

"You ever been to Europe?" he asked.

I shook my head.

"Me, either. Forty-two and I've never been anywhere. You believe that? I'd like to go once before I check out. Just once. Climb to the top of the Eiffel Tower and stand there and look down on the lights of Paris. I hear it's quite a sight."

SIXTEEN

CANARYVILLE was a couple of blocks off the highway, a few miles south of the Loop. It was a small working-class enclave, one of those places where a low-level city job was almost considered a birthright. Finding one that required little or no actual toil was the neighborhood equivalent of hitting the lottery. The checks kept coming forever, or until your clout disappeared.

The place had once been almost exclusively Irish. But now there were pockets of Appalachian whites, a sprinkling of Mexicans, and a couple of stray Italian families that had somehow got lost on their way to Twenty-sixth Street.

Huge trucks were everywhere. They lumbered by in every direction, crept under viaducts with their flashers going, double-parked in front of diners, made wide turns, blasted their horns, and sent dark streams of diesel exhaust into the air, turning a sunny autumn afternoon into just another gloomy Canaryville day.

There was an elusive fragrance hidden behind the stench of diesel fuel, some sweet scent that I couldn't quite identify.

I turned into an alley behind Emerald Avenue. There was a shuttered factory on one side. Across the way stood an old two-story barn. If you pulled into the trash-cluttered parking area behind the factory, it might appear to be the perfect spot to take a shot at your own truck. A perfect spot, if you didn't happen to notice the fluttering window shade on the first floor of the barn.

I parked right under the window, got out, and watched the shade drop back into place. I opened a freshly painted gate and stepped into a small, well-tended yard. A sidewalk, bordered by flowers, led to a tidy brick house, a small postwar bungalow.

I looked around for the old farmhouse that must have once accompanied the barn. But it had been torn down or remodeled beyond recognition, or it was somewhere blocks away, just a short walk across the old pasture.

A handwritten sign, tacked to the barn, said: "Bikes For Sale." I pushed a doorbell. "It's open!" a gruff voice called.

It was a big, open room, which smelled of oil and damp, rotting wood. All the shades were pulled down tight, the windows closed. Daylight splashed around the edges of the shades and seeped in through numerous cracks in the exposed wood-slatted walls, leaving the room in a misty half-light.

An exhaust fan was making a racket up in the old hayloft, but it seemed warmer inside than out. The floor was crowded with secondhand bicycles. Adult bikes were on one side, kids' bikes on the other. The center of attention was a beautiful red-and-white Schwinn with a shock absorber on the front fork. It was sitting all alone on a stack of forklift pallets, bathed in the glow of an aluminum work light.

The walls and the rafters were dotted with old license plates and city street signs. Unadorned bicycle frames hung here and there. Shelves and milk crates were crammed with bike parts, chains, sprockets, handlebars, seats, and pedals.

An old man was working on a rusty three-speed. He was wearing a long-sleeved thermal shirt, baggy jeans, and heavy work boots. But that wasn't quite hot enough. He'd added a khaki hat to keep any heat from escaping. It was soaked with sweat.

"Mr. Purcell?" I asked.

"That's the name," he said without looking up. "Don't wear it out."

"I want to ask you a couple of questions about what happened out back last week."

He sighed loudly, spun the front tire of the bike, watched it wobble for a moment, then picked a towel off a workbench and wiped sweat from a pasty, liver-spotted face. He looked damn good for seventy-five, and he still had a bit of thunder in his voice. "Where are all you guys when the local hoodlums are trying to kick the door down?"

I didn't say anything to that. If he wanted to think I was a cop, now wasn't the time to complain.

"Here." He picked a wrench off the workbench. "Make yourself useful. Tighten that wheel."

I tightened one nut. "Other side," he said. I followed directions. "Can't give it that last turn anymore." He held out a trembling hand and we both watched it shake, then I dropped the wrench into it.

I held out my own hands and he handed me an oil-stained rag and I added a little more to it. The rag had a nice smell about it.

"Little honest work never hurt anyone," Purcell said, as if he could read my mind.

"How much you want for that old Schwinn?" I pointed toward the bike with the shock absorber.

"Not for sale," he said, and I could hear him saying the same words a thousand times before.

"How 'bout that?" I pointed to the one he'd been working on. It was another Schwinn, a woman's model, with blue-and-white fenders and a wire basket on the front.

"Rest are all the same," he said. "Thirty for kids' bikes, fifty for adults. But I don't sell out of the neighborhood."

"No?"

"Not anymore. Had a couple of fellows coming every couple of weeks. Turns out they were selling 'em up north as antiques, two, three hundred dollars a pop."

"Really?"

"Two, three hundred dollars. I remember when you could buy a car for that kind of money. A good car."

I pointed at the bike with the shock absorber. "Must be worth a small fortune," I said.

"Like I said, it's not for sale. Now let's hear these questions you were talking about. I ain't got all day."

"I'm here as a friend of Officer Grace."

"Grace. Who he?"

"Guy who started this whole mess." I pointed toward the alley. He looked confused. "I'm not sure I get you."

"Officer Grace," I said. "He was driving that pickup truck."

He sat down on an old kitchen chair. Suddenly he almost looked his age. "He's a cop?" he asked softly.

I nodded.

"Well, what'd he shoot that truck for?"

"Long story," I said.

"Think a cop would have more sense than to buy Japanese."

"I agree," I said.

"Never will understand that. Killed lots of boys. Marched my uncle to death. Bataan. To his death. And I'm supposed to buy their cars and their toaster ovens and their microwaves. Forgive and forget. Not this boy." He pushed himself up from the chair and pointed a finger at his chest. "Not this boy."

"I agree," I said again.

"So what was so wrong with that truck, he had to shoot it?"

"Wish it was that simple," I said. And I told my story.

It was basically the same one Grace had told the police. The station wagon had run a light and crashed into his truck. When Grace got out the driver of the wagon started shooting and then took off. Grace shot back, then ran to his pickup. But his rear bumper had been knocked loose in the crash. By the time he got it tied up, the Chevy was long gone.

"That doesn't make a damn bit of sense," the old man said when I was done. "If they really took a shot at him, why'd this Grace fellow have to pull in here?"

"You have to remember this happened on the other side of the highway," I said. The other side of the highway was black.

"Yeah?"

"The guy took a shot and missed," I said. "Grace shot back, but he was the only white guy anywhere around."

"Oh, I see what you're getting at," he murmured.

"Tracy just wanted a little insurance in case everybody forgot to mention that the other guy fired first."

"Tracy?"

"Tracy Grace. Known him since we were kids."

"So I messed your friend up, did I?"

"Not your fault," I said.

"His own damn fault, you ask me."

"You're right," I said, and I went into one of my standard spiels. "But they're trying to throw him off the force, Mr. Purcell, and he's a good cop. He made a bit of a mistake here and he knows it. But it would be a shame to see him lose his job."

"So it's not too late," he said, and there was a promising twinkle in his eyes. "That's why you're here."

"Well . . ."

"So tell me what I can do."

"Well, if your memory wasn't so good, it might help. Maybe you're not sure you really saw a gun. Maybe what you heard was a car backfiring. Maybe Tracy just stopped to take a leak."

"Be surprised how often that happens," the old man said. "Son of a bitches think it's an outhouse back here some nights."

"Maybe I could get a statement out of you today," I said.

"A statement," he said, and the word hung there a long moment; then he tried it out again. "A statement. Yeah. Maybe you could. Tell me this: what's a cop make nowadays?"

I shrugged. This was something I tried never to think about. "What's that got to do with anything?"

"Forty, fifty grand, somewhere in there," he answered his own question. "Kid next door's been on three years he's over forty already. But your friend's been on a good long time. So he does better than that. Let's call it a grand even. What do you say?"

"Huh?"

"One week's pay. It ought to be worth that?"

"You're putting me on, right?"

"I know I'd be willing to pay a little to keep those big, fat checks coming in."

"I know you're putting me on," I said. "Christ, we could both go to jail for something like that. And anyways, Tracy hasn't got it. He had to take out a second mortgage just to pay his lawyer."

"Five hundred," he said softly.

"I'll tell you what," I let him off the hook. "We'll buy one bike. North Side prices, two hundred, and forget about delivery."

"Two-fifty." He was back in familiar territory.

"Sold."

"You had me going there for a while." He smiled.

I pulled my roll out and gave it a quick count. "I'm a little short," I said.

"If you want, catch me at work tomorrow, Division of Sign and Marking."

"Jesus, you're seventy-five and you're still working?"

"Seventy-five? Where'd you get that? Be fifty-eight January the third."

"Somebody gave you a couple of years," I said.

"You really thought I was seventy-five?" he asked, and something strange happened to his eyes. He sat down slowly. "Christ," he whispered, "I'd be the oldest guy in the neighborhood, you know that?" He held out his hands and we both watched them shake.

I opened the door and the sunlight was almost blinding. "I'll be right back," I said, but he didn't appear to hear. The sun had found his hands. Shadows flickered on the walls.

There was a truck stop over on Halsted Street, a place left over from Canaryville's boom days, when the stockyards had started right here. I found a bank machine inside and slipped my card into it.

A thin guy in jeans, cowboy boots, and a leather vest was talking into a nearby pay phone. "The money ain't here in two hours, you can find someone else drive that piece of shit back." He slammed the phone down, then turned to watch as the bank machine spit out a stack of crisp twenties. "Goddamn, that looks good," he said.

"If only I could keep it," I said.

"Damn, I hate the East." He kicked a trash can and walked away.

There were several trucks idling outside, sending more diesel exhaust into the haze. The sweet scent was stronger now, sickeningly sweet. I could almost put a flavor to it but not quite.

Purcell was back working on the bike. I counted out $250 and dropped it on the workbench. "I'm waiting on a call," he said, and he left the money sitting there. "Smoke 'em if you got 'em."

I lit a cigarette and sat on the kitchen chair and watched the smoke rise to the exhaust fan and disappear. I wondered if Purcell had someone who came in regularly to give the nuts that final turn.

"What's that smell?" I asked after a while.

"Just try to ignore it," he said. But then a few moments later he lifted his nose into the air. "I think that's supposed to be raspberry. Artificial flavor factory, other side of Halsted. It's funny, in the old days, people always complained about the smell from the stockyards. But if you lived here you hardly even noticed. Same smell every day. These flavors keep changing. The butterscotch is the only one smells real, everything else just chemicals, you ask me."

The phone rang. Purcell picked it up. "Yeah," he said, then listened for a while. "Gang Crimes south," he said. "Maybe I can get 'em to come up here. . . . No, just kidding. I'll tell you later. Thanks, Frank."

He hung up. "Thought you might be pulling my chain, your friend's a cop," he said. He picked up the money, counted it, and slipped it into a pocket.

"Never be too sure," I said. "Mr. Purcell, I'm an investigator for the law firm of Siegel and McGovern. I'd like to ask you a few questions."

He reached out to shake my hand. "I heard you might be by," he said. His hand was cold and trembled lightly. His lips twisted into a cozy, knowing leer. He winked and I wondered what my own face revealed.

SEVENTEEN

No wonder Becky didn't trust me, I thought, as I headed north. I'd spent the last few years collecting volumes of lies for Shelly. Why would anybody trust me? I probably reeked of fraud and deception.

I had a sudden impulse to hold Purcell's statement out the window and let the wind take it. But the urge passed quickly. I'd be out $250 for the bike, plus a couple of billable hours. And, worse, I'd be letting the Police Board win.

My clients right or wrong. Who cared if they shook down drug dealers, shot little old ladies for jaywalking, or emptied their weapons at cars fleeing fender benders? We were all on the same side of that thin blue line. Wasn't that what mattered?

Of course, Purcell's statement wouldn't necessarily be enough to keep Tracy Grace on the job. But it would muddy the water a bit. The Police Board would also look at Purcell's previous statement and listen to a tape of his 911 call. The Office of Professional Standards would take their own statement from Jimmy—if they ever found him, that is—and if the new statement conflicted with the old, well, that wasn't necessarily bad news.

The conflicting statements would give the Police Board an easy out. The rank and file generally professed nothing but hatred for the board. But frequently they'd give a cop the benefit of the doubt. Not always, but often enough to keep people like me in business. People who knew how to manufacture doubt.

I drove downtown, dropped the statement in the night drop at Shelly's LaSalle Street office, then headed for Bucktown.

Lights were burning in the windows above the Gare du Nord. I parked, killed my lights, picked up the phone, and started to dial Becky's number.

The front door of the Gare du Nord opened and a man came out with a piece of paper flapping in his hand. He was tall, muscular, and black. He came down the steps lightly, without a care in the world. His eyes passed over the Olds without a flicker of interest. But that was just part of the show. He hadn't missed a thing.

He taped the paper to the restaurant window—MISSING/RE-WARD were the only words I could read—then walked to the side entrance of the building, reached toward the doorbells, and disappeared inside. I put the phone down. A few minutes later, I crossed the street.

A picture of Jimmy Madison was on the top of the poster. He was standing on the breezeway at the Horner Homes. **For information leading to the whereabouts of James Madison. Big reward,** was in bold letters and underlined twice.

The phone number looked familiar. I flipped through my notebook and found it. The business card had said: "William Harris, private detective." But the brothers at the tire shop had called him Wet Willie. I turned and walked into the restaurant.

It was almost seven and the place was fairly crowded. It was a mixed group, mostly suits and ties and dresses, but there were several pairs of jeans and even one cowboy hat.

The hostess was an older woman, small and very French. She seemed disappointed to see me. When I pointed toward the nearly empty bar, she suddenly cheered up. She smiled, bowed slightly, and gestured. I interpreted this to mean that I would be welcome at the bar, but only at the bar.

The bartender was working the levers at a big, steaming espresso machine. She looked my way, smiled, and held up one finger.

Someone was singing "Ten Cents a Dance." I thought it might be Abbey Lincoln, but with the noise of the room it was hard to be sure. Whoever it was knew how to break hearts.

I dropped a twenty on the bar and lit a cigarette. The bartender arrived. "What'll it be?" she asked, making it all one word. She smiled to let me know it was just a gag.

"Beer," I said. I could joke, too.

"Would you care to elaborate?" She pointed toward a placard with a list of beers, along with wines sold by the glass.

I shook my head. "You decide."

She was tall and slender, with narrow hips. Her hair wasn't much longer than a crew cut. She wore a plain white T-shirt that hung with barely a ripple and a black vest and pants. She opened the sliding door of a cooler, looked down, then back up. "I'm thinking domestic," she said, and came up with a bottle of Huber.

"Wow," I said. I hadn't seen Huber in years.

She held the bottle with both hands, as if she were presenting a fine wine. I nodded my head. She opened the bottle and poured just a bit into a highball glass. I tasted it and nodded my head again. She smiled and filled the glass.

A waiter came up. "Ordering!" he called. The bartender went to work. She was good. Fast but not flashy. She didn't use a shot glass and her pours were generous, but not enough to send you crashing into a tree on the way home.

The waiter waited with a pout on his face. He was a smooth-looking guy with a streaked blond pompadour. He was dressed in simple black and white, just like the bartender, but he didn't look a bit sexy. He looked like a priest balancing a lemon meringue pie on his head. He went away with his drinks.

The bartender emptied my ashtray. "Great song," I said. Sarah Vaughan was singing "Broken-Hearted Melody."

"I hate it." She crossed her arms, ready for a fight.

"How can you hate Sarah Vaughan?"

"They play the same tapes over and over and over and over."

"Well, that just means you gotta bring your own in."

"Jazz only. It's so boring. I like real music."

I shrugged. "You need better speakers."

"I need more than that," she said, and she went away and left me wondering.

I was almost through with my beer when she came by to polish the bar. "What's with that poster outside?" I asked.

"This is so spy-versus-spy."

"Huh?"

"One detective following another."

"Who's a detective?"

She pointed at me.

"Really?" I said.

She nodded. "You were following Becky yesterday."

"I was?"

"You parked right there." She pointed out the window. "And then you came over here"—she pointed toward the side entrance of the building—"and started scribbling in a notebook. And then you pretended to read the newspaper."

"And you turned me in."

She shrugged. "And then Becky hired you. And your name is Nick. And you're really nice. And you used to be a cop. And your last name is something Greek, but you're not really Greek."

"You know my whole life story. I don't even know your name."

She reached out her hand. "Patrice," she said.

Her hand was cool, her fingers long and narrow, no rings or other jewelry. I didn't want to let the hand go. "Now about this other detective?" I asked, and the coolness slipped away.

She shrugged. "He asked if he could put a poster in the window. I said it was OK."

"What's he doing upstairs?"

"I imagine he's talking to Becky. She's so lucky. She's got two big detectives to protect her." She winked and walked down the bar and started polishing a cognac snifter.

She stretched to slide the snifter into a rack above the bar. Her vest hung open and I could see the slight curve of her breasts. There looked to be more hair under her arm than on top of her head. Maybe I'm not old-fashioned enough. But from where I sat, the look was very, very sexy. I swiveled around to keep from getting overexcited.

On the wall next to the front door there was a large, dark oil painting. A couple is sitting in an otherwise empty restaurant. Plates clutter their table, along with empty glasses of every variety and a flock of empty wine bottles.

The couple is obviously very drunk. Their clothes are disheveled. They sit hunched over a huge, smoldering ashtray, crumpled cigarettes in their hands. A shiny green frog is on the table between them, and next to the frog is a stack of tiny bowls, all empty. The man is waving his empty glass at a waiter. The waiter is pretending not to see.

I walked over and read the card under the painting: "One For My Baby And One More For The Toad, by Ruth Sinclair."

The bartender came up behind me. "It's great, isn't it?"

"That's a lot of work for one joke," I said.

"I can tell you've never worked in a restaurant," she said.

A few minutes later, the sound of not-a-care-in-the-world footsteps came down a nearby stairway. I got up and headed to the back, to a pay phone just outside the kitchen door.

I turned toward the front as Wet Willie walked past outside. I dropped some coins in the slot and dialed Becky's number.

"Hey, yourself," I said after she answered. "Look, I'm in the neighborhood. How about a drink?"

"I'm not really dressed. Why don't you come up? We can talk here. Ring the bell that says: 'Sinclair.' "

Back at the bar, Patrice held up my nearly empty bottle. "Another?" I shook my head. "You are such a coward." She picked up my twenty and carried it to the cash register.

"What time do you get off?" I asked as she set my change down. "I'll buy you a drink at a nice place."

She shook her head, shrugged.

I shrugged back. "Can't blame a guy for trying."

"How about tomorrow night?" she asked.

"Say when."

She gestured at her outfit. "Is this OK or do I need a change of clothes?"

"I know the perfect place," I said.

"I'll bet you do," she said. "Come by about ten-thirty."

"One more floor!" Becky called as I stopped on the third floor for a rest. I followed her voice to the back of the hallway, where a wooden ladder had been bolted at a somewhat relaxed angle. It was outfitted with sides and railings.

"You're out of shape," she said when I got to the top. She was wearing jeans and a white smock, both spattered with paint. Her hair was tied in back.

"What is this?"

"It's an old attic that my friend Ruth turned into an art studio. You should see the light."

It was a big open room, with skylights set into a peaked ceiling. There was a great view of the Kennedy Expressway. Inbound traffic was barely moving.

A large canvas was sitting on an easel. It was partitioned into faint squares. The outline of a familiar-looking building had begun to emerge over the squares, just lines and shadows in very thin paint. "Your dad's store," I said.

"Oh, good, so it can't be that bad. Or did you see the picture?" A large photocopy of the photograph I'd seen earlier that day was sitting on a wooden crate next to a bottle of wine. The photocopy was also partitioned into squares.

"You're a painter?"

"A little. I almost went to art school. I went back and forth my whole senior year. Art school, premed. Art school, premed. I finally decided I could always go to art school later, you know, if I didn't like medicine or something. But it'd be real hard to get into medical school later if art didn't work out."

"Makes sense."

"But you know, I always have to have a painting going. It helps me think, I think. You just get lost in it sometimes and . . . I don't know. My friends make fun of me. They'll be cramming for an exam and I'll be painting away." She picked up a wineglass and took a swig. "Oh, sorry. You want some?"

"Sure," I said. "Why not?" Whiskey, beer, and wine, all I needed was pretzels and I'd have the four food groups.

She walked toward the back, where a stove and refrigerator shared a large platform with a sink and a bathtub, and returned with another glass.

"Have you ever heard of St. Anthony's Medical Center?" I asked.

"No. What about it?"

"It's right behind your father's store." I pointed off canvas. "I heard a rumor that your father owns it."

She shook her head, shrugged, and took another sip of wine. "I don't know. I never heard of it. But I really don't know. The more I think about it, the less I know."

"What?"

"Everything. Maybe you're right. The house, the cars, the tuition. I never really thought about where the money comes from."

"Who have you been talking to?"

She took a sip of the wine. "Oh, just you know." She picked up a slender brush and added another line to the canvas. "What do you think happened to Jimmy?" she asked after a while.

"Hard to say," I said.

"What if he's dead?"

"You think he's dead?"

"I don't know. It's just so hard to imagine him just walking away. The idea of him doing this on purpose doesn't make sense."

"Lots of things don't make sense," I said.

"But you think eventually?"

"What?"

"It will."

"Every case comes to some kind of end. But sometimes the end is you just give up. When I was a cop, we didn't usually get all the answers. That's actually the exception, when you can say, 'This is exactly what happened and why.' "

"How long were you a cop?"

"Just shy of fifteen years."

"Do you miss it?"

"I try not to think about it."

She lifted her glass. "I've got another bottle after this."

"I hate to turn down free liquor, but I've got an appointment in twenty minutes."

"Is it about my dad?"

"Another case," I said. "Look, tomorrow morning I thought I'd try and find Irv Kaplan's widow. Want to come along?"

She shook her head. "I can't."

"I can wait till afternoon, if that's better."

She shook her head again. "Call me tomorrow night, OK?"

EIGHTEEN

TEDDY'S was hidden away in a factory zone off Elston Avenue. There was no sign out front, no name, just a flush of barroom neon barely visible through hazy Plexiglas.

There were a dozen cars parked at the curb. Most had a small Fraternal Order of Police badge somewhere near the rear license plate. A bumper sticker read: SUPPORT YOUR LOCAL POLICE/THEY ARE ARMED AND DANGEROUS.

I rang the doorbell and positioned my face so it could be seen through the small window. A buzzer sounded and I pushed the door and went in to Dean Martin, "Everybody Loves Somebody Sometimes."

There were a dozen drinkers crowded around the front corner. Only three were in uniform, but they were all obviously cops. They were singing along with the jukebox, laughing, and telling stories. But the sound level dropped as I entered. Several of them gave me that blunt gaze that men with badges have been giving strangers since before the invention of gunpowder.

Teddy was behind the bar. He was tall and thin, and as gray as a corpse. He lived above the place and the sun rarely found him. He was well past retirement age, but his plan was to keep pouring until he dropped.

"Hey, Nick, where you been?" he asked, and that was enough to let everybody know I was one of their own.

"Hold on. Let me check!" one of the guys down the bar shouted, and the entire crew roared with laughter.

I picked a stool near the far end. "What's the celebration?" I asked as Teddy reached for the bourbon.

"They haven't let me in on it," he said. "You know, just 'cause you're not on the job doesn't mean you're not welcome."

"Come on, Teddy. I know that."

"What do you hear from Andy?" he asked. My old partner's going-away party had been held in this very room.

"If he's lucky, two more years."

He shook his head in disgust. "Fucking feds."

"I'll drink to that," I said, and I did.

Teddy moved down the bar and spread more drinks around. I went over to the jukebox and punched the numbers for "Autumn Serenade."

It was an old factory bar and Teddy had done little in the way of remodeling. The walls were covered with cheap wood paneling and photographs of cops. There were cops who had become actors, like Dennis Farina. And actors who had played cops, like Betty Thomas. But most of the pictures were from parties. There were pictures from Andy Kelly's going-away party and from my own legal defense fund benefit. In both cases Teddy had donated the booze and we'd taken a donation at the door.

The floor was faded vinyl. When the exhaust fan over the front door kicked in, the smell of bathroom disinfectant filled the room. Even without the fan, the place always smelled faintly of Lysol. But it was a great place to unwind after a particularly tough shift. To tell war stories in private and wait for dawn. Teddy usually stayed open until daylight, unless the local watch commander called to tell him it was time to close.

I was still nursing my drink when the doorbell rang. Teddy looked toward the window. "Now who's this?" he whispered. He didn't want just anybody spending money in his saloon.

"Probably the guy I'm waiting for," I said, and Teddy pushed the buzzer and a pale redhead walked in with a big smile plastered on his face. He was an inch or two under six feet, with the well-developed chest of a weight lifter. But he'd been neglecting his legs. He looked like the guy on the outside of the peanut can.

The group by the front turned his way and then a woman in uniform waved: "Hey, Trace!"

His smile got even wider. "Paula, baby. How they hanging?"

Paula stood up. "Hold on. Let me check." She reached down, felt her crotch, and shrugged. "Oh, well, too bad. Looks like they got those, too."

The entire group collapsed in laughter. They couldn't talk. They fell off their stools. Drinks and stools were knocked over. A couple of guys ended up on the floor.

Grace stood there with a puzzled look on his face, but none of them paid any attention. They were lost in their private joke. After a moment he turned my way. "I hope you're Nick." I nodded my head and waved him over. We shook hands. "I'm not usually that funny," he said.

"Don't worry," I said. "They've been doing that every couple of minutes."

Teddy cleaned up the spills, then came down our way. I made introductions. "Last time I was here was for a benefit for Bob Foley," Grace said.

Foley was another of Shelly's clients. One night he'd decided a gangbanger needed a little street justice and locked him in the trunk of his squad car. This is not as unusual as it might sound. The unusual part came when Foley forgot to let the banger out at the end of his shift. By the time the next shift found him, hours later, the banger had almost frozen to death. Foley was now operating a hot dog stand on the west coast of Florida. I'd been told he had the best Italian beef in the state.

"Oh, sure," Teddy remembered Grace. "Light beer, right?"

"Hey, good memory," Grace said. "And a Jack on the side. Tonight I need a real drink."

"The POW camp would drive a nun to drink," I said. Teddy raised an eyebrow. "One of Shelly's," I explained.

"Now isn't she a beautiful lady?" Teddy smiled and winked as he dropped a beer in front of Grace.

"Like any other broad," Grace said. "She's beautiful until you have to start writing her checks."

We all drank to that. Grace dropped a ten on the bar and pushed it toward Teddy. "Out of here," he said.

Teddy pushed the money back and gestured down the bar. "Day watch at Fourteen would like to buy you fellows a drink."

We raised our drinks and the group down the bar raised theirs. Teddy walked down and pulled some money from a huge pile.

"Oh, here, before I forget," Grace said, and he handed me an official Chicago Police Department envelope. I slid the report out enough to see "Kaplan, Irving" printed in the box marked: "Victim."

"Thanks," I said, and I slipped it into an inside pocket. "You have any trouble getting it?"

He shook his head. "The sergeant takes a nap every afternoon. I could photocopy an entire file cabinet and he wouldn't know."

"I owe you one."

"Just get me out of that pit."

"Right." I raised my glass and we both drank.

"Let me ask you something," he said. "I couldn't help noticing, this Kaplan guy got hammered in the same store that station wagon was from, right?"

"Yeah."

"So what's that about?"

"I don't get you."

"I mean you're working for Shelly, right?"

I nodded my head.

"So what's this Kaplan got to do with my case? I think I've got a right to ask. I'm the guy who's gonna get stuck paying the bill."

"Relax. The meter's off."

"And if there is some connection, I'd like to know about it. I mean, I'm in enough trouble already."

"I just got a little curious. You know how it goes. Once a dick, always a dick."

"OK," he said. "Just wanted to make sure."

"You miss it?" he asked a while later.

"What?"

"The job."

"Every fucking day," I told him the truth.

"Yeah. I don't know what I'm gonna do if they boot me."

"Just keep your fingers crossed."

"I mean where else you gonna make this kind of money, drive around all day, fucking off?"

"You know how much the pay was when I came on? Eleven grand."

"Jesus Christ, why would you bother?"

I tried to buy the day watch a drink, but instead they bought the house another round. Paula carried her drink down to say hello.

She was a shapely blond. Her hair was cut short, but it was long enough so there was a bit of a bounce and it wasn't a dye job. Her eyes were blue. She was wearing wire-rim glasses that didn't appear to have much of a correction.

"Nick," Grace said. "Meet Paula, my future ex-wife."

"In your dreams, Trace."

"Nick used to be a dick," Grace said. "Paula's on the list."

"Next class," she said. "If they ever call it."

"Where do you want to go?" I asked.

"Violent Crimes. Where else?"

"Good girl," I said. Violent Crimes is what they now called Homicide.

"What's the party all about?" Grace asked.

"Oh, it's right up your alley, Trace." She looked my way. "But I don't know if I should tell it. . . ."

"I'm like a priest," I said.

"He's OK," Grace said. "He's working for my lawyer."

"Well, what happened," Paula said, "a couple of the guys got a burglary call. Neighbor saw somebody coming out the back door with the TV. The guys get there. There's a broken window off the porch. The door's open, but nobody's home. A neighbor comes over and gives 'em the owner's work phone. They call, and he gives them permission to go in. 'What'd they get?' he wants to know. 'The TV, the stereo. Did you have a microwave?' 'Yeah,' he says. 'Not anymore.' 'Did they get the three grand I had hidden in the freezer?' "

"Oh, Jesus," Trace groaned.

Paula pretended she was holding a phone to her ear. " 'Hold on,' " she said. " 'Let me check.' " She opened a freezer door. " 'Sorry, looks like they got that, too.' "

"See why I love this fucking job?" Grace said.

I pulled one of Shelly's cards out and handed it to Paula with a wink. "You might need this someday."

She looked down at the card, then up at me. The smile stayed on her face, but her eyes narrowed a bit. "Thanks," she said.

"You're something else, Nick," Grace said. "You never rolled a stiff, right?"

"Just what I could find under the couch cushions," I said, and it was the truth. I'd never been a money guy.

"Yeah, I believe that," Grace said.

"You mind if I pick your brain about the detective division?" Paula asked.

"Go right ahead," I said.

"I gotta take the monster for a walk," Grace said, and he headed for the washroom.

The smile dropped from Paula's face. "What a fucking snake," she hissed.

"You'll be a good dick," I said.

"Why do you say that?"

"You're a good actor. That's half the job."

"I'm sick of acting. That's what I've been doing all night. That's what I've been doing for years. You really think I approve of stealing someone's life savings?"

"You were doing a pretty good imitation."

"Yeah. Sometimes I don't know if I'm acting or not."

"When you're a dick you won't have to act with your partners. That's for everybody else."

"I'm just so sick of it. Here. You're gonna like this. Guess who I'm married to?"

"The superintendent?"

She shook her head. "A nurse," she said, and she shrugged. "Got it all sort of backward, didn't we?"

"World's spinning backward," I said.

"You know, I could never tell him that story." She lowered her voice almost to a whisper. "He'd want me to turn them in and I could never do that, not in a million years. Why is that?"

"The way it is," I said. And the way it had always been and would always be. You didn't turn your partner in. Even if he did steal some poor sap's last dime.

"And he wouldn't see the humor, either. I mean, forget whether it's right or wrong. It really is a funny story."

"Sure," I agreed. "But I wouldn't want to hear it in a courtroom."

As if on cue, someone down the bar said, "Hold on. Let me check. Ooops. Looks like they got that, too."

"You know, I think he'd actually want a divorce. And you know something? I wouldn't blame him."

"That'll just bring us a little closer," Grace said as he walked up. He put his arm around Paula and tried to pull her close.

She shook him off. "Trace, if you only knew." For a moment, I thought she was really going to tell him. But then the actor took over. She smiled at Grace and sent a wink my way.

"You're not a real cop unless you've been divorced at least once," Grace proclaimed.

"I couldn't agree more!" a cop shouted from down the bar.

"Hey, is my wife still here?" another asked.

"Hold on. Let me check," somebody answered. "So sorry. Looks like they got her, too."

Paula gave a little wave, picked up her drink, and walked down to join the revelry.

I swallowed the remains of my drink and got up to leave.

"Have another," Grace said.

"I better get out while I still can," I said.

"Just one," Grace said. "I want to hear how you worked it with that Purcell guy."

I switched to beer and told him about buying the bicycle that would never be delivered.

"That cocksucker," he spit. "Two hundred and fifty bucks. You tell him the guy was a shine?"

"Just be glad he flipped."

"What kind of white man pulls something like that?"

"One with your money in his pocket."

"Hey, I did a pretty good job on that car, didn't I?"

"What car?"

"That fucking station wagon. Did you see the pattern on that tailgate?" He jumped off his stool and down into a shooting stance. *"Boom! Boom! Boom!"* he shouted, and the whole room turned to watch. "You should have seen those shines on Forty-seventh running for cover."

"You believe they're trying to throw this guy off the force?" Paula asked, and she flashed a smile.

"Get everybody another," someone else said, and a few seconds later Teddy dropped two cool ones in front of us.

Mine went down as easy as water, always a bad sign.

I finally got out of there, leaving Grace with the day watch. The pile of money still had a long way to go.

Outside, I walked over to have a look at Grace's truck. The

passenger window had been replaced. But there was a big dent in the front right quarter-panel and another just beyond the passenger door. A deep gouge ran from the second dent all the way back to where the bumper was held up with several loops of rope.

KEEP HONKING, a bumper sticker read. I'M RELOADING.

NINETEEN

I was living on Clarendon Avenue that year, on the border between a small but wealthy lakefront neighborhood and the
melting pot neighborhood of Uptown, a sprawling place full of
poverty, immigrants, and refugees, who were slowly being
squeezed by creeping gentrification.

The building wasn't much, a ten-story apartment hotel that had
been built during the boom of the twenties and barely kept in
repair since.

I'd moved in three years before, after my marriage had fallen
apart. It was that kind of place. There was almost always a vacancy,
and each apartment came furnished with its very own Murphy bed.
All you needed was sheets and blankets and you could sleep there
the night you signed the lease, or try to sleep while scenes from
whatever you'd run from played out in the darkness.

I'd started with a three-month lease, figuring I'd find something
better before it was up. But I never even looked before renewing
for another six. By the time that lease had run its course, I'd read
the writing on the walls and signed for a full year.

When I was sober I usually took the stairs and counted my heavy
breathing as exercise. But when I'd been drinking I'd take a chance
on the cantankerous gated elevator if it was anywhere around.

When I came in just before midnight—whiskey on my breath
and a six-pack under my arm—the elevator was waiting in the

lobby. I pulled the door open and pushed the gate aside, and then waited while they both closed behind me.

The ascent was slow and loud and then the car stopped with a jerk and I pushed my way into a long, dim hallway, where a series of dark doors waited. Peepholes reflected muted light. Brass knockers waited for visitors who seldom came.

The carpeting, long-worn stripes of maroon, blue, and gold in a heavy-duty industrial grade, looked as old as the building itself. The place always smelled faintly of burlap and long-dormant dust. There was another smell, too. A sour smell of people living alone for too long; of people waiting it out behind closed doors, with their hot plates and Murphy beds and flickering TVs.

I turned the key, like I had a thousand times before, pushed the door, and the moment it was cracked I knew something was wrong, but by then it was already too late.

I looked up to find a skinny black guy with tight, smoky eyes and a gap in his teeth as big as a tollbooth hurrying my way.

I tossed him the six-pack and went in low, right into his partner who'd been waiting on the dark side of the room. All I saw was shiny wing tips. Something hard hit me on the back of the head and the shoes came closer, then danced out of the way.

I awoke with the world's worst hangover. I'd really done it this time, I decided when the only memory I could dredge up was of that big, dark painting at the Gare du Nord. Christ, drinking with a frog. Where had I run into that crowd?

I sat up and dropped my head into my hands. My hair was matted. I opened my eyes and looked at my hands. They were caked with blood. It all came flooding back. I wasn't a drunk. I was a victim.

I staggered into the bathroom and took a look in the mirror. It wasn't pretty, but at my age it rarely is. It took me a few minutes to clean myself up and to determine that I was no longer bleeding; then I went out to assess the damage.

They'd done a pretty thorough job, pulling out drawers, books, and papers. They'd found the concealed drawer in the bottom of the wooden wardrobe, but they'd left my collection of guns and ammo sitting there in plain view. They'd emptied the last few inches from a bottle of Old Grand-Dad.

I did my best to clean the place up. The six-pack had broken apart and the cans were scattered about. When I picked them up, I found two empties. The sons-of-bitches had stood over me toasting what, I wondered.

As far as I could determine, the only thing gone beside the beer was that few inches of whiskey.

It didn't make any sense. If they'd come to kill me I'd have been through the tunnel and past all those long-gone relatives and friends and probably on the express heading down.

If they were burglars they would have taken the guns.

I checked my coat, and the Irv Kaplan homicide report was still in the pocket. I unfolded it, then skimmed through it without finding a reason to pause. I went through it again, slowly.

The police had talked to Jimmy and Westerfield, of course. They'd talked to Clyde and Jesse Moore. They'd also found a CTA bus driver who'd seen the hit man heading toward the drugstore, briefcase in hand. A fancy foreign car was parked on the street behind him. The bus driver thought it might have been a BMW or a Mercedes.

I took a long, hot shower, sitting on the floor with the water pounding on my head. When I came out of the bathroom I realized that something was missing.

Years of dust surrounded the spot where the photograph had hung. It was an eight-by-ten shot, framed and matted, of me and my folks the day I'd graduated from the police academy. *Why would anybody steal that?* I wondered as I checked to make sure it hadn't merely fallen.

It was the last photograph of me and my father together. He'd died a few months later. If you knew him, the illness was evident in his eyes, which were shining a bright, deep, unnatural blue. But if you didn't, he probably looked like a million dollars. The cancer had eaten away years of excess pounds.

I wouldn't notice it for months at a time and then the picture would catch my eye, and just like that, I'd be paging through my list of regrets.

But why would anyone steal it? Who cared but me? And then I had another thought.

I strapped on a shoulder holster, tucked a Smith & Wesson .38 inside, grabbed my jacket, and opened the door. I went down the hall and four flights of stairs and out to my car.

There was a balmy breeze coming off the lake, a few blocks east, and there were plenty of people out and about, enjoying the weather. There wouldn't be many nights like this. Winter was just around the corner.

My first stop was a late-night liquor store where I picked up a replacement for the pilfered whiskey. I slipped the bottle into the glove box, then headed for my office.

I parked around the corner, then walked up the alley and entered the building through the service door.

I stood there listening to the building's gentle hum. A half-dozen dentists had offices upstairs, and the place reeked of pain.

I went up the stairs as quietly as I could, then down the hall to my office. I unholstered the gun, then slipped the key in and kicked the door open.

There was nobody there, of course. There rarely is when you're ready. So you stand there like a fool, pointing a gun at an empty room. Anything move, I'll plug you full of holes.

But nothing did, so I put the gun away.

It was just a single room with a wooden desk and credenza, two gray-metal file cabinets, a matching bookcase, three chairs, and a dilapidated sofa. Everything was right where I'd left it. Except for some cigarette butts, crumpled papers, and Styrofoam coffee cups that the cleaning crew had swiped from the wastebasket.

There was a framed copy of my private investigator's license on one wall and, next to that, a framed photograph, a souvenir of my years as a homicide detective.

Three of us were standing in front of a crime scene, a second-hand appliance store on Roosevelt Road.

I was in the middle, between my longtime partners, John Casper and Andy Kelly. It was impossible for me to look at the photo now without seeing the demented glint in Kelly's eyes, that crazy, hard-core glint that never went away.

At the time, I'd enjoyed it as much as anyone, the hard-edged humor behind it.

The photograph itself was one of Kelly's minor practical jokes. If you looked closely, you'd notice that he had three arms. Unknown to everybody else, Kelly had borrowed one from the carnage inside the store. He'd conned us outside and had then conned a newspaper photographer into taking the picture.

We were obviously having a good time. Three young guys in the prime of their careers, laughing and smoking, relaxed, not a care in the world. Hell, even the corpse had a cigarette going.

Now every few weeks, I'd decide to throw the photo out or to break the glass and use it as a dartboard with Andy Kelly as the bull's-eye. But then I'd change my mind and just leave it hanging there, a reminder that if you hung around with the right people almost anything could happen.

The partnership had come to a sudden end not long after the photograph, the aftermath of another practical joke. If you could call bank robbery a joke. The FBI didn't seem to think so. That stunt had sent Kelly to a federal penitentiary and had got me tossed off the force.

I stood there looking at the photograph. It had been a long time since I'd been glad to see Andy Kelly. I actually smiled back, and then I laughed at my ridiculous fears.

Back at the apartment, I'd decided that somebody was trying to steal my past. And when they had every single trace, they'd tell me I'd never been a cop. I'd never been married. I'd never been anything but what I was today: a private eye with few friends, no steady woman, and a poverty-level income.

"Those are delusional dreams you're having, Mr. Acropolis," they would say. "A leading indicator of mental illness is the inability to distinguish dreams from reality."

Well, maybe so, Doctor, but then again, maybe not.

I pulled the office bottle out, turned off the lights and opened the window and let the breeze and the sounds of the city in.

You could see all the way downtown from here, to the soaring towers of the Loop. I lifted my glass in a toast to all those pretty lights. Lights that I knew camouflaged a world of cubicles, most of them as dreary as my own.

TWENTY

I WOKE on the office sofa with the morning sun dancing along the windowsill. Down in the lumberyard a power saw was whining. The telephone was in my hand. I put the receiver to my ear and heard Frank Stringfellow say, "FBI just walked out of here."

"Who?"

"FB fucking I," he said.

"What's up?"

"They won't tell me."

"Jesus," I said as I stood up.

In the lumberyard, men who built things for a living were loading supplies into pickups and vans. Their talking and laughter seemed louder than usual. Heat rising. Inviting. That's where I should be, I decided, not for the first time. I'd hammer in the morning. I'd hammer in the evening.

"What do you mean, they won't tell you?"

"Just what I said," Stringfellow said. "They want to know what I've been doing on Madison Street. I tell 'em I only go to watch the Bulls. 'A little west of there, Frank,' they say. 'Oak Park?' I ask. 'Not that far, Frank. Not that far. Westerfield's,' they say. 'That ring any bells, Frank?' Jesus, don't you hate when they call you by your first name?"

"Westerfield's?" I said as evenly as possible.

"Yeah. What's my interest in Westerfield's?"

"They tell you what it is?"

"No. But I already knew 'cause I had another visitor just before them. Black guy claiming to be a PI. After he left I checked the directory and the phone book, no listing. So I called Professional Regulations. They never heard of him."

"He still got all his teeth?" I asked.

"Pretty good set. Why?"

"Something last night," I said. "He have a name?"

"Harris. William Harris."

"So what'd he want?" I asked. But I already knew the answer. Wet Willie wanted the same thing the FBI did. He wanted to know what Stringfellow's card had been doing at the tire shop.

"Same thing as the FBI," he said. "What am I working on Madison Street? What's my interest in Westerfield Pharmacy? What do I know about some kid named Jimmy something or other?"

"Jimmy," I said.

"Westerfield's?" he said. "Why does that name sound so familiar? I know I heard it somewhere the last couple days."

It was time to change subjects. "We're in the wrong line of work, Frank, you know that?"

"Speak for yourself, Nick. Speak for yourself."

"I love watching the lumberyard. Guy loads up his truck and goes out and builds something."

"Nick, he's probably going to fix somebody's toilet."

"I was gonna call you today. I got a line on that truck."

"City Movers," he said. "Forget that. I'm on it. Look, you got time to run around and find out what you can about this Westerfield place?"

"I could probably squeeze you in, Frank. But tell me more about the FBI."

"Nick, there's nothing to tell. They just kept busting my chops, accusing me of lying and laying down all the usual threats."

"What threats?"

"You know, how they can make things rough if I don't cooperate. They've got friends at the IRS."

"That's low," I said.

"Look, Nick, help me out on this and I'll forgive you for that fuckup in Rogers Park."

"The least I could do, Frank," I said. "Hey, did these FBI agents have names?"

"Kramer and Johnson. You ever notice how none of 'em ever have real names?"

"I'll get on it right away," I said.

"I wish I could remember where I heard that name," Stringfellow said, and the line went dead.

I put my shoes on, closed the window, and drove home. My apartment hadn't looked this clean in months. I started coffee, then showered and shaved and poured myself a cup.

I dialed Irv Kaplan's number and talked to his widow, then called Becky. "Last chance to meet Mrs. Kaplan," I said.

"I think I'm going up to see my mother," she said. "Maybe if she knows I know . . ."

"Sure," I said. "Maybe."

"She must know, right?"

"What?"

"About Irv Kaplan?"

"Only way to find out is to ask."

"But what if she just lies?"

"Well, if you catch her at it, that'll tell you something, too."

"I'll call you later," she said.

I poured another cup of coffee, then pulled out the Irv Kaplan homicide report and took another look.

It was four pages, concise and to the point. The point was they didn't have a suspect or a motive. "THIS INVESTIGATION IS CONTINUING," was typed on the bottom of the report. The report was dated October 23, two days after the murder. If there'd been any follow-up, it hadn't made its way downtown to the POW camp.

TWENTY-ONE

ARLINGTON Heights was part of the endless suburban sprawl in the land beyond O'Hare International Airport.

If you didn't look too closely, the Vista View Condominiums looked a bit like the Horner Homes. It was the little things that made the difference. There was grass out front, neatly trimmed and surrounded by a miniature picket fence. The sidewalk had been swept sometime in the past year, probably in the past couple of days. I didn't see one piece of broken glass, although I spotted a couple of cigarette butts under the bushes by the front door.

In the hallway, the doorbells worked. The mailboxes had not been pried open. The intercom hummed and the buzzer buzzed. Lightbulbs glowed, and the elevator smelled faintly of some pleasant perfume.

Upstairs, there were framed reproductions on the walls and springy carpeting on the floor. A door opened near the end of the hallway and Berenice Kaplan stepped out. She was around seventy, I guessed. Her hair was frosty white. Her glasses were bifocals. Her smile seemed genuine.

"I'm so glad you could come," she said. "I'd probably still be sleeping. That's all I seem to do. My doctor tells me it's depression. But I don't feel depressed. I know I should be depressed. So maybe he's right. But I don't feel it."

She led me into a pleasant living room and asked if I wanted tea and then went to put the kettle on.

There were scores of pictures on the walls. One was an old black-and-white, a bride and groom standing on a beach. Behind them you could make out the curve of Lake Shore Drive, the Drake Hotel, and high above everything the Palmolive Building.

Her hair had been jet-black back then and hung just past her shoulders. Irv Kaplan was in uniform, with sergeant's stripes on his sleeves. His smile let you know he thought he was the luckiest guy in the world.

"I was a war bride," the recipient of the smile said behind me.

"Korea?"

"Oh, how nice," she said. "It was a little before your time. We were married in March 1943, just before Irv shipped out." Tears welled up in her eyes.

"I know you've been through all this before, but can you think of any reason why someone would want to kill your husband?"

She sat down on the sofa and shook her head. "I keep thinking back to the time he locked those two drug addicts in the store."

"When was this?"

"We kept getting robbed, you see. They always wanted morphine or some such. Well, one day Irv saw them coming, these same two fellows who had robbed us before. So as they're walking in the front door we slipped out the back. Irv ran around and locked the front door and I ran next door and called the police. Oh, those fellows, they were so mad. They couldn't get out. They tried, but they just couldn't."

"When was this?" I asked.

"Oh, quite some time now. I remember it was in the winter. These fellows always used to pick the slow days. I think it was 1965. No, 1964. Oh, we used to laugh about that."

"Can you think of anything more recently?"

She shook her head. "I just keep coming back to those two

fellows. My husband wasn't the kind of man who made enemies. And if he did I think I would know. I was his best friend for fifty years."

"Any problems with neighbors, anything like that?"

She gave me a look that made me feel foolish for asking. I went on anyway. If you're going to be a successful detective, boys and girls, you have to ask the hard questions. "Problems about noise, parking spaces?"

She smiled and shook her head.

"Did he have life insurance?"

"I didn't kill my husband, Mr. Acropolis."

"Of course not," I said. And if there were anything unusual, the insurance investigator would already be snooping around. "You really don't have any idea what could be behind this?"

"I keep thinking it must have been a mistake."

"The killer asked for your husband by name," I reminded her.

"There's more than one Irving Kaplan in this world."

"Did your husband gamble?"

"Oh, he'd bet a horse now and again. But I don't think he ever bet more than ten dollars. He'd usually wait until the last races, so he wouldn't have to pay to go in. I used to go with him occasionally. Oh, one time we did bet more. There was a horse, Berenice's Bundle. Oh, we thought we were going to be rich. I think we bet fifty dollars. It came in last. That was the most we ever lost."

"He didn't bet with bookies?"

"No."

"Did he play cards?"

"Pinochle, when we had the store. There used to be a whole group of them that played back then."

"Where was this store?"

"In the city on Chicago Avenue. Kaplan Drugs and Sundries. It's still there, only now Gene Westerfield runs it."

"He owns it or he runs it?"

"Both. He bought us out. He really saved our skin. We might have lost everything if it wasn't for him."

"Why?"

"See, the state wouldn't pay us. Public Aid. They were almost a year behind and we just couldn't afford it anymore."

"What did Gene Westerfield do?"

"He and Irv drove all the way down to Springfield, to the big Public Aid office, and Gene talked to some people he knew and that was that. We had a check the next week."

"Your husband and Gene were friends?"

"Well, Gene's father was Irv's first boss. It's funny how it turned out. Westerfield's was his first and his last job. Irv used to laugh about how he'd ended up right back where he'd started."

"That's interesting," I said. "It was Gene's father's store. I didn't know that."

"Oh, he was quite a fellow, Henry Westerfield. And nobody called him Hank, either. He was a tough old so-and-so. Irv worked for him all the way through school. We had that and the GI Bill. That's how we saved enough to buy our own store."

"It must have been hard for your husband, working for someone after owning his own store."

"Oh, he and Gene had their little disagreements," she said. "But Irv always said Gene Westerfield was a genius. He knew the business was changing and he wasn't afraid to change with it. When Public Aid came in, we just saw it as a lot of extra paperwork. Gene Westerfield saw it as a golden opportunity."

"How's that?"

"That's what Irv said. After he went to work for Gene. Irv said we'd been sitting on a gold mine all those years and we'd never even known it."

"Did your husband consider Gene Westerfield an honest businessman?"

She gave me a look that she probably used on naughty grandchildren. "Let me tell you something about Gene Westerfield, Mr. Acropolis. He didn't have to help us collect from the state. He could have stood by and watched us go belly-up and he could have bought our store for next to nothing. Instead he helped us collect and then when Irv got sick and we wanted to get out he offered us top dollar. Does that sound dishonest to you, Mr. Acropolis?"

"Sounds pretty fair," I had to admit.

"If you want to talk about honesty," she said, "let's talk about the state of Illinois. Do you think it's honest for them to withhold your money for months and months and months, while you have to keep paying the rent and keep paying the suppliers and keep paying the electric and the insurance and all the other payments that you have to keep paying whether the state pays you or not? Is that honest, Mr. Acropolis?"

"Doesn't sound like it," I said.

"And then when they do pay, they give you a list and say, 'We've rejected this prescription, that prescription, and the other prescription,' and they refuse to pay. And they won't even tell you why. Does that sound honest?"

"Doesn't sound like it."

"Is it honest for the drug companies to charge the small stores more than the big chains? Is that honest, Mr. Acropolis?"

"Doesn't sound like it," I said again. "You say your husband was sick?"

She nodded. "Lung cancer." The words came out in a whisper. "Sometimes I think it's almost a blessing." Tears welled up in her eyes. She took off her glasses and dabbed her face with a handkerchief. "I know he wasn't ready to go. But I can't help thinking of all the pain he was spared. We watched Irv's brother go through hell." The tears rolled down her face.

"I didn't mean to upset you."

"Oh, you're not upsetting me, young man. I just cry sometimes. But I think you're barking up the wrong tree. Gene Westerfield is one of those rare men who really do care about other people. Why, after Irv died, he came to sit with me two different nights. He and his wife. And he felt so bad because it happened in his store. And when he left he handed me an envelope, 'to help with the funeral expenses,' he said. Five thousand dollars was in that envelope, Mr. Acropolis. Now, I don't know what kind of funerals they have in your family . . ." She put her glasses back on.

"That was very generous," I said.

"See, he didn't want me to feel bad taking charity. And I wouldn't have taken it from just anyone. But Gene Westerfield is the kind of man that doesn't make you feel bad."

We sipped our tea for a while, and then she put her glasses back on and walked me to the door. "You made my day," she said. "It's nice to have a man around, if only for a while."

"Thanks for seeing me," I said.

"I think I'll take a nap." She smiled and closed the door.

On my way out, I knocked on the building manager's door. The Kaplans had been in the building for years, he said, and had never caused any problems.

"He always had a smile for you," the manager's wife said. "I feel so sorry for Berenice. She seems so lost alone."

TWENTY-TWO

D R. Zailradenik lived in Morton Grove, on a block of neat, well-kept three-flats. A few of the buildings had colorful awnings hanging over big picture windows that sat front and center. But that was about the only spark of individuality.

There were no porches, just small cement slabs a single step above the sidewalk. On one, an old woman sat knitting her life away.

The Buick hadn't looked too terrible on Madison Street, but up here it looked like a refugee from a junkyard. There didn't seem to be a body panel without some kind of damage. Long ago somebody had written: "Wash Me!" in the dirt on the trunk. The words were barely visible beneath new layers of dirt and mud.

The car was angled toward the curb, but it had stopped a few feet short. A Ford was parked behind it. It was parked even with the curb, but about two feet out, as if to hide the slant of the Buick.

I opened a screen door, walked into a small hallway, and rang the bell for Zailradenik. A door to the basement apartment opened and a man stood there. "Yes?" He was decades younger than the doctor but had those same wide shoulders, that same long and narrow face.

"Is Dr. Z. around?"

"What's this about?" he asked.

"I wanted to ask him some questions about Eugene Wester-field."

"Look, my dad doesn't know anything. He's a sick man. You guys are wasting your time."

I pulled out my wallet and showed him my license. "How about telling me who's he been talking to?"

"You name 'em, they've been here. The FBI. The Illinois Department of Public Aid. Professional Regulations."

"What do they want?"

"They ask him questions about Westerfield and St. Anthony's Medical Center, and when he can't come up with answers they like they threaten to indict him or to revoke his license."

"Your father works at St. Anthony's?"

"Not anymore."

"What happened?"

"Have you ever met my father?"

I shook my head.

"Well, if you had, you wouldn't have bothered coming. I haven't heard him say anything sensible in a year. What's your interest in all this?"

"A clerk at Westerfield's has gone missing."

"And you think my father knows where he is?"

"I also wanted to ask him about Irv Kaplan."

"Well, look, I can assure you my father doesn't know anything. Irv Kaplan. I saw that on the news and I went and told Westerfield my father quit and I brought him home."

"What's Westerfield's connection with St. Anthony's?"

"It's his place. Although, according to the FBI, my dad owned it, at least on paper. I guess there's some law against cross-ownership. So it's illegal for Westerfield to own the drugstore and the medical center because they do business with each other."

"So your father was the front man?"

"Well, that's according to the FBI. I don't know if I'd put much faith in what they say. When I told Westerfield my father was through, it didn't seem to bother him."

"What was your father doing down there Monday?"

"He probably just went for a ride. He can't do anything else. He can't remember anything. But he still knows how to drive. You put him behind the wheel of a car, suddenly he looks like his old self again, and he remembers how to get around. I know what you're thinking. I should probably take his keys, right?"

"What's wrong with him?"

He shrugged. "He's old. You know, he was always so smart, so sharp, so strong. But as soon as he lost it the sharks were waiting. You wouldn't know it to look at him but he owns four thousand pay phones."

"Really?"

"The problem is, they don't exist. Or if they do exist, there's a couple thousand other suckers think they own them, too."

"Oh."

"A Ponzi scheme. You use Peter's investment to pay Paul and rope more suckers in. The return was so high my father actually remortgaged the house. That's how they ended up here."

"How much?"

"Two hundred thousand, maybe a little more. So he went back to work. He wouldn't even tell us it had happened. And who would hire a broken man, a broken-down old doctor, except a crook?"

"Do you have any actual proof that Westerfield's a crook?"

"He hired my father. He let him examine patients, prescribe drugs. No honest man would do that."

"That's not much," I said.

"You know what my father was doing that day I went to bring him home? He was signing blank prescriptions. One after another, all day long. Pad after pad after pad."

"Maybe he filled them in later," I said.

"You better meet my dad."

I followed him down a short flight of stairs into a living room packed tight with oversize furniture. There was an entire dining room set, including buffet, server, and breakfront. The table was tight against a wall. The chairs crammed together like passengers in a rush-hour train. A Tiffany-style lamp sat on a refectory table. There was a thick Oriental rug on the floor, a coffee table, two side chairs, a bookcase, a rolltop desk, and a floor lamp with a cut-glass shade.

It was furniture that had been built to last, but it hadn't been purchased with this room in mind. The walls were covered with cheap wood paneling. The side windows were glass block.

There wasn't much room for moving about. Dr. Zailradenik and his wife sat on opposite ends of the sofa, a big red leather job, probably the only piece of furniture younger than the building itself. They looked like refugees waiting for a truck that would never arrive.

"Mom," the son said, and he reached out to help her up. She looked as old as the doctor. She was wearing a long black skirt and a white blouse, and she had on a pair of those thick high-heeled shoes that had been popular decades ago. She walked toward the back of the apartment.

Dr. Zailradenik ignored us. He sat watching an old console TV; a soap opera was going with the sound off.

"Dad, this is Mr. . . ."

"Acropolis," I said.

"He wants to ask you some questions about Eugene Westerfield."

He looked as confused as he'd been in the weeds behind Madison Street. He was still searching for some hidden sign. "Westerfield," he repeated flatly.

"How long did you work for him?" I asked.

"Westerfield," he said again. "Gene Westerfield." I thought he might be waiting for the name to connect in his mind. But all I saw in his eyes was emptiness and, behind that, fear.

He was wearing good wool slacks and a white dress shirt with the sleeves rolled. A thermometer was clipped to his shirt pocket, next to a pair of eyeglasses. He was all dressed and ready to go. He looked from me to his son—not really seeing either one of us, I thought—then he turned his attention back to the silent TV.

"Seen enough?" the son asked.

I turned and walked up the stairs. The son followed.

"The FBI keeps threatening to send him to jail. You know what, it would almost be a relief. It's killing my mother. It's like living with a ghost."

TWENTY-THREE

JOHN Olmstead was waiting for me in front of Jerry's, a deli on Grand Avenue. He was the picture of a hardworking reporter, a notebook in one hand, a pen in the other. He was about thirty, I guessed. His tie was loose, his shirt open at the collar. He had a speech all prepared.

"I talked to Mike Brewer," he said. "He wasn't exactly sure what you're investigating, but he said he asked around and everybody says you're a straight shooter—that's his term—so I don't mind talking, but I'd like a promise that if your investigation leads to something that we, by 'we' I mean the *Chicago Tribune*, might be interested in as a story—"

"Sure," I said. "You get an exclusive, if there is one."

We went inside and then we carried our sandwiches and coffee down to the river walk. "So how'd you get on to Westerfield in the first place?" I asked after a few bites of corned beef.

"A couple years back, the paper sent me down to Springfield, to dig through Public Aid vouchers and find out where the money was going. We broke it down into categories. The ten highest paid doctors, medical centers, and then chain and independent pharmacies."

"Where was Westerfield?"

"He just made the independent list. Tenth. But his was the only Chicago store. I went out with a photographer and when I saw that neighborhood . . . Well, it just didn't make any sense. Here was this store in the middle of nowhere doing all this business. Westerfield refused to answer my questions. But we ran a picture of his store with the story and was he ever hot. He said we implied he was a crook."

"Did you?"

"We never said it directly. We just said, look, these few stores took in all this money. But we did talk about welfare fraud in the story. We used some figure out of Washington. They estimated that fraud and abuse cost the welfare system billions of dollars each year."

"Billions?"

He nodded. "Fifty billion dollars, I think that was it."

"What was Westerfield's cut?"

"Just under a million. Nine hundred and ninety-four thousand, something like that."

I whistled. "This was in one year?"

He nodded. "He's closed Sundays and holidays, so we figured it out. He was taking in over three thousand a day."

"That's an awful lot of money," I said softly. And if that was from the one drugstore, how much did Westerfield get from St. Anthony's? And what about the Kaplan store? And what about Prospect Drugs? Did Gene get a cut of that, too?

"After the story came out, we started getting all these phone calls—crooked doctors, crooked pharmacies, optometrists, you name it. One of my editors had worked with Mike Brewer before, so we started giving information to him. And he started giving a little back. One of the things he told us was that the numbers at Westerfield's had fallen to about five hundred dollars a day."

"He was scared," I said.

"So I wrote another story just saying that the business at Westerfield's had dropped considerably since the first story. Well, now Westerfield called again and he was really mad this time. Said first we implied he was a crook because he billed too much, now we were implying he was a crook because he billed too little. 'Well, tell me you're not a crook,' I said."

"Don't tell me he did the Nixon line?"

Olmstead looked confused and I realized he was probably too young to remember Richard Nixon telling the world he wasn't a crook.

"What he did was, he invited me to lunch. Of course, I explained that I had to pay my own way. And then he suggested some fancy place and I had to explain that I couldn't afford that on a reporter's salary. So finally we decided on Manny's. Do you know it? It's really good."

"Great potato pancakes," I agreed.

"You know, I never even heard of potato pancakes until I moved here. I don't think people in Chicago know how lucky they are."

"So Westerfield told you his story and he's not a crook."

"Well, we never really got into that," he said. "Westerfield didn't seem to . . . What we mainly talked about was the things he's done for the community. It's really quite a story."

"Like what?"

"Oh, there's this young black man that he's putting through medical school."

"Jimmy Madison," I said.

He nodded. "And there are these old black gentlemen across the street that he basically takes care of."

"Jesse and Clyde?"

He nodded again. "But I think maybe the biggest thing he's done is just staying in that neighborhood after all the other stores left. Those people really need him."

"What people?"

"See, that's what I didn't understand before. People come from all over the West Side to that store. Do you know there used to be four Walgreen stores on Madison Street, but when the neighborhood changed from white to black they all shut down?"

"I think the riots might have had a bit to do with it," I said.

He gave me that confused look again. "My editor said something about riots. When did that happen?"

"Well, '68 was the big one." Who could ever forget 1968 in Chicago? "Then there was a smaller one in '65, I think, and then the anniversary riot in '78."

"What happened?"

"The tiller man didn't get down the pole. . . . No. No. No. That was earlier. '78 a stolen car was being chased by police and it hit two little boys. That's what started it."

"And what happened?"

I shrugged. What happened with any riot? "They burned down the neighborhood. Looted the stores."

"How about the other riots?"

"Well, '68 was after the King assassination. That was the big one. '65, that was where the tiller man didn't make it down the pole and the hook and ladder left the station without him. The truck jumped a curb and killed a couple of people."

"The tiller man?"

"The fireman who steers the back of the hook and ladder."

He smiled and I could see him storing it away.

"Sounds like you bought Westerfield's story," I said.

"And you sound like Mike Brewer. He thinks Westerfield is playing me for a sucker."

"What did Westerfield say about Irv Kaplan?"

"That was the last time we talked. He was scared. He said he didn't understand what was happening. I told him to go to the FBI and tell them the truth."

"Which was?"

He shook his head and shrugged. "Whatever it was. See, we'd talked about the FBI before. Gene thought I'd given them information about him."

"Had you?"

He shook his head again. "Then, it turned out, he wanted me to talk to them for him. He wanted me to try to negotiate a deal."

"What kind of deal?"

"I never found out. I went to my editors and they said we couldn't because we'd become part of the news rather than just covering it. But one of my editors said the best thing Westerfield could do was find someone else to give to the FBI. When I told Westerfield, he said I sounded like his lawyer. And then he made a joke. He said that was the problem with being boss. There was no one above to turn in."

"So he just admitted he's a crook," I said.

"We were supposed to meet again, but then he called to cancel. He said he had to figure out what happened to Irv. He thought if he knew who was behind the murder he could work something out."

"So he thought it was business-related?"

"Definitely."

"Did you write about the murder?"

He shook his head. "No. See, that's not my beat. I tried to tell my editors what I thought happened, but—"

"What is your beat, Public Aid?"

"I'm on education now. See, they like to move a young reporter around so he gets a feel for a bunch of different beats. Then they can just plug you in wherever they need you."

"So what were you doing on Madison Street the other day?"

"I was hoping to talk to Westerfield. I had an idea."

"What?"

"He could give his friends in Springfield to the FBI."

"What friends?"

"I don't know. But I know he has them. Mike Brewer stopped payment on sixty thousand dollars' worth of bills and Springfield went ahead and paid Westerfield the money anyway."

"Why did he stop payment?"

"Mike said there was a pattern in the prescriptions that showed abuse, if not fraud."

"What kind of pattern?"

"The same exact combinations of drugs prescribed to hundreds of patients. Prozac and something else. Identical prescriptions. And when Brewer tried to question the patients, he couldn't find most of them. They were all crack heads and prostitutes."

"Sixty thousand worth of Prozac," I said. "That's depressing."

"You know what I think happened?" Olmstead asked. "I think the mob decided to muscle in. They read our story and they saw that million dollars and they wanted a piece of the pie."

"Did Westerfield say he'd been approached?"

"No. That's why he was so confused. No one had threatened him. No one had—"

"Maybe somebody just wanted Irv Kaplan dead."

"That's what I said. And Westerfield said Irv was a nobody. He was sure it was a warning. Are you working for him?"

"I can't really tell you who—"

"No. I know. I used to read a lot of detective stories in college. But I think you are. I think he hired you to find out who killed Irv Kaplan. You don't have to say anything. But would you do me a favor? If you do happen to see him, would you tell him my idea about his friends in Springfield?"

TWENTY-FOUR

I TOOK Grand Avenue over the highway, then pulled to the curb in the heart of an old Italian neighborhood. This was where Frank Nitti, Capone's right-hand man, had come from, where Richard Cain, another ex-cop gone bad, had ordered his last sandwich.

Doctors and lawyers, stockbrokers and architects lived here now. But there were still plenty of Italians around, and the successors of Capone and Nitti could still be found sipping coffee in some of the strip's quieter restaurants. Had they heard of Westerfield's million and decided the easiest way to cut themselves in was to give Gene a message he wasn't likely to forget?

I couldn't quite talk myself into Olmstead's theory. Why go to the bother of a hit man when the threat of one might work just as well? But if they were going to send a hit man out, couldn't they find a white guy somewhere? Even with Harry Aleman rusting away in prison, I couldn't quite see the Chicago mob using a black hit man. Equal opportunity hadn't come quite that far.

I stood in line for a loaf of sourdough and some tomato bread, crossed the street for a coffee to go, then got back in my Olds and continued west.

According to Olmstead, Westerfield was convinced the Kaplan hit was intended as a warning. Maybe Westerfield was right, but maybe he was just another crook with a guilty conscience. Maybe

Irv Kaplan had his own enemies. Or maybe he'd arranged his own execution. He wouldn't be the first person to decide that a bullet was preferable to death by cancer.

At Western Avenue, Grand angled northwest. The World War II tank that had guarded the intersection for decades was gone. I found it in a park a few blocks down. On its island at Western Avenue it had always looked ready to swing into action and start picking off passing tractor-trailers. In the park, it was just another war memorial.

I turned left at Chicago Avenue and a mile later slowed down. Kaplan Drugs and Sundries was another decrepit-looking ghetto drugstore. It was sandwiched between an auto body shop and a package liquor store. Out front, a security guard was standing alongside a double-parked squad car. The cops and the guard all seemed to be having a good time. Behind them a collection of thirsty-looking winos were holding up the wall at the liquor store.

If Westerfield had got a million from his store on Madison Street, how much had he got from this one, from the gold mine Irv Kaplan had never realized he'd been sitting on?

The Fifteenth District station was about two miles west of the Kaplan store, a bit shy of the Oak Park line. I could never step into one of the old houses without thinking about the stories they might tell. But if station houses could talk, this one would probably plead the Fifth Amendment.

Every decade or so, half the station seemed to find itself under indictment. The last group had been charged with shaking down, protecting, and robbing local drug dealers. Nobody called Shelly, and they'd all been convicted. Not that one thing had anything to do with the other, but I hadn't made a dime and I hadn't shed any tears. Petty shakedowns, like off-duty traffic altercations, not only made cops look bad; they made them look stupid.

The usual crew of fat boys and misfits was holding court behind the front desk as the afternoon watch drifted in. I followed them into the roll call room, where they were forming into racially and sexually segregated groups. I kept my eyes open for a name tag saying: "Gabriel" or for anyone I knew, but I didn't spot either.

Gabriel was the cop that might have been on duty at St. Anthony's the day Jesse thought he saw the hit man stop by.

There was a pile of Daily Bulletins on a desk, and next to that a stack of Training Bulletins. "Special: Depression, Suicide, and Department Members," the headline read. "DOES THIS SOUND LIKE YOU? Do you stare at the walls for hours on end, unable to focus on your work? Do you miss days of work because of vague medical complaints? Have you lost interest in your work for no apparent reason? Have you lost confidence in your abilities?"

I walked out front, lit a cigarette, and watched traffic pass. It was a deteriorating commercial strip in a lower-middle-class black neighborhood. But unlike Madison Street, most of the neighborhood was still there. This was not always a blessing.

Just across the street was an apartment building where a few years back a rookie patrolman had been killed by a fifteen-year-old with a Glock .9.

I flicked my cigarette into the gutter and walked back inside.

"Nick!"

I turned and he had that same awkward smile I'd first seen at the police academy. "Lenny," I said, and I spotted the chevrons on his sleeve. "You made sergeant. Christ, that's great."

He extended a limp hand and I did my best to shake it without letting it slip away. He was one of those guys who seemed to have no business on the force. He'd been voted most likely to drop out of the academy. He should have been driving a Good Humor truck or working as a camp counselor or as a teacher or in a library. Instead, he was a cop in one of the city's toughest districts. And somehow he'd made sergeant, which meant he'd exceeded my final rank.

"You're looking good, too, Nick," he said, and then he started to stammer like someone in the receiving line at a wake. "I w-w-was sorry . . . s-s-sorry to hear about-t-t . . . about all your t-t-troubles."

I waved it away. "What'd you do to end up out here?"

He waved that one away with an embarrassed smile. "Same old Nick. Hey, I heard you were . . . I heard you were . . . I heard you were doing something."

"Private investigator, working a lot of Police Board stuff."

"Oh, yeah. So how's that?"

"Pays the bills," I said. "Hey, you know a guy named Jack Gabriel?"

"Yeah, he's on my watch. I mean we're not tight or anything, but—"

"You think you could introduce us?"

"Sure. Hold on a sec. Let me see if he's here yet."

Lenny was back in a minute. Gabriel was right behind him and I knew immediately that things were not going my way.

Gabriel was at least six-four, maybe 230 pounds. He had a paunch but just a bit. Most of it was muscle. His eyes were light gray, so light they appeared almost colorless, and they didn't seem to track together.

Lenny started to make introductions, but Gabriel cut him off. He pointed a thick finger my way. "You want to talk to me?"

"If you've got a minute," I said. "I was talking to—"

"You can skip all that. I know all about who you were talking to, so just ask your questions."

We were drawing a bit of a crowd. The fat boys at the desk had stopped jawing away. Cops on their way to roll call suddenly decided to stop and have a drink of water.

"Can we do this somewhere else?"

"No. No. No. This isn't gonna take long. Let's just do it."

"Well, what I wanted to ask you about was Irv Kaplan."

"Never heard of him."

"He was a pharmacist—"

"And if I had heard of him, I wouldn't tell you anything. And if my little toy sergeant here"—he gestured toward Lenny, who was looking more and more like a Good Humor man; he might have been listening to one of his favorite kids tell an off-color joke— "were to order me to tell you, I would go straight to the lieutenant. And if he told me to obey I would go find the watch commander's hiding place, and, well, if he told me I would go to the commander, and if he told me I would call FOP, and if they told me, well, then I guess I'd just lie."

"Jack, Jack," Lenny kept trying to interrupt.

"Lenny," I stopped him when Gabriel was done. "It's not that important."

"Listen to your friend, Len-n-n-n-ny," Gabriel said.

"You know, I used to be on the job," I said, and color came suddenly into his eyes.

"Yeah, you used to be a big-time homicide dick, but you ain't no more. They threw you off the job. So now you're just another weaselly-ass civilian. So why don't you take your weaselly civilian ass out of my—"

I turned around and turned Jack Gabriel off.

Lenny followed me out to the street. "Nick, I'm sorry. I don't know what that was all about."

"Lenny, it's not your problem. Now go back in there and tell him that I'm just some guy you knew in the academy and apologize for—"

"Forget that," Lenny said, and for an instant he almost looked like a real cop.

"Lenny, if I worked out here I'd want him on my side," I said. I would want all the Jack Gabriels in the district on my side. "You know I'm right." It took Lenny a while, but he finally came around. It wouldn't pay to have Jack Gabriel as an enemy.

"But look, what about your questions? I mean—"

"Lenny, he doesn't have any answers that I can't get somewhere else."

"Yeah, probably."

"Now go back in and tell him you're sorry."

"You really think I should?"

"It'd be better for everybody, Lenny, believe me."

"OK. You were always smarter than me."

"You don't have to flatter me, Lenny."

"No, really. You know when I used to see you on TV, you'd be at some big murder and there'd be all the cameras and the reporters and the deputy sup and everybody, and I used to tell everybody that that was my friend Nick."

"We're still friends, Lenny."

"Yeah, I know, but you should still be on. You know that. Everybody knows. You got a raw deal, Nick."

"Thanks, Lenny," I said. "Thanks for remembering."

I wanted to pet him, but I was afraid he'd go back with his tail wagging. We shook hands instead.

I headed straight west on Chicago Avenue. At Austin Boulevard I crossed into Oak Park and I relaxed in the seat.

Maybe Gabriel was just a hard-ass with a particular dislike for private detectives. Or maybe I'd stepped on his toes once, back when I was a big-time homicide dick. It was the rare murder when we didn't have to throw some sight-seeing cops off the scene. Everybody always wanted to see the gore.

But Gabriel had known all about my visit to the medical center behind Westerfield's and all about the talk I'd had with his friend Officer Dolan.

I found a shady spot on a block of big single-family homes, pulled over, and started on the tomato bread. "Everybody knows you got a raw deal," I said to nobody in particular, and then I sat there and ate the whole damn thing.

TWENTY-FIVE

A T the Horner Homes, the wrecking crew had called it a day, leaving the nearly demolished building sitting in a mist of dust and sunshine. A high Cyclone fence surrounded the ruin, but two packs of not-quite-teenage boys had slipped inside. They were doing a little demolishing of their own.

One group stood on the ground, throwing rocks at the few unbroken windows. Another group had made it to what was now the top, about five stories up. There was nothing but sky above them. They managed to loosen an entire three-section window, frame and all, and send it tumbling down the side of the building. The boys on the ground diverted their rocks; the boys up top cheered and slapped palms. Glass shattered.

On Lake Street, in front of a different high-rise, slightly older boys were waiting in the shadows under the elevated tracks, whistling and calling to passing cars. When a car stopped, a boy would run up, take the order, snatch the cash, and disappear into the lobby. Seconds later he'd reappear, still running, to dump his cargo. An entire transaction usually took well under a minute.

And the cars would roll down Lake Street, would roll out of Horner, out of the ghetto completely, sometimes all the way to the suburbs. And the ghetto candy, that extra-added spice that some people just couldn't live without, would be shared with friends and lovers. A reward for getting through another tough day.

And I couldn't look down on anybody. I just happened to prefer my rewards in liquid form.

I parked in the lot where I'd spotted Becky's car. There weren't many adults around, but there were kids everywhere. Kids on bikes or playing basketball or just running around. Little kids toddling along in diapers. Teenage girls with babies that I hoped were not their own.

Two guys in motorized wheelchairs were sitting side by side next to the basketball court. They were both in their teens or early twenties. *Had they been friends before being shot?* I wondered. One kept shouting, "Yo, Jobo! Yo, Jobo!" Nobody seemed to be paying any attention.

"Watch your car, mister?"

I turned. He couldn't have been more than seven, with huge dark eyes set in a chocolate pie face. He was in short pants and a dirty T-shirt. His shoes were untied. He held out a grubby hand, and I dropped a quarter into it.

He looked at the quarter, then up at me. "That ain't no money," he said, and he squinted a bit, like he'd been watching too many Clint Eastwood movies, and held out his hand for more.

"It's a deposit," I said, and I showed him a dollar. "When I come back, if the car's OK, this is yours."

"Still ain't no money."

"How old are you?"

"Eighteen," he said. He sounded like he actually believed it.

"You don't have to be so tough," I barked. But who was I kidding? I turned and left him with a scowl on his face.

I took the stairs. Only the very brave or the very stupid, the crippled, the old, and the gangbangers who ran the drugs and the buildings, took the elevators.

It was always better on the stairs. The stench of urine wasn't as bad as the heavy fragrance trapped in the closed elevators. And it was usually stale urine. There was nothing worse than being trapped in an elevator with the escape hatch gone and the lights out and a group of gangbangers pissing from above.

That'll keep you on the stairs for a long, long time.

And the stairs weren't bad. Most of the lightbulbs were broken or missing, but I had a penlight to lead the way. The breezeway doors were propped open, letting in some light and air. The steps were worn cement. The walls were government-issue cinder block, marked with gang graffiti and a couple of painted tombstones. RIP PLAYER DOG, one of them read, and like a regular tombstone there was a date underneath. Player Dog had been gone three long years. Was this the same Player Dog that Jimmy Madison had picked up hitchhiking just last week?

I rested every couple of floors. When I finally reached the eighth floor, I stopped to catch my breath again. From here it was easy to see the confines of the Horner Home, a little red-and-gray patch in the heart of the city. It was bordered by the el tracks and an industrial zone to the north. To the south sat the doomed Chicago Stadium, the United Center, and a sea of parking lots.

All the movement below was like that in a prison yard. Nobody went far. Maybe across the street to the windowless grocery/liquor store with the armed security guard on the door.

Once upon a time, these projects had been seen as an improvement over the ramshackle slums of the forties and fifties. Now the old slums seemed almost quaint in comparison. But there was no going home.

The shiny United Center looked close enough to reach out and touch. The kids working away at the basketball courts downstairs all had their hopes and dreams, their hoop dreams, but Michael Jordan had not come out of a place like this. You didn't end up in that kind of shape without lots of good, healthy food and plenty of fresh air and exercise.

And the logistics of getting either in the Horner Homes seemed to doom the effort before it started. How many shopping bags could you carry up eight flights of stairs?

And fresh air, the cheapest commodity of all, wasn't cheap at all in a place where letting your kids run around outside was akin to saying, "Go play in traffic."

When the gangbangers went to war or just decided to celebrate, it was the innocent bystanders who died as often as not. Zip guns and Saturday night specials were a thing of the past. Drug money had bought real firepower to children. But it hadn't brought the training required to handle the high-powered guns proficiently. Andy Kelly had once suggested that the city offer weapon-training programs to cut down on the slaughter of innocent bystanders.

It was just another gag, of course, and nobody paid any attention. But sometimes it took a nut like Andy to see the simple truth. If you really wanted to save innocent lives but couldn't manage to keep guns out of the hands of children, the least you could do was teach them to shoot straight.

But this was not a program you could envision the mayor announcing at his next city hall press conference.

There were a couple of babies in diapers crawling along the breezeway. A little girl on a tricycle was shouting orders. The babies didn't seem to mind.

The first two apartments were boarded up. One of the doors had been pried open, then boarded up again.

A little boy was napping in the open doorway of the next apartment. There was a dead mouse in an overturned trap a few feet from his head. The smell of filth and poverty wafted out. A TV blared in the background.

I knocked on the next door. It opened almost immediately. But only to the end of several safety latches. It was the same woman I'd seen yesterday morning, Jimmy's mother. She had an expectant look on her face, but it soon disappeared.

"Yes?" she asked in a suspicious voice.

"My name's Acropolis. I'm working for Rebecca Westerfield. I was downstairs yesterday."

She nodded. "I know who you are."

"I'd like to ask you some questions about your son."

"Jimmy," she said softly.

"Did Missing Persons come out?"

"They were here," she said.

"Do you mind if I come in?"

She pushed the door closed in my face, undid the safety latches, then opened the door about halfway and stepped out of the way. She closed the door behind me and then locked it again, safety latches and all.

We were in a small living room. The furniture looked like a Nelson Brothers special—a sofa, a love seat, and a chair all in the same coarse plaid, a couple of end tables, and two lamps. Everything was clean and scrubbed, including the vinyl tile floor.

A gleaming wood-and-glass corner frame held a depiction of the Sacred Heart of Jesus. A simple metal crucifix hung over the sofa.

The windows were covered by solid wood shutters protected with two-by-fours in stockade locks. It was all painted the same white as the walls.

"I wished you'd called before coming," Mrs. Madison said. "This is homework time."

I followed her into the kitchen. The boys I'd seen yesterday were sitting at an old Formica table, along with a girl of maybe fifteen. There were open schoolbooks and papers scattered around.

"Children, this is Mr. Acropolis. He's a friend of Becky and he's going to help us find Jimmy."

She paused like a teacher waiting for the class to respond, and they didn't disappoint. "Hello, Mr. Acropolis," the two boys said in unison. The girl looked up but didn't say anything. She gave me a gaze that I couldn't quite read, a dark look that seemed much too old for her years.

Back in the living room, Mrs. Madison gestured for me to sit down. I pulled out my notebook. "Can you tell me about the last time you saw your son?"

"Jimmy," she said.

"I'm sorry," I said. "Can you tell what you remember about the last time you saw Jimmy?"

"I was helping the boys with their homework and Jimmy was in his room studying. The phone rang and Jimmy answered it. I assumed it was Latisa calling." She gestured toward the kitchen.

"Latisa is your daughter?"

She gave me a small, bittersweet smile and shook her head. "Latisa is Jimmy's girlfriend. She's . . . She's . . . Well, she's been very helpful since Jimmy's been gone."

"How old is she?"

"She's nineteen." She must have seen my surprise. "She's had a hard life, Mr. Acropolis. But sometimes when she's here with Jimmy or with the boys, it all just rolls off her. I used to think she was the wrong kind of girl for my Jimmy, but . . ." She stopped.

"It wasn't her on the phone the other night?"

"No. She called after Jimmy left. And that's when I realized he didn't say what he usually says when he goes to visit Latisa. 'I'll be back for dinner.' This time he said, 'I'm just going downstairs.'"

"And?"

"He never came back. They took him. Somebody took him."

"Who?"

"I don't know. Latisa sent her brothers out and they found some itty-bitty ragamuffin who saw Jimmy getting into a car."

"What kind of car?"

"The boy's five years old, Mr. Acropolis. How would he know what kind of car? He ought to be home with his mother."

"Why would someone take Jimmy?"

"The store. Something to do with Mr. Gene's store."

"He was there when Irv was shot?" I said.

She nodded.

"Do you have any idea why Irv was shot?"

She shook her head.

"What did Jimmy say?"

"He was upset. But he didn't talk about it. No. He was more than upset. See, that was part of his safe world, the store and Mr. Westerfield, school. It's one thing to have something like that happen out here. But it wasn't supposed to happen there, too. I think that was a shock to him. To find that there really is no safe world."

"There's a good chance this is all tied together," I said. "Jimmy's disappearance, Irv's murder, Gene Westerfield's vacation."

"I know."

"Jimmy must have said something."

She shook her head. "It was troubling him. And then he seemed on the verge of saying something. That's how Jimmy is. He gets it right in his own mind before he speaks. And now I think he was ready the other night. But I . . . Oh, I don't know. I was busy with the boys and, well, lately I haven't wanted to pry so much. Him and Latisa. A boy gets a certain age he doesn't want to tell his mama every little thing. You have to let a child have wings."

"Sure," I agreed. And I remembered Jimmy hesitating before he'd signed the statement. Neither one of us had asked a few simple questions.

"Oh, I wish he was right here in my arms," she said, and she hugged herself tight.

"Did Jimmy say anything about being in an accident?"

"An accident, when was this?"

"Last Tuesday."

"This is the first I've heard of it," she said.

"Do you have any idea what he might have been doing on Forty-seventh Street?"

"Oh, he goes all over when he makes deliveries to the stores."

"Where, Sixty-third Street, Madison?"

"Now Mr. Gene, he has stores all over the city."

"And Jimmy does what?"

"He take things from store to store."

"What kind of things?"

"Mostly paperwork. Or if one store would run short of something."

"Do you know where these other stores are?"

"Why are you so interested in Mr. Gene's stores?"

"Just curious," I said. "As far as Becky knows, her father only has the one on Madison."

"Parents don't always tell their children every little thing. But you listen to me: Mr. Gene's a good man and a good father. Here, let me show you something."

She led me back through the kitchen, where Latisa was holding up homemade flash cards. The boys were racing to answer first.

We entered a small bedroom. There was a set of bunk beds with ships' wheels at the ends, a roll-away bed, and a small desk piled with textbooks and papers.

"Do you know who paid for all these books?"

"No." I shook my head.

"Mr. Westerfield. And you know who's paid Jimmy's tuition all through college?"

"Mr. Westerfield," I said.

"And you know who gave Jimmy a part-time job where he could spend half his time studying?"

"Mr. Westerfield," I said again.

"And do you know why?" Mrs. Madison asked. "Do you know why Mr. Westerfield has been so good to the Madison family?"

I shook my head.

"Well, I don't, either," she said. "But Mr. Westerfield, why, he's been helping the Madison family so long, I don't know what we'd do without him."

She walked to the room's only window, parted the curtains, and looked down to Lake Street.

"I don't know why we ever moved here," she said softly. "Nothing good happens here. Madison Street was so nice, before we burned it down like fools."

I had a sudden flash of everybody holding hands on Madison Street, and the old stores and the theater reflected in the drugstore window.

"I do not let my children play outside, Mr. Acropolis. Do you know what that's like for little children, to be locked up like prisoners? Do you know what it's like for Jimmy to be sitting in here night after night looking at these books and then listening to what goes on outside? Do you know how many nights I've come in here and found him staring out this window?

"They think they're having fun down there, Mr. Acropolis, selling their drugs and playing gangster. Little boys playing gangster, cops and robbers with real guns. And they hate me and they hate my Jimmy, and they hate my little boys. Because once you give up on life, once you give up on ever getting out of here, you don't want anybody else to get out, either. They won't let you get ahead. That's what happened to our Jimmy. They saw he was going so good and they couldn't stand it. So they pulled him down."

"I'm sure he'll turn up," I said.

"That's nice of you, to try to make his poor mother feel better. But I don't think you have any more hope than I do, and I've all but given up. Now if you don't have any more questions, I'd like to get back to my little boys, because I got to get them ready. I got to prepare them for the worst, because they love their big brother like nothing else in the world."

"If you knew the names of any of the other drugstores, it might really help."

"Jimmy would just say Ogden Avenue or Garfield Boulevard or somewhere," she said. "I don't remember any names."

I wrote the street names in my notebook. "Can you think of any other streets?" I asked.

"Halsted, Sixty-third, Forty-third, Roosevelt, Cottage Grove, Chicago Avenue, Homan. State Street. Stony Island."

"Do you mind if I talk to Latisa?"

"You'd be wasting your time," she said. "Believe me."

"Why's that?"

"Latisa doesn't have much regard for white people, even in the best of times. And this is not the best of times."

I said good-bye to the boys, nodded at Latisa, who nodded back, and then Mrs. Madison locked me out of the apartment.

The breezeway was empty. The children were gone, but the mouse was still dead in the trap and the TV still blared.

Downstairs, I found my car right where I'd left it. The little boy had grown up a bit and his wardrobe had improved. He wore a black leather jacket and shiny cowboy boots. "I paid him off," he said, and he held out his hand. I'd seen the same man last night, taping a poster to a window at the Gare du Nord.

I reached into my pocket and pulled out a dollar.

"A dollar?" The man was as tough as the boy. "What's that?"

"I told the kid I'd give him a dollar for watching the car."

He snatched the dollar out of my hand. "Little son of a bitch told me five. Damn, should have known better." He looked around, but the kid was gone. "That was a nice trick you pulled on Madison."

"What's that?"

"That business card. I hope that Stringfellow isn't your friend. He didn't know what I was talking about, but it took him forever to convince me. Yeah, chased all the way out to Oak Brook 'cause of a little bitty business card. I'm gonna remember that."

"Wet Willie, right?"

"See, you everywhere just a little ahead of me. Why don't you tell me where you're going, save me the trouble of tracking you down?"

"Why would you want to track me down?"

"Looks like we're working the same case. I'm just trying to figure out who hired you."

I didn't say anything. We looked at each other for a while.

"What were you doing on Madison Street?" he asked.

I shook my head, shrugged.

"What were you and Jimmy whispering about? What did Jimmy sign? What's so important about that station wagon? Who paid you to take those pictures? What was in that envelope that Jimmy gave Rebecca Westerfield?"

"Why didn't you ask her last night?"

"See what I mean?"

"So what's this case you're on?"

"Jimmy Madison," he said, and he pointed upstairs. "His mama hired me to find him."

"Don't you need a license, do this kind of work?"

"You planning to turn me in?"

I shook my head. "But I don't see how I can help you."

"Oh, you can help all right. You got those friends in high places."

I got in the car. Before I could close the door, Harris slipped into the opening, leaned down, and whispered in my ear, "Anything bad happens to Jimmy Madison, anything, and I find out you're part of it, all the friends in the world ain't gonna mean a thing."

I let the car creep forward, then stopped. "Where's your wing tips?" I asked.

He stepped back from the car. "You don't like my boots?" He did a quick shuffle, turned, and walked inside.

TWENTY-SIX

A DENSE haze hung along the horizon as the sun descended. Through the blue of my sunglasses, West Madison looked as cool and forsaken as the high plains at dawn. I kept expecting riders on horseback, tumbleweeds bouncing out of the prairies.

With the tint, Westerfield's had a somewhat hallucinatory look. I thought I might wake up and Jimmy would be back behind the counter. Maybe this time, I'd ask that simple question.

I tooted my horn and Clyde and Jesse waved and smiled. I had the feeling this was one of the high points of their day. Did they ever change a tire?

That familiar whistle came from one of the guys under the stink trees. He managed to add a bit of a mocking tone, and I made a note to go over and say hello someday. I pushed the Olds up over the crumbling curb and through the weeds.

The back door of the medical center opened and Dr. Lutton stepped out and headed straight for a burgundy Cadillac. "Dr. Lutton!" I called as I pulled alongside.

He glanced my way but didn't slow down. "Come back tomorrow," he said as he unlocked the driver's door.

"I talked to you yesterday," I said.

He stopped and looked my way. "Yeah. Now what the hell did you want?" He had the bedside manner of a fully cocked hypodermic.

"I wanted to ask you about Irv Kaplan."

"Oh, Jesus."

"It shouldn't take long."

"Well, you're gonna have to buy me a drink," he said. He got in the Caddy and pulled away.

I followed him west down Madison, through more of the same tinted landscape. I assumed we were heading for the highway, but a few blocks later Lutton pulled to the curb across from a Budweiser sign. A smaller sign said: "Mitchell's."

I parked and followed him across the street. The bar stood all alone, another survivor. Dr. Lutton didn't bother knocking. He kicked the bottom of the door until a buzzer sounded.

It was a small neighborhood place, cool, dark, and inviting. But there wasn't a customer in sight. Most of the light seemed to come from assorted beer signs, some brands long out of business. The Hamm's bear was ice-skating around on an old Christmas display. From the land of sky blue waters.

There was a bar along the far wall, maybe fifteen stools and a curve at the front, and a half-dozen three-sided booths in back.

The bartender was black, of course, somewhere near fifty. He looked like an old-time bartender, with a long apron around his waist and a black vest. His bald head gleamed. As we approached the bar he sailed a bottle of vermouth over a metal canister. "You're gonna be buying me a new door one of these days, Doc."

"Doors I can afford, Mitch," Lutton said. "It's waiting for that first drink I can't stand."

Mitchell set a martini glass in front of Lutton, dropped an olive in, then filled the glass to the brim. He looked my way.

"Bourbon," I said.

"Straight up?"

"Rocks," I decided.

Lutton was having a silent conversation with his martini. He took a sip, then devoured the olive. He raised the glass and held it out at arm's length but didn't drink. Mitchell rolled his eyes as he set my drink down. Lutton finally brought the glass to his lips, then downed the martini in one long pull.

"Ahhhh," he said, and he held the glass out again. After a while he set it down softly and pushed it toward the rail. "First of the day," he whispered. "Always the best."

I dropped a twenty on the bar. "Let me get the doc, too."

"You don't know me well enough to call me Doc," Lutton said. "Hell, I don't even know your name."

I told him my name.

"And you're some kind of cop, right?"

"Private."

"So I don't have to talk to you?"

I shook my head as Mitchell dropped my change on the bar. He speared another olive, then filled Lutton's glass again.

"So why the hell should I?"

"You might want to help find the guy killed Irv Kaplan."

"I'd like to find the son of a bitch all right," Lutton said. "I'd like to find him and do a little surgery. I'd come out of my surgical retirement for that."

"Amen, Doc," Mitchell said. "Amen."

"Were you guys friends?"

"Were we friends? You hear that, Mitch? Was I Irv's friend?"

"They only came in together three nights a week," Mitchell said. He poured himself a cup of coffee.

"You got any theories on who might—"

"Theories? I'm a doctor, Acropolis. I believe in science, not theories. I'll tell you one thing, though."

"What's that?"

"I wish the son of a bitch had gotten Westerfield instead, and that's the god's honest truth."

"What do you have against Gene?"

"Oh, the sanctimonious phony. You're not gonna tell me you actually fell for his bullshit, are you?"

"Haven't met."

"Well, maybe you'll get lucky and you never will."

"Everybody else tells me what a great guy he is."

"Yeah, he's got a lot of people snowed. He'll help you out, but he expects something in return. You got to kiss his big fat ass. I'm just too old for the game. Been around too long."

"He ever help you out?"

He waved that away and took a sip of his drink. "Let's talk about Irv. Now there was a man. You know what he used to do? Crazy son of a bitch used to jump out of airplanes. Mitch, too."

"Don't make me a hero, Doc," Mitchell said. He took a sip of coffee. "I made a lot of jumps, but they were all practice. Irv jumped behind enemy lines and made it back home. That's something to be proud of."

"Mitch lost his war," Lutton said. "He's never got over it."

Mitch held up his coffee and grinned. "Ho, ho, Ho Chi Min." He looked like he'd got over it just fine.

"You a vet?" Lutton asked.

I shook my head.

"Why not?" he barked.

"War's over, Doc," Mitchell said. "Let's not fight it again."

"How about you?" I asked Lutton.

"Irv went right over my head the morning of June sixth, 1944. That date mean anything to you?"

I nodded my head. D day.

"I helped set up the first field hospital in Normandy," Lutton said. "I had to leave medical school early to get there, but I got there, by god. Largest invasion in the history of the world."

I let that sink in. "How'd you end up here?"

"Like Mitch said, the war's over. Not much demand for seventy-year-olds in the medical field."

"Come on," I said. "You're not really that old?"

"Cut the crap, Acropolis," he said. "Get to the point, if you have one."

"All sorts of funny stuff happening," I said. "Irv gets hit; then

Westerfield and Jimmy disappear. There's got to be some connection."

"Well, I'll be damned if I know what it is."

"Lot of money going through that store," I said.

"Oh, that's it," Lutton said, and he pointed his cigar my way. "You're one of those Public Aid investigators."

"You don't have to be a Public Aid investigator to know that a million dollars is a lot of money."

"Which million is this?"

"That's what Westerfield billed Public Aid last year just from the drugstore," I said.

"Well, here. Let me give you Gene's side. I've sure heard it often enough. There's the lights, the gas, the real estate taxes, payroll taxes, workmen's comp insurance, health insurance. The list just goes on and on. Gene's probably lucky if he walks with a hundred gees, the poor guy."

"Yeah, but that's just the drugstore. I haven't got the figures for the medical center yet."

"Party line says there's no connection."

"Come on, Doc."

"You know who owns the place? You met her yesterday, Nurse Hennessy."

"What happened to Dr. Z.? I thought he was the owner."

"Yeah." He smiled. "But he got to where he couldn't sign his name anymore. That's all he ever did. Five hundred a week to sign his name in all the right places. But then he started coming in, just staring at the wall. They'd stick a pen in his hand, but all he'd do was doodle."

"So how come you didn't take his place?"

"I don't sign my name just anywhere."

"No?"

"And I don't order unnecessary tests and X rays or prescribe unnecessary drugs."

"No?"

"I went out to grab a sandwich one day, come back, six of my patients are standing in line outside the X-ray office, including a pregnant gal. I hadn't even seen 'em yet. I came this close to smacking Westerfield. And then the X-ray tech tells me, 'Relax; there's no film in the camera.' That's Westerfield to a tee; there's no film in his camera."

"So why do you keep working for him?"

"If it wasn't for me, nobody'd get any medical care in that place. I must send twenty people a week to County Hospital. Sick people. Cancer, emphysema, cirrhosis, you name it, they've got it. But if I wasn't there, they'd be going home with a couple of prescriptions after getting their toenails clipped by that clown who calls himself a podiatrist. Yeah, I need the money. But I could get it somewhere not quite as bad. But if I did, what would happen to them? And you know what, I'd miss this place, too." He shook his head. "Although it hasn't really been the same without Irv."

"Did you talk to the police?"

"Sure."

"What'd you tell 'em?"

"I just answered their questions, whatever they were. Oh, yeah, they wanted to know if I thought Irv might have hired his own killer."

"Why would he do that?"

"Lung cancer," Lutton said.

"You think he paid someone to murder him?"

He shook his head and smiled. "We used to talk about suicide all the time, right, Mitch?"

"They used to go on and on so bad they'd get me drinking. And I almost never drink until last call."

"You get to be my age, you'll be thinking about it, too. And if you're lucky . . ." He stopped and took a long drink. "But doctors and pharmacists use pills. Irv wasn't about to waste his money on a hit man when he could get all the pills he needed free."

"How long did he have to live?"

"Who knows? Six months. Two years." He shook his head again. "If he was going to kill himself, I would have known. We weren't just friends, you know. We were partners."

"Partners? Business partners?"

"Sure." He winked at Mitchell. "Don't tell me you never heard of West Side Field Hospitals Incorporated?"

I shook my head.

"Yeah. That's 'cause we never got it off the ground. Oh, well. It's still a good idea."

"You were gonna open your own hospital?"

He nodded. "On wheels."

"Really?"

"Yeah," he said, and suddenly his eyes were alive. "And, believe it or not, it's what they need out here. You see, it's not just Westerfield. Even somebody who's trying to do a good job, it's damn near impossible in a neighborhood like this.

"Half the sick people never go anywhere near a doctor, and a lot of those who do wait until they're almost beyond help. But a field hospital. You go to them. You go out into the neighborhood and you find the sick people. One day you're on one corner, one day on another. You send out announcements letting people know where you're going to be. And if they're too sick to come out to the van, you go to them."

"Was Westerfield going to be part of this?"

"Oh, we talked about it. We didn't want to set up a new business just to experiment. But who could trust Gene to play it straight? And then Irv died. Oh, well. What the hell. I'm too old to do it alone."

"I still think it's a great idea," Mitchell said, and he turned to me. "You'd be surprised how many people walk in here and buy a bottle just to use as a painkiller."

"Remember that guy the other day?" Lutton asked me.

"Who?"

"When you were in the clinic. The guy with the swollen head."

"The drunk?"

He nodded. "See, this is typical West Side medicine. A few weeks back, he had a minor ear infection. One look, I prescribe antibiotics. Next patient. A couple of days later, the ear clears up. So he stops taking his medicine, even though I specifically warned him about that. But why listen to your doctor when you can sell the pills on the street? Well, now the infection comes back. But now it really comes back, because the antibiotics killed all the other germs. So does he come back to the clinic? No. He drinks for days and days until even the whiskey won't kill the pain. Then he comes in. I've seen people die from stupidity like that.

"But, see, the field hospital, you go to him. You don't give him the entire prescription. You go out every day and you give him his pills. And you're there the next day, too. It's a lot of running around, a lot of work. But it's real health care."

"Makes sense," I said.

"I'll bet we could save five hundred strokes a year out here just by getting people to take their blood pressure medication."

"I hate to stop all this happy talk," Mitchell said, "but sun's down. Time for all the honkies to go home."

Lutton drained his drink and stood up. "Mitch doesn't let us stay after sunset."

Somebody knocked lightly on the door and Mitchell pushed the buzzer and a couple of CTA bus drivers walked in. "Hey, Doc," one of them said. "How's it going today?"

"Same old, same old," Lutton said. "And I do mean old." He dropped some money on the bar. I slid a few bills toward the rail, waved to Mitchell, and followed Lutton out to Madison Street.

TWENTY-SEVEN

Back at my office, I threw some junk mail in the wastebasket and put my feet up on the window ledge. The phone rang.

"Nick, guess who died?" Shelly asked in a cheerful voice.

"I'm gonna pass," I said. This had never been my favorite game. The people you wanted dead always seemed to live forever.

"The old man," she said.

"Daley?"

"Purcell."

"He wasn't that old," I said, and I had a flash of that barn full of bikes and Raymond Purcell's hands shaking in the sunlight. "Where'd you get this?"

"A little bird at OPS," she said. OPS was the Office of Professional Standards.

"Your little bird know the cause of death?"

"The important thing is, we got the last statement."

"Do me a favor, Shel, try to find out what happened."

"Nick, what's the diff?"

"I'm just kind of curious."

"Speaking of curious, Trace called me this afternoon."

"Yeah?"

"He's a little worried about you."

"I'm touched."

"OK. The truth is, he's worried about himself. But I don't blame him. He told me you're looking into some homicide that happened at that drugstore."

"Why's that bother him?"

"I guess what he's worried about is the newspapers' getting interested in the drugstore. The murder. That guy who's missing. If they start sniffing around and find out about Trace's accident . . . Well, you know how witnesses tend to come out of the woodwork once the TV and the newspapers get ahold of something."

"He should have thought about that before he decided to play cowboy on Forty-seventh Street."

"Nick, you're supposed to be on his side, remember?"

"Yeah." I remembered. "You know, Shelly, I almost threw that statement out the window yesterday. Christ, I wish I had."

"Nick, what's up? What's going on?"

"Don't you find it a bit odd that one witness disappears and another dies right after I take statements from them?"

"Oh, come on. You can't be serious."

"Just do me a favor and find out how Purcell died."

"I mean, Tracy might not be a choirboy," Shelly said. "But I don't quite see him . . ." She stopped without finishing.

"He's a snake, is what he is," I said.

"He might very well be, Nick. But try to remember: he's our snake. This is what we get paid to do."

TWENTY-EIGHT

S o where are we going?" Patrice asked as we walked out of the Gare du Nord.

"I was thinking of the Key of C."

"What's that?"

"Sexy little nightclub," I said.

"I can't believe I've never heard of it."

"Jazz," I said, and she rolled her eyes.

I opened the door of the Olds and she slid into the front seat. "I could stop home and change," she said.

"You'll fit right in," I said. She was wearing a black cardigan sweater over her uniform T-shirt.

"You're sure?"

"Trust me."

The Key had been there as long as I could remember, and just about everybody fit in. They overcharged for their drinks and paid their musicians as little as possible. The room was a dump, but years ago they'd figured out that if they kept the lights down low nobody would notice the years of decay. This also helped at closing time. The regulars knew to get out before they brought the house-lights up.

They got away with all this because they were one of the few jazz joints with a 4:00 A.M. license and they did a late set every night. The musicians who worked the early clubs would come to the Key to unwind, and if things got rolling the best players in town, or from out of town for that matter, would be sitting in, all at no cost to the owners, who made most of their money in those late hours.

The doorman was a house fixture. He'd worn a beret for years and had always looked like an aging hipster. Lately he'd switched to the world's worst toupee, and now he was just another old guy trying to appear young. He was sitting next to a sign that read: COVER $7. The house wits said that's what the toupee had cost.

I went for my roll, but he waved me past as usual. "Always good having you in the room," he said, and I thanked him like I always did. And I meant it. He knew I'd lost the badge.

Patrice gave me a look. I winked.

The best thing about the joint was the row of booths that climbed an alcove opposite the stage. They were dark three-sided jobs, installed years ago by some long-forgotten genius, who couldn't possibly be related to the current owners.

We picked one about halfway up, which put us on a level several feet above the band. I slid in beside Patrice. A piano trio was working its way through an easygoing version of "It Never Entered My Mind."

The waitress came by. She was probably pushing sixty or maybe a little past, a slim woman, with rhinestones on the corners of her eyeglasses and an accent about forty years out of some West Virginia hollow. I ordered Old Grand-Dad in a snifter. Patrice asked for red wine.

"Honey," the waitress whispered, "what they call wine in this place, the 7-Eleven calls vinegar. I highly recommend a mixed drink."

"Vodka and soda," Patrice decided. "Wow. That was great," she said when the waitress was gone. "I wish I had the balls to say things like that."

"You probably don't have to, where you work."

She rolled her eyes.

"Never mind. I don't want to know."

Patrice took her time looking around the room. "This is right out of *Blue Velvet*," she whispered.

"Bobby Vinton?"

"Who's that?"

"Isn't he the guy who sang 'Blue Velvet'?"

"I was thinking of Dennis Hopper."

"The painter?"

She rolled her eyes again.

"Is that good or bad?"

"What?"

"Blue Velvet."

"Sexy," she said.

"I told you."

"But dark."

"They go together, don't they?"

"Sometimes," she said. "But light's OK, too."

"I'll try to remember that."

"Aren't you a little old for me?"

"I try not to think about stuff like that."

"How old are you?"

"That's exactly the part I try not to think about," I said, but then I told her the truth. "Forty-five."

"I'm twenty-eight."

"That's a nice age," I said.

"That means you were seventeen when I was born."

"I think I remember that day," I said. "I was in high school and I had this strange feeling."

"I was born in July."

"That's right," I said. "Summer school."

"Probably every year," she said. They all had my number.

The waitress dropped our drinks and went away. "Relax," I said. "Let's just relax and have fun."

"Why do I have the feeling you've said that a million times?"

I lifted my glass in a toast and found her free hand. There was something about drinking Old Grand-Dad out of a snifter that always made me feel I was putting something over on someone. The grand-dad himself, perhaps. It certainly wasn't Patrice. She had an amused look in her eyes.

We sat that way for a while, sipping our drinks and holding hands. Patrice seemed engrossed in the band. They did a nice rendition of "Dancing in the Dark," then finished the set with a red-hot "The Night Has a Thousand Eyes."

"Wow," Patrice said.

"See? It doesn't have to be boring."

Patrice nodded her head. She released my hand, sat up straight, and grinned. "So did you really rob a bank?"

"Oh, boy," I said. Here it was again. "Where'd you get that?"

"Oh, here and there," she said.

"Shit," I said, and I stood up and dropped some money on the table. "Come on. Let's get out of here."

Patrice didn't want to go. She put a little pout on her face but then gave me her hand.

"So about this bank robbery business," I said once we were outside.

"Hey, it's no big deal," she said.

"No. It is a big deal."

"I think it's sort of intriguing."

"Patrice, I hate to disappoint you. But I didn't rob any bank."

"Nick, it was on the front page."

"Oh, Jesus," I said softly, and I backed up to a brick wall.

"It's OK." Patrice slipped into my arms. "Hey, we've all done stuff," she whispered. "I mean, people with nothing to regret, those are the biggest bores in the whole world."

"You heard this from Becky, I take it."

"Nick, let's go back inside and have another drink, and we'll forget I ever brought it up. Let's not spoil the night."

"How about a ride instead?"

We got in the Olds. I opened the glove box and cracked the seal on the bottle of old Grand-Dad and took a swallow.

"Easy, boy, easy," Patrice said. She pushed the armrest up and moved close. I handed her the bottle and she took a small, ladylike sip. I found some jazz on public radio.

"It was a long time ago, Nick," Patrice said.

"What?"

"The bank robbery."

"But nobody will let me forget it."

"You shouldn't still have your ego invested way back there."

"My ego?"

"Who you are, Nick. Who you are," she said. "We're not the past. We're here right now. Yesterday doesn't mean anything."

"Is it really that simple? You just turn it off?"

"It's already turned off. That's the point. You can't change it. You just have to accept it and go on."

We sat there for an hour or so, sipping the whiskey, barely talking, listening to the music, and steaming up the windows. It was the best kind of ride.

"Why don't we go to my place?" I said when the time seemed right.

"Oh, I wish I could," she said softly.

"OK, I'm easy. Your place."

"There's something I should have told you," she said. "I sort of have a boyfriend."

"Sort of?"

"See, it's over, but it's not. We can't quite break away."

"Forget the past," I said.

"See, it's hard. We live together."

"Your place is definitely out," I said.

"What's wrong with right here?" she whispered.

TWENTY-NINE

A N hour later, I was on the highway heading northwest. An air horn mourned. Black smoke floated into a starry sky. I followed a line of long-haul trucks, but I wouldn't find out where they were going tonight. I rolled down an exit ramp, picked up the phone, and dialed my old partner John Casper.

"Jesus, Nick, what's up?" He didn't sound very awake.

"I'll buy you a drink at Teddy's," I said.

He groaned. "Stop by here," he said. "Teddy's is like a time machine. Every time I walk in the door, next thing I know it's six in the morning."

The house was a block off Northwest Highway, in a peaceful neighborhood just inside the city line. The area was full of cops and firemen, who all had to live within the city. Most of the breaking of the peace was done by their children.

I went around back, like the old days, and Casper opened the door and led me into the kitchen. It was turning out to be a night of bad toupees. "What's that on your head?" I asked.

He ignored me and opened the door leading to the basement. "Fix yourself a drink. I'll be right down."

This was the kind of neighborhood where every house had a basement rec room. There was a bottle of Old Grand-Dad on the bar, an ice bucket, and a pitcher of water. I poured myself light, then swiveled around. There was a sofa and chairs, a TV, and a card table. The aquarium was now without fish or water. The washer and dryer were hidden in back, beyond western-style swinging doors.

This had been our retreat when even Teddy's wasn't dark enough. Sometimes we wouldn't talk at all, just drink and smoke and try to forget whatever had led us here.

Andy Kelly, the third member of our team, was usually the first to leave. He was single, but he generally had something going on. And he was the kind of guy who could get away with calling at three in the morning and inviting himself over.

I'd pass out on the couch, more often than not, and Casper usually managed to crawl upstairs. The hangover was often a blessing. This was the kind of pain that was easy to understand.

I was on my second child's portion when Casper came down and popped the tab on a beer. "So what're you working?"

"Couple things," I said. "I'm doing an off-duty traffic altercation for Shelly."

He shook his head. "Another psycho, I presume."

I gave him a brief rundown without mentioning names.

"Isn't there some law against obstructing justice?"

"Laws against everything." I shrugged.

"I honestly don't know how you do it. I mean most of these guys should probably be in jail."

"You can't take individual circumstances into account."

"Says who?"

I shrugged innocently. "That's what the Police Board said in my case. I'm just playing by their rules."

"Oh, Nick, get over it."

"That's easy for you to say."

"You know what gets me? Andy's been inside for years and he's not feeling sorry for himself and you're walking around a free man and all you can think about—"

"Andy Kelly robbed a bank. He's supposed to be in jail. I didn't rob any bank."

"When you gonna drop this smoke screen, Nick? You're not out because of a bank robbery. You're out because you lied."

"I suppose you would have turned him in?"

"In a heartbeat. Why would I lie to protect a man who jeopardizes my career and my family? That thin-blue-line crap only goes so far. Cover your ass, Nick. That's the name of the game. So stop giving me this you-didn't-rob-any-bank bullshit. Nobody said you did."

"Well, at least I know you're not tapping my line."

"Somebody said you robbed the bank? Where the hell would they get that?"

"Oh, I don't know, front page of the *Sun-Times*, maybe the *Tribune*, any of the TV stations."

"Yeah, but it all got straightened out."

"John, people don't remember those stories on page forty."

"Well, fuck, just tell 'em what happened." He had all the answers. "Keep a copy of that page-forty story in your wallet."

I dropped another ice cube in my glass and added bourbon.

"So what's all this have to do with Irv Kaplan anyway?" he asked.

"Can we hold off on that for a while?"

"You're working for Shelly, right?"

"I can't tell you who I'm working for."

"Nick, everybody knows you're my old partner. You could really put me in a box on this."

"Look, there's nothing I know that your worst dick couldn't get in an hour."

"So save me the trouble of sending one out."

"How many people were in that store when Kaplan got hit?"

"Kaplan, the guy who did him, Westerfield, and Jimmy Madison."

"And the only one you can find is Kaplan and he's in the ground."

"Where's Westerfield?"

"Supposedly on vacation."

"Why supposedly?"

"There's people who don't believe it."

"Your client?"

"I can't say."

"And they think?"

"They don't know."

"Who's running the store?"

"Gone Fishing."

"Oh, hell, I better send some guys out." He didn't sound very happy about the idea. "You're not holding out on me, are you?"

"Speaking of holding out," I said, "why didn't you tell me Kaplan had cancer?"

"You seem to be doing OK without my help," he said.

"That's kind of funny. Who'd put a hit on somebody who's only got a couple months to live?"

"This isn't a rational business, Nick. You know that."

"A black guy with red hair, that's kind of unusual, too, don't you think?"

"See, you didn't need our files after all."

"That's where I got it, John."

He started to say something, then stopped. "The POW camp," he said softly.

"I tried to get it from an old friend, but he turned me down."

"Nick . . ."

"What I'd really like is the runner," I said. The runner was the street file, passed on from detective to detective. It never left the area. It was destroyed as soon as the case was closed.

"And you told me you weren't reading the newspapers, Nick. Street files don't exist." There'd been several unsuccessful lawsuits through the years, with defense attorneys asking that the unofficial files be turned over.

"I just can't figure out why you didn't work this thing."

"Nick, we worked it until there was nowhere to go."

"Well, you got places to go now. Westerfield's gone. He might be dead. Jimmy Madison's gone. He might be dead."

I filled my glass again. Casper popped another beer. Nobody said anything for a while.

"Hey, how's your old buddy Stringfellow?" Casper broke the silence. "You still pick up work from him?"

"Now and then," I said.

"Good old Frank."

"Yeah."

"Lot of nights down here," he said a while later.

"Yeah."

"I really miss you guys."

"Sure."

"No. Christ, we had some times, didn't we?"

"Yeah." We had.

"It's weird, some of these young guys, they're from some other planet. I got two guys don't even play poker."

"Probably sick of losing."

"No. No. They never learned to play."

"Come on. Dicks?"

"I'm not kidding. They never learned to play."

"Oh, well."

"It's funny." He laughed, a short fake laugh. "I hear more from Andy in jail than I do from you."

"He's got nothing else to do," I said. "Just thank your lucky stars he's not calling collect."

"I didn't know he called you."

"No," I said. "I didn't mean that. It's just that's what a lot of these clowns do. End up bankrupting their families with collect calls. No, Andy just writes me a letter about once a month and I toss it right into the trash."

"You don't read his letters?"

"Straight into the garbage." I sailed an invisible envelope across the room.

"How can you do that?" Casper slammed his beer on the bar.

"It's always the same letter. How great he's doing. The weight he's lost, all the weights he's lifting. Three hundred push-ups a day. Clean living. No cigarettes. No booze."

"But that's great!" Casper said.

"He'll get out and he'll be a hundred times better than when he went in, and I'll be a wreck."

"You better look in the mirror, Nick. You're already a wreck."

"That's when I'm gonna pop him," I said.

"Pop him?" Casper whispered.

"Sure. He's out. He's having a good time. Finds himself a girl, a job, everything's coming up roses. That's when I'm gonna walk up and shoot him right in the fucking head."

"Jesus Christ, Nick," Casper said. "You're not a happy man."

"No," I said, and I splashed more bourbon in my glass. "But I will be, John. Mark my words. One of these days I will be."

I went away somewhere. When I came back I noticed my glass was empty. I filled it with ice and bourbon and listened to myself talk. "You make me sick, John. Your perfect little house and your perfect little family, and your perfect little record to go with your perfect career. Don't you ever get tired of being so fucking perfect?"

"See, what you don't understand, Nick, with guys like you for partners, I had to be perfect. I mean, what'd I have? A psycho and a . . ."

"A what, John?"

"A budding pedophile."

"What the fuck does that mean?"

"What do you call Shelly?"

Shelly, my lawyer turned lover. Now she was just a client. "You better get your dictionary out, John. She was over twenty-one."

"What, by two days?"

"You know, I think you're fucking jealous."

"You're old enough to be her father, Nick."

"But I'm not her father. And her father, by the way, is fifteen, sixteen years older than me."

"And the poor mope's in the joint and his daughter's looking for a replacement and there you are robbin' the old cradle."

"I wasn't replacing her father, John, believe me. And anyway, it's one of the few advantages of getting older."

"What?"

"Younger women. Try dating someone fifteen years younger when you're twenty-five. See where that gets you."

"Oh, that's supposed to be a joke, I guess."

I found two shot glasses, filled them to the brim, and set them on the bar between us. "To Shelly," I said.

"You know I don't drink whiskey anymore," Casper said.

"You're gonna have a shot with me or I'm gonna knock your ass right off that stool."

"This I want to see."

"To Shelly," I said again.

He hesitated, but then he picked up the glass. "To Shelly," he said, and we both downed the shots.

Now it was Casper's turn to fill the glasses. "To Andy Kelly," he said.

It was my turn to hesitate before lifting the glass. "To Andy," I said, and I started to laugh.

"What's so funny?"

"Now we're fucked," I said.

"What?"

"We're fucked. I'm gonna have to sleep on the couch and you're not gonna get laid for a month. Couldn't you just have some balls and not let me force you into drinking whiskey?"

"Have another," he said, and he filled the glasses and we held them up for every homicide detective's favorite toast. "To life," Casper said.

"L'Chaym," I agreed.

THIRTY

CASPER'S two boys jumped me in the morning. They'd grown enough, in the years since I'd last seen them, that rough-housing was no longer much fun. Maybe my hangover had some-thing to do with it. My series of hangovers.

After a while I begged them to stop, and sometime later they actually did. I sent them upstairs to check for their mother; then I took a few more punches and slipped out the back door.

At home, I showered and shaved. I was making coffee when the phone rang.

"Nick, Frank," Stringfellow said.

"What's up?"

"What's up? Whadda you mean, what's up? What'd you find out about that drugstore?"

"It's all locked up," I said.

"That's all you've got?"

"I'm just waking up, Frank," I said. "Give me a minute, huh?"

"Sure. Sorry, Nick. I know it's not even ten o'clock. What was I thinking?"

I had to give him something. I tried the truth first. "Look, there was a murder in that store a few weeks back."

"A murder?"

"Yeah. Contract hit, looks like."

"What's this got to do with me and the FBI?"

"Here's the thing," I suddenly realized where I was going. "The hit man fits the description of the guy you're looking for."

"Leslie Crawford?"

"Bingo," I said. Crawford and the hit man were both well-dressed black males. There were probably only a few hundred thousand in town. That would get the FBI's interest up.

"Nick, he's a shakedown artist. Not a hit man."

"Didn't you tell me this has something to do with the medical field?"

"Yeah. He's shaking down a doc."

"What's the shakedown?"

"Remember the old joke, what do you call the medical student who graduates last?"

"I don't know," I played along.

"Doctor," he said. "Anyways, that's my client. Graduated dead last from East Chicago, Class of '72. And it's not something he likes to advertise. So he gets a phone call a few months back. Guy threatens to inform his patients about his class rank unless the doc sends him two thousand dollars."

"And the doc did it," I said.

"No. No. No. Give him credit. He told him to go fuck himself, and then he wouldn't take any more of his calls. He figured it was bullshit. Somehow this clown had come up with his class rank, but how was he gonna get the names of his patients?"

"But he did," I said.

"Fucking modems, it's like giving some of these guys a key to your office. Anyway, a few weeks after the turndown he sends the doc a copy of a letter that he claims he sent to ten patients. The letter's pretty funny, actually. It's on the doc's stationery, with a pretty good forgery of his signature. All about how twenty-some years ago he graduated at the bottom of his class. And although some people thought he was doomed to be a second-rate physician, through a lot of hard work, and knowing the right people, he had built up a successful practice. And he now wants to thank his patients for sticking with him through thick and thin, blah, blah, blah. It's better than that. But that's the gist."

"So did he actually send the letter out?"

"Oh, yeah. Within a week, three of the ten patients had their records transferred. The rest never called at all."

"So he paid."

"But now the bozo wants ten grand. Now that should have told the doc where this was headed. But he talks him down to five and then pays him off."

"And then he wanted more."

"And that's when the doc calls me."

"Well, you're probably right, Frank. He doesn't sound like a hit man. But you never know. Maybe Kaplan refused to pay and—"

"Who's Kaplan?"

"The guy who got hit on Madison Street."

"He's a doc?"

"Pharmacist."

"Come on, Nick. Who cares if a pharmacist graduated last?"

"Hey, Frank, you asked me to find out what I could about that drugstore. I'm doing the best I can. You know, I got something going for Shelly, too."

"Well, keep track of your time, Nick. I only want to pay my own."

"This one's on the house, Frank."

"The house? Whadda you mean?"

"I can't charge you."

"Of course you gotta charge me, Nick. I mean, Jesus, you're in business, right?"

"Frank, I'm just trying to help you out. All the work you send my way. I owe you a little. FBI comes knocking at your door, it's the least I can do."

"Well, hell, I don't know what to say, Nick." For a moment I thought he was going to cry, but then he coughed instead. "That's mighty white of you," he said. "Mighty white. Maybe I can send a bit more work your way."

"I'm not complaining, Frank."

"No. No. No. I know. But sometimes I get some nice gravy I gotta farm out. I'm gonna remember you, pal."

"Well, thanks."

"Keep up the good work, Nick," he said, and the line went dead.

I sat there staring at the phone. If Frank ever found out that I'd given his business card to the brothers at the tire shop . . . Oh, well, maybe it was better not to think along those lines.

And the FBI might be only the beginning. Casper had asked about Stringfellow last night. He had tried to make it sound casual, but I wouldn't be surprised if one of his detectives had handed him a list with Stringfellow's name on it. Well, at least they were back on the case.

THIRTY-ONE

I COULDN'T face another day on the West Side, so I headed north instead, gliding along under a wispy blue-and-white sky.

I took the scenic route up Sheridan Road, winding through Evanston and into Wilmette, occasionally catching a glimpse of the lake just out of reach beyond towering trees shading those huge single-family sanctuaries, where the garden path kept right on going, winding down to the water's edge.

I thought of Mike Brewer, standing at the bar at Berghoff's dreaming of Paris. Yeah, I had my own little dream; if you had a few days to kill and the right sidekick, it might be worth the thousand-mile drive around Lake Michigan.

This would be the perfect season, the tourists and the heat of summer gone and that first touch of winter about to sail in, on some midnight breeze.

Hell, the right companion—Patrice, for instance—you might stretch it out a bit, find a cabin on the coast of the Upper Peninsula and stockpile it with plenty of firewood and enough brandy to get through winter's first true snow. And then run like hell, laughing and singing, the heater blowing full blast and winter an ominous gray in the rearview mirror.

The Westerfield house was no cabin, of course, and Wilmette was a long way from Michigan's Upper Peninsula. But there were all those beautiful trees, most still sporting those endless autumn colors, and bushes and flowers, and the rustic unpaved driveway with dark stones crunching under my tires. This was as close as I generally got to the great outdoors.

I went up the front stairs and pushed the doorbell and then one of the wooden porch swings. It had almost stopped moving when the door opened just a touch. "Yes?" she said softly. She barely looked my way.

"I'm a detective from Chicago," I said, and flashed my ID. "Is Eugene Westerfield in?"

She had that same troubled look that I'd glimpsed the other day from inside Becky's closet. There were dark circles under her eyes. Her hair wasn't quite in place. Her dress was wrinkled. She couldn't decide what to do with her free hand, the one that wasn't holding the door open.

But she wasn't that tired. "Do you mind if I look?" She held out the hand. I flipped the ID case open again. She gave me a faint smile. "A *private* detective," she corrected me, and there was something familiar in her voice.

It must run in the family. "Mrs. Westerfield?" I asked.

"My husband's out of town. If you like, I'll have him give you a call when he returns."

"Sure," I said. I slipped a business card out and handed it over. "When would that be?"

"A week. Possibly two."

"This is a business trip?"

She looked down at my card, then up. "Mr. Acropolis, I don't see how that is your concern."

"You're right," I said. "Sorry."

"I'll make sure he gets this." She held up my business card and started to close the door.

"Maybe you could help me," I said. "A car registered to your husband was in an accident last—"

"Mr. Acropolis, I'm very sorry, but I really have nothing further to say. Perhaps you should talk to my husband's attorney."

"That might help," I said.

"Sheldon Banks," she said. "He's downtown. Dearborn Street, I believe."

"Thanks," I said. The door had almost closed when her accent finally registered. "You grew up on the West Side, right?"

The door opened. "What did you say?" She almost looked awake.

"You sound like you're from the old West Side."

"The *old* West Side?"

"You go to Austin High by any chance?"

The surprise turned to suspicion. "You're asking me to believe you pulled that out of thin air?"

"You can take a girl out of the West Side, but—"

"Oh, please," she said, "don't say it." And she actually laughed. "And where did you go?"

"Austin, but only my first two years," I said. "So I was right?"

"Yes, Mr. Acropolis, it appears we have something in common." She gave me that same small laugh. "I went to Austin until the middle of my senior year."

"I'm going to say '66," I said.

She nodded. "Very good. That was my graduating class, but I never quite got there. I transferred out in the fall of '65."

"The first riot," I said. "The lunchroom riot."

She nodded again. "First and last for me."

"My sophomore year," I said. "And that one little riot was all it took for my parents to start looking for a house out of the neighborhood."

"My parents didn't wait. They never let me go back. I never forgave them for that. It all seems so silly now. The next day, there I was up in the great north woods."

"Wisconsin?"

"Skokie." She laughed. "That's what we called it, all the kids from the West Side, the exiles. The great north woods. It might as

well have been Wisconsin. I had to go to summer school to graduate. How embarrassing."

"Seems to me I went every year."

"Yes," she said, and she gave me a real smile. "And you probably
wore a leather jacket and combat boots and got in trouble with the
police."

"No combat boots," I said. "I was always afraid someone might
take them seriously."

"Yes. That was always there, wasn't it?"

"What?"

"Vietnam. It's funny. I look back now and it's like two completely separate worlds. In one world there were all the innocent
things about growing up, the dances and the boys, girl talk, the
Beatles. And then in the other world there was Vietnam, the race
riots, Bobby Kennedy, Martin Luther King. And for some reason
I can never get the two worlds together. Does that happen to you?"

"All the time," I admitted.

"Really? You're not just . . ." She left it hanging there.

". . . trying to trick you into answering my questions?"

"Yes," she said.

"Tell you the truth, I think I'd rather talk about high school.
How about lunch?"

"Oh, Mr. Acropolis," she said sadly, and I had the feeling that
I'd just gone and ruined everything.

"There must be a restaurant around here somewhere."

"This has been very nice actually to think about something . . .
to remember back then . . . but—"

"You know I've got Austin High in my blood. My parents met
there."

"At Austin? Really?"

I nodded. "Nineteen-forty."

"How interesting," she said, but I knew I was losing her.

"So what do you say, a hamburger, fries, and a chocolate phos?
Just like the Green Grill."

"The Green Grill? Oh, my god!" Her face came alive and for a moment she was back in that long, narrow room on West End Avenue. "You know I was only there once, but . . ." She stopped suddenly.

"It was off-limits," I seemed to remember.

"Off-limits? I don't remember that. But it was very . . ."

"Dark," I said.

"Risqué, I think. That's the word, in a very nice 1950-ish sort of way."

"So what happened at the Green Grill?"

"What makes you think anything happened there?"

"Something in your eyes."

"Yes," she said. "You're a detective. You watch people's eyes, don't you?" And for the first time she didn't try to hide her distress. "That must be a very useful skill."

"Sometimes."

"You know, maybe it would be nice," she said, and she seemed to suddenly relax. "A hamburger and fries. There's a place in down-town Wilmette, Bill's Fountain. It's not the Green Grill, but—"

"Sounds great," I said.

She looked down at her hands. "I'll need a little time, I'm afraid. Is—"

"Whatever you need," I said.

"An hour?"

"An hour's fine," I said. "I'll take a little tour. See how the other half lives."

"I might even have a phosphate," she said. She smiled, a wan little smile that could have meant almost anything, and closed the door.

THIRTY-TWO

I CRUISED downtown Wilmette for a while, then found a parking space across from the movie theater. I dialed Stringfellow's number. "Didn't you tell me Crawford was some kind of computer expert?" I asked when he came on.

"That's the assumption."

"You know, there wasn't any computer stuff in that apartment, Frank. Nothing."

"You expect him to leave a computer sitting there?"

"All that garbage, none of it had anything to do with computers. There weren't any disks or computer paper or computer books or magazines. The only magazines I saw were skin rags. I thought the whole point of having a computer was you got good porn."

"Where you going with this, Nick?"

"What kind of car does Crawford have?"

"Mercedes-Benz."

"Black, right?"

"Yeah."

"There was a bus driver saw the hit man on Madison Street. He was pretty sure he was coming from a black Benz or BMW. You really ought to call John Casper over at Area Four, tell him you might know the boy who did Irv Kaplan. Might solve your whole problem. And don't be afraid to use my name."

It might solve a few of my problems, too. And I wasn't going to feel bad feeding Leslie Crawford to the wolves. Not after his stunt with my tires.

"What's Casper doing at Area Four?"

"They made him a lieutenant. He took Hayes's place."

"Jesus, Nick, if you'd stayed on that might of been you."

"Thanks for reminding me, Frank. Thanks for reminding me."

I dialed my answering machine. "Nick, I'm sorry about that stuff I told Patrice," Becky said. "Call me, OK?" Mike Brewer was next. He had the vouchers from the day Irv Kaplan died. But he was leaving his office at two and wouldn't be back until Monday. Could I pick them up before that? I called him back and we agreed to meet at my office at two-thirty.

"So how was your tour?" Mrs. Westerfield asked as she slipped into the booth at Bill's Fountain.

"Every time I get up this way I think the same damn thing."

An easy smile flashed across her face. "And that is?"

"Rich people sure know how to live."

"Oh, they like to think they do," she said.

"I mean, it's like the fifties all over again. All the little shops. This place." I gestured around the restaurant. "Christ, Mrs. Westerfield, they've even got a matinee at the movie theater."

"Janet, please."

"Nick," I said. "It sort of reminds me of the West Side back in the old days."

"Oh, but it's all so phony, isn't it? Like something preserved in a museum. A room where someone you never heard of died."

"Sure. Another amusement park. I was having this same conversation about Berghoff's the other day."

She pointed a finger at me. "I forbid you to say anything derogatory about the creamed spinach."

"Never."

We talked about Austin High for a while. She told me her story about the Green Grill and, not surprisingly, it involved a boy.

There was the lunchroom riot, which neither one of us had witnessed, although we'd both been in school that day. And then there were all the other riots and catastrophes that had befallen the school since our time.

"A couple of years ago," I remembered reading in the newspaper, "Austin had the highest dropout rate in the city. Seventy percent."

"That's inexcusable," she said.

We sat there munching on our hamburgers and fries. She really did order a phosphate. What the hell, I had a malted.

She'd put on some makeup and a fresh dress, fixed her hair, and it had done wonders for her looks. But her eyes still held that troubled, wary look. I had the feeling there were two different people sitting across from me. The second one was watching both of us with equal suspicion.

"Did you ever wonder what would have happened to the West Side if everybody had just stayed?" she asked.

"I used to play that game."

"It doesn't get you anywhere, does it?"

I shook my head.

"Do you ever get out that way?" she asked after the waitress cleared the plates.

"When I was a cop I was there quite a bit."

"You were a police officer. That doesn't surprise me. Why did you give it up?"

"It was actually the other way around. They gave me up."

"Oh, I'm sorry," she said. She never asked, but for some reason I ended up telling her what had become the story of my life.

"It all started when the superintendent issued a directive that we no longer had to wear our guns off duty."

"Why?"

"Well, the truth is, too many off-duty cops were getting involved in bad shootings. Shootings that weren't quite justified. A lot of

barroom stuff. If you're ever in a saloon and there's off-duty cop-
pers around, you better be very careful who you start making time
with."

"I'll try to keep that in mind," she said.

"This new directive said that if we thought we might be drinking
we should leave our guns at home. Well, that meant that we never
had to carry a gun off duty. 'Hey, I thought I was gonna be drinking.' So that was it. As soon as I read the directive, I started leaving
my gun home."

"You don't look like the kind of man who would shoot innocent
people."

"That's nice of you to say, and I don't want to give you the wrong
idea; I've never shot anybody. But the right circumstances, especially with enough alcohol, you never know what might happen.

"And it's not just innocent people you have to worry about. Say
you're sitting in a bar and a fight breaks out. The bartender knows
you're a copper with a gun. So now he wants you to go do his work
for him. I say, break up your own fights. Or maybe the same bar
gets stuck up. Half the customers know you have a gun. So you
can pull it out and get in a shoot-out and maybe get yourself or
somebody else killed—for what, a couple hundred bucks?—or you
can sit there and now half the bar thinks you're a coward. There's
no way you can win in a situation like that."

"It seems to me you could solve the problem very nicely by not
spending all your free time in saloons."

"There's that West Side accent again," I said. "The only person
who had any problem with all this was one of my partners, Andy
Kelly. It just drove him crazy that I was walking around unarmed.
He kept coming up with scenarios where I was going to be sorry
I didn't have a gun."

"For instance?"

"Oh, I'd come upon a mass murderer in a public place, you
know, a McDonald's or a post office, and if I just had my gun along
I could drop the guy and save all these innocent lives. My all-time

favorite was his Mother's Day Massacre. This is where a lone gun-
man goes berserk in a restaurant on Mother's Day and starts
shooting all the mothers and he's heading right for the table where
I'm sitting with my very own mom. . . ."

"With an imagination like that, you'd think he'd be writing for
the movies."

"Well, he's got plenty of time for it now."

"Oh, really?"

"Yeah. One payday I was waiting in line at my bank and Andy
walks in with his Nixon mask on and robs the place."

"He didn't!"

"He did," I said. "And then on the way out, he walks right up
to me, just in case I haven't already recognized him in his favorite
mask, and he says, 'Now don't you wish you had your gun, Nick?'
And he walks out with his big haul. Seven hundred and eighty-one
dollars."

"That's unbelievable," she said, joining a long line of people who
had used that very word to describe Andy Kelly's most memorable
practical joke. "What did you do?"

"What could I do? I pretended I didn't know him. I lied. I said
I didn't know who he was and I hadn't heard what he'd said. I
mean, you can't turn your own partner in."

"Why not?"

"You just can't," I said. "You either understand that or you don't.
I can't explain it to you."

She thought it over, nodded. "OK," she said.

"They knew I was lying, of course. Everybody in the whole goddamn bank heard him say my name. The FBI wanted to charge
me with bank robbery. They were convinced I was in on it. When
Andy found out I'd been arrested, he turned himself in."

"So if you'd told the truth?"

"Yeah, Andy still would have ended up in jail. The difference is,
I would have been the one to put him there."

"But you'd still be on the police force."

"You sound just like my wife. We used to go round and round with that."

"She forgave you?"

I shook my head. "Ex-wife, actually."

"Kids?"

"No."

"That makes it easier, I'm sure."

"Sure."

The waitress brought coffee, and we took our time adding cream and sugar.

"The feds could have charged me with something, lying to the FBI or whatever, but they didn't bother. But the superintendent was another matter. He decided I should be charged with bringing discredit to the department and impeding a criminal investigation, and that's my tale of woe."

"So why are you wearing a gun today?" she asked, and she gave me that same long, direct look I'd got from her daughter down at the Horner Homes.

"Well . . ." I said.

"Something about the North Shore?"

"The truth is, something happened the other night."

"Something?"

"Something that made me think having a gun handy might be a good idea."

"Does this something have anything to do with my husband's business?"

"I'm not sure. It might. I'm working several different things, so—"

"Is that unusual?"

"Generally how it happens. Feast or famine."

"Do you have time for one more?"

"I might," I said cautiously. "As long as it doesn't conflict with anything else. What's the problem?"

"My daughter has suddenly decided to drop out of school and move into the city."

I took my notebook out and opened it to a blank page. I looked at the page for a while; then I closed the book and put it away.

"And that means?"

"Well, the truth is, I crossed paths with your daughter the other day and we had a little talk and—"

She drummed her fingers on the table. "Mr. Acropolis, I'm a mother," she said after a while. "I'm concerned about my daughter. She really has no business running around down in those neighborhoods. You must know that."

"I pretty much told her the same thing," I said. "Maybe if you had your husband call her."

"Mr. Acrop . . . Nick, that's just not possible. I wish I could explain, but I can't. She was up here yesterday with a man named Harris. He claimed to be a private detective, but when I asked for identification he could only produce a business card. Do you know him?"

"We've met," I said. "What I've heard, he doesn't have a license."

"I tried to warn Becky, but of course what daughter listens to her mother?"

"Look, I can check him out for you, if you want."

"I'd be willing to pay you," she said.

I shook my head. "I'll do you a favor and find out if he's legit at all. Just because he doesn't have a license doesn't mean he's a crook. The rules are a little different on the West Side nowadays."

"I'd appreciate it," she said. "Are you working for Becky?"

"No." I looked her straight in the eye and tried not to flinch. "But that's your last guess."

"Becky told me she was staying in a place called Bucktown; are you familiar with it?"

"The new Lincoln Park."

"Really." This seemed to cheer her up. "I was afraid it might be dangerous."

"Bars, bands, and bistros. It's one of those swinging neighborhoods that kids love."

"You don't approve?"

"I just wish I was young enough to enjoy it."

"It's funny," she said. "I have the strange felling that I might actually be able to trust you. Maybe it's just Austin High. Do you think I'm mistaking sentimentality for trust?"

"Why don't you try me?"

"I might sometime. I might. Well, this has been very nice, Nick. Thank you."

I paid the check. We walked out, then around the corner to her car. She unlocked the door and opened it.

"If you happen to see Becky again," she said, "I'd appreciate it if you'd do what you can to keep her out of harm's way. She's just a child, a sheltered suburban child, and . . ." She stopped, shrugged.

"I'll do what I can," I said.

She held out her hand and when I took it she leaned in and gave me a fleeting kiss on the cheek. "You're a sweet man," she whispered; then she got in the car and drove away.

THIRTY-THREE

I HEADED back south and the kiss lingered like fine perfume. The sun splashing through the trees and occasional flashes of the lake were all I needed to get me dreaming of my round-the-lake trip. Patrice was still along for the ride, but now Janet Westerfield was there, too, in my build-your-own-dream-girl kit.

Take those sad, dark eyes—what was it I loved about that sadness?—and that perfect skin, and mix it with a dash of pout and a little tease, and then sprinkle in a bit of that boyish look and you'd probably destroy all the good things you'd started with.

But it passed the time until Shelly called. "My little bird says Raymond Purcell fell out of a loft in his garage. That make any sense?"

"It's an old barn with a hayloft. You tell Trace the news?"

"He is the client, Nick."

"How'd he take it?"

"Well, he wasn't crying, but he wasn't jumping up and down, either."

"Did he sound surprised?"

"I'm not going to dignify that," she said. "He's not your biggest fan, by the way."

"Why?"

"Have you been listening to the radio?"

"Just daydreaming."

"Turn on Newsradio Seventy-eight," she said, and she was gone.

I waited through a traffic report and the weather and then the local news came on. "A West Side medical student is missing. James Madison, a twenty-five-year-old University of Illinois student, has been missing since Monday evening when he left his Henry Horner Home apartment and failed to return. Madison, a former Whitney Young honor student, works part-time at a West Side drugstore. This same store was the site of a yet-to-be-solved murder October twenty-first. Killed execution-style was Irving Kaplan, sixty-nine, a part-time pharmacist. Police suspect a link between the Kaplan murder and Madison's mysterious disappearance. In other murders, police say they are close to an arrest in the slaying of—"

I switched the radio off and dialed Area Four and asked for Casper. "News fucking radio," he said when he came on. "Is that your idea of a joke?"

"Wasn't me, John," I said. "I tried to get the *Trib* interested the other day, but they didn't bite."

"They're biting now," he said. "I've been on the phone all morning."

"The joy of lieutenancy."

"Look, be straight for a second: you got anything at all on this Kaplan business?"

"And if I give you something good, you let me see the runner?"

"Nick, I can't let you go through our files. Anyway, there's nothing there. You think I'd be asking otherwise? You must have something."

"You talked to those brothers at the tire repair shop lately?"

"Should we?"

"You might want to ask if they've seen that hit man again."

"How long you been sitting on this?"

"It's not a hundred percent," I said. "One guy says yes; the other one says no. But it might be worth checking."

"Thanks," he said softly.

"Did Frank Stringfellow call, by any chance?"

"No. Why?"

"I better let him tell you. Hey, you ever hear of a guy named William Harris, also goes by Wet Willie, black, private eye, no license."

"You're kidding, right?"

"What am I kidding about?"

"Harris is the guy got Hayes sacked."

"How?"

"Hayes sent him up years ago. Willie confessed to rape/murder, but then he claimed Hayes tortured it out of him. He got himself a good lawyer, and when DNA came along they talked a judge into letting them test the blood and semen. Guess what? Nothing matched. So Willie walks after ten years inside. He gets some money from the state; I don't know how much, but it's enough to open a big Laundromat out on Madison Street. That's where the Wet Willie thing comes from. But Willie's not happy washing clothes. He comes up with his own religion: get Hayes. He puts together a whole string of guys that Hayes sent up. They all claim they're innocent. They all claim they were tortured into confessing. Blah. Blah. Blah. But Willie hits pay dirt with a couple. The DNA doesn't match. They reopen the cases. A couple of 'em walk. Willie's a hero in the black community, et cetera, et cetera, et cetera. Then the stewardess gets tons of press and there's Hayes with another confession. So Willie gets on the case and lo and behold, he discovers that the mope who confessed was in county jail when the stew got done. So Hayes is out on his ass."

"Sounds like he might deserve it, John."

"I don't know about that. But what's he doing his own interrogations for? Let the dicks do their job. So I take it Harris is after me now."

"Why would he be after you?"

"What else is he doing in this?"

"Looking for Jimmy. I think the mother hired him."

"Well, just to be on the safe side, I'll try not to beat a confession out of anybody."

"How come he doesn't have a license?"

"He's an ex-con, Nick. Even private eyes have to have some standards."

"I thought the conviction got tossed."

"Yeah, but he had others. You think Hayes would try to hang a rape/murder on a choirboy?"

"You don't want to know what I think," I said.

"You're the last guy in the world to talk," he said, and the line went dead.

I dialed my answering machine. There was another message from Becky: "Call me, OK?"

Lenny, my old friend from the police academy, was his usual stuttering self: "N-n-n-ick, give me a c-c-c-all. I don't know if it's anything, b-b-ut . . ."

Next up was a Sergeant Lopher of the Twenty-second District: "I'm a friend of Ray Purcell. If you get a chance, give me a call."

I punched in the number and the same voice answered. "I don't know if you've heard the news," he said after I identified myself.

"I heard Raymond Purcell died," I said.

"Yeah. Well, look, what I wanted to ask. When you were out there, you happen to see a real fancy-looking bicycle? A Schwinn."

"The one with the shock absorber?"

"It was there Tuesday?"

"Yeah, I asked him about it. He told me it wasn't for sale."

"He was saving it for his grandson when he got old enough. Kid's only five."

"The bike's missing?"

"Yeah. One of the neighborhood punks probably walked off with it in the confusion. Oh, well."

"What was Purcell doing up in the loft?" I asked.

"I've been wondering that myself. A few months back I helped him clean it out. Mostly just garbage. Old bike parts. Ray was a bit of a pack rat. But we pulled it all down, threw a lot of it out. He had Parkinson's disease. That's why his hands were always shaking. Going up and down that ladder was getting pretty tough. I went up there yesterday to take a look. Still clean as a whistle. But the exhaust fan was unplugged. So maybe that was it. He might have been having problems with the fan. But when I plugged it in, it worked just fine."

"Or maybe somebody hid up there, unplugged the fan, and waited for him to come up the ladder."

"Yeah, I thought about that, too. Probably wouldn't even have to push him. Just stand up and say boo. You got any suspects?"

"No," I lied. "How about you?"

"Who'd want to kill a guy fixes old bikes and sells 'em to kids?"

Neither one of us said anything for a while. The car behind me tapped the horn and I looked up to find the light green. I made a left turn and headed onto Lake Shore Drive.

"I've probably been a cop too long," Lopher said. "Always looking at the worst in people. Chances are he just lost his balance. But look, you come up with anything that points some other way, be sure to let me know."

"Likewise," I said.

We said good-bye and then I dialed Becky.

"Look, I want to apologize for telling Patrice that stuff. I'm really sorry."

"You know, you can't believe everything you read."

"I know," she said. "But sometimes my mouth works faster than my brain."

"I take it you got that from Harris."

"Nick, does it really matter?"

"You know he's not a real detective. . . ." I stopped myself. "Forget I said that."

"For a second I thought you might be jealous."

"I just suspect anyone who's out there spreading lies."

"Like me, you mean?"

"The difference is, you didn't know it wasn't true."

"Well, maybe somebody else didn't, either."

"This isn't getting us anywhere," I said.

"What are you doing today?"

"I'm on my way to pick up some Public Aid vouchers. People who filled prescriptions at your father's store the day Irv Kaplan was murdered."

"What are you going to do with them?"

"See if any of the people remember anything special about the store that day."

"Can I come with you?"

"I don't think that'd work out."

"Why not?"

"Well, for one thing, you look too much like a college kid, which is what you are."

"Oh, are you going to pretend to be a cop again?"

"I'm not going to pretend anything. I'm just going to let people make whatever assumption they want. But if you're along, they're going to assume something funny's going on."

"I can look like a cop."

"Oh, come on."

"No. Really. Ruth's got all sorts of clothes. Are you picking me up or what?"

"Forget it," I said.

"Why?"

"Because," I said. *Because I just promised your mother I'd keep you out of harm's way.*

"You know, I'm not a child," she said.

"Nobody said you were. Look, come by my office in an hour or so. We can look through the vouchers. See what we find."

"Ten-four," she said.

THIRTY-FOUR

MIKE Brewer dropped a file folder on my desk. "You asked about a Dr. Lutton the other day. I don't think he's gonna be around long."

"Why not?"

"Too straight, and he's not prescribing much. What I hear, he's an old ear, nose, and throat guy from the infirmary at the U of I. He retired years ago; then his wife died and he went back to work. Most of his patients only get one or two scripts. And worst of all, at least for Westerfield, he's prescribing generic most of the time. I can't figure out why Gene lets him get away with it."

"He's a tough old guy," I said.

"Must be. Here, let me show you something else." He pulled a stack of photocopies out of the folder. "Remember I was talking about patterns? Well, here's one. Sixty-five people got prescriptions that day. And everybody got more than one except a few of Lutton's patients. Twenty-two people ended up with an antacid. And you thought poverty was the big problem on the West Side. No. It's indigestion, at least according to Gene. So we're supposed to believe that more than a third of the people who walked into the store that day suffered from indigestion. But it's like the kid with the tummy ache who doesn't want to go to school. It's awfully hard to prove otherwise. This is typical, low-level abuse. You find something we're paying a reasonable price on and push the hell out of it. And if you're smart, you'll stick with things like that. You over-utilize the system. Because you're never going to jail. But fraud's an entirely different animal. Fraud, you don't deliver the goods at all. If we suspect that, we stop payment immediately, and if we think we can prove it, well, that's a criminal case."

"I hear that sometimes even if you stop payment, Springfield goes ahead and pays."

He didn't say anything for a moment. "Yeah. And sometimes I get superparanoid thinking about things like that. But, you know, the state of Illinois is a huge government bureaucracy. And it's filled with people who want to do as little work as possible. It might just be incompetence."

"Sure," I said.

"The thing is, Gene left himself a little open this time. Every-body who got the antacid was also billed for a hot water bottle. Now my bet is very few of those people actually ended up with one, and if I wasn't on my way downstate, I'd be out there checking myself. Because that's clear-cut fraud. So look, if you actually do interview these people, ask to see the hot water bottles and let me know how it goes."

"Sure," I said.

"See, usually I have to wait months before I see these." He thumped the photocopies. "They can't all lose their hot water bot-tles in three weeks, can they?"

"What's going on in Springfield?"

"Sixty-five people filled prescriptions the day Kaplan was mur-dered."

"OK."

"Sixty-six people the day before. Sixty-four the day after."

"Average sixty-five customers a day."

"And for the two weeks before the shooting Westerfield was right about average."

"That store had to be closed for hours after the hit."

"I never even thought of that," Brewer said.

"Evidence guys are never in a hurry. Never. And Westerfield ends up having an average day."

"But then the rest of the week he's way down," Brewer said. "Just a handful of scripts a day. But he's sure making up for it. The volume's gone through the roof."

"How much?"

"The patient volume has more than doubled, and the volume of prescriptions has nearly tripled. I want to take a closer look; that's why I'm going to Springfield. But what I hear, he's grabbing with both hands. It's like the last hurrah. I think he's trying to get as much as he can before we turn the gravy train off."

"Why now?"

"We've got a new computer system just about ready to go. Everything's going to be on-line. You don't get paid unless you get approval from us up front. We're still testing it. But if everything goes according to plan, it'll be up and running by the first of the year. Westerfield knows all about it. Everybody does. We've been sending out memos and test software for months. They know it's over. And Westerfield's not the only one filling his pocket. Volume's up all over the city. Probably the entire state. I'll tell you something, I don't think Gene's ever coming back."

"Why not?"

"If these numbers are real, there's no way he can justify them. He must know the party's over. My guess is he's funneling the money to wherever he's hiding. Probably somewhere out of the country."

"What do you know about Kaplan's pharmacy on Chicago Avenue?"

"Doesn't ring any bells," he said. "Any relation to Irv?"

"It was his until a couple of years ago."

"That's interesting," he said, and he pulled a notebook out and scribbled a line. "Who owns it now?"

"I'm not sure. But I talked to the widow the other day. She said a few years ago the state owed them all sorts of money. And Westerfield helped Irv get the money from the state."

"Yeah, Gene knows how to work the system. Did I ever tell you about the time he paid me a visit?"

"No."

"Yeah, two, three years ago. I stopped payment on a batch of his bills and he shows up unannounced one day."

There was a knock at the door. I went around the desk and opened it and Becky was standing there. She was wearing a black leather jacket over a maroon pants suit. She had a scarf tied around her neck, loads of makeup on her face, and a Chicago Police Department baseball cap on her head. She looked like the kid at the Halloween party who still hadn't figured out what to be.

"Hey, partner," she said, and she winked. "Am I on time?"

"Unbelievable," I said softly.

"What?"

"You're a little early, actually. But come on." I waved her into the room. "Mike, this is Becky. Becky, Mike."

Brewer stood up and they shook hands. "Nice to meet you," he said. If he was shocked by her appearance he didn't show it.

Brewer turned back my way. "I was sure he was going to try to pay me off, so I got one of my bosses and a security guard; then I had them send Westerfield in: 'OK, say anything you want.' He turned and walked out the door. Never said a word and he never came back, either. But you know now I regret doing it. I should have let him offer me a payoff, not that it would have ever stood up in court. But at least I would have seen with my own eyes that that's how he operates. I mean, I know he's a crook, but the only proof I have is on pieces of paper like this."

He dropped the photocopies in front of me. "Well, I better get moving, if I'm gonna beat that traffic." He closed his briefcase. "And I'll add Kaplan's pharmacy to my list. And you see if you can actually find any hot water bottles."

"Sure," I said.

We shook hands. He waved to Becky and walked out the door.

Becky looked from the door to me, then back to the door. Nobody said a word. She took her time looking around the office. Time passed. I could hear a power saw whining down in the lumberyard, a train passing on the commuter line two blocks away.

"I think the hat's overdoing it a bit," I said.

She took the hat off and flung it across the room. It bounced off a wall, then fell silently like a fly without wings. More time passed.

"Whose side are you on?" she asked softly.

"I'm on your side."

"So who was that?"

"He's a Public Aid investigator."

"And you're giving him information about my father."

I pointed to the photostats. "He's giving me information. And he was investigating your father long before I came along."

"And he doesn't have any evidence, but he thinks my father's a criminal. Isn't that what he just said?"

"You could interpret it that way. Sure. But look, he told me something interesting. He says a week or so after Irv's murder the volume of business at your father's store went way up. Doubled, almost tripled, something like that."

"And?"

"That's about the time your father dropped from sight."

"So what does that mean?"

"I don't know. Maybe nothing. But the timing suggests there could be some connection."

"What?"

"I don't know."

"You're not much of a detective, are you?"

"Look, do you want to help with these or not?"

"Whatever."

"If you don't, it's fine with me."

She turned away, then spun back around. "OK. What are we doing?"

"First, let's pull out all the scripts for hot water bottles. Then we'll go through the phone book and try to find addresses."

I split the photocopies into two piles. "What's the big deal about hot water bottles?" Becky asked.

"The question is whether they've actually been delivered. Brewer seems to think not. He wants me to check and see if the people actually got them. It might help prove whether—"

"My father's a crook."

"Or not," I said.

"OK," she said.

We spent a couple of minutes sorting through the photocopies, then several more flipping through the phone book.

"So where do we go first?" Becky asked when we were done. "I have to be back by six-thirty."

"Forget it," I said.

"What? Don't I look like a cop?" She got up and picked the hat off the floor.

"It has nothing to do with how you look."

"Well, what?"

"Becky, these are dangerous neighborhoods. What if something happened to you? How would I ever explain that to . . . to everybody?"

"Nothing's going to happen," she said.

"That's what my friend George Milano said when he went to Vietnam."

"Look, if my father really is . . ." She pointed the way Brewer had gone. "Don't I have the right to see it with my own eyes? I mean, you've been hinting for days that he's nothing but a criminal. Well, here's your chance to prove it."

"Becky—"

"I'll just follow you. You can't stop me."

"If my Olds can't outrun that Honda—"

"Why are you so afraid of me?"

"Becky—"

"That's it, isn't it? You're afraid of me. Why?"

"I'm afraid of something happening to you."

"Nick, if I never did anything I was afraid of, I'd still be in kindergarten."

We sat there staring at each other. I shook my head from side to side. Becky moved hers up and down.

"We ready?" Becky broke the silence.

I stood up. "Oh, Jesus."

"How do I look?"

"Well, like I said, I think the hat's overdoing it, but other than that . . . You have a fanny pack, by any chance?"

"Ruth has some."

"That would help. A lot of the women use them instead of holsters."

"You're going to give me a gun?"

I picked my stapler off the desk. "This ought to work."

She held out her hand and I handed the stapler over. She pointed it right back my way. "Hands up," she said, and she flashed a tiny smile.

I picked up the photocopies, locked up the office, and we went down the hall to the elevators.

We took separate cars to Bucktown. When I pulled up, Becky and Patrice were standing on the steps of the Gare du Nord. Patrice was in her waitress getup and she looked as sexy as ever.

"I'll be right down," Becky said, and she headed upstairs.

"I had fun last night." Patrice slipped right into my arms, like she'd never gone away.

"Me, too," I said, and then neither one of us had anything else to say. "How's your boyfriend?" sounded too much like the mope who would never get the girl. "How big's your boyfriend?" sounded like a guy who wasn't sure he even wanted her.

Someone tapped on the window. "Oh, that's for me," Patrice said. She gave me a quick kiss. "Stop by some night," she whispered.

"Sure."

She shrugged. "Up to you."

"Hey, I'm not the one with the boyfriend," I said, but by then she was already inside.

Becky was down moments later. She'd ditched the hat and replaced it with a black headband. The fanny pack was a shiny blue vinyl. The weight of the stapler looked just about right.

She unzipped the fanny pack with one hand, reached the other inside, and held it there. "What do you think?" she asked.

I thought I was probably out of my mind. But what I said was, "Whatever you do, don't pull that stapler out."

THIRTY-FIVE

THE first address was on Jackson Boulevard, just a few blocks south of the Westerfield store. I spotted the building we wanted, but there were gangbangers everywhere. "Let's skip this one," I said. "Who's next?"

We went over the highway to Flournoy Street. There were only three buildings left on the block. The one we wanted was a crumbling three-flat. I pulled in front and killed the engine. "Who's here?"

"Somebody named Lizzy James," Becky said. "She got antacids, a hot water bottle, plus four other prescriptions."

"Don't try to look tough," I said after we got out of the car, "just sort of disinterested. You don't really want to be here. You're just backing up your partner, OK?"

She smiled. "OK, partner. Let's go." I thought I detected a note of nervousness in her voice. Maybe it was in my ears.

The stairs were treacherous, the wood rotted and cracked. One railing was missing, the other loose. The front door was standing open. It led into a small dark hallway. The door to the first-floor apartment was cracked a half-inch. A sliver of light and the sound of a TV drifted out.

I trained my penlight on a row of mailboxes. The locks were all broken or missing. "L. James" was one of several names written above the bell for the first floor. I pushed it; nothing happened. I knocked hard on the open door and it opened another inch or so.

The TV stopped. "What you want?" a man shouted, and I could hear the fear hiding behind the toughness. If we were the real police, now would be the time to chamber a round into the shotgun and let him listen to that distinctive sound. Of course, he didn't know we weren't the police. And I didn't know if the police wanted him or not. Ignorance is not always bliss. Sometimes it's sheer stupidity.

I slipped my gun out and pushed the door open with a foot.

He was a big healthy-looking guy, and he was almost completely out of the room. He was wearing a pair of jeans and nothing else. He was standing at the back of the living room, his right arm hidden by the hallway alcove. He had the thumb of his left hand stuck in the front pocket of the jeans. There was a tattoo on his shoulder, one of those homemade jobs that help pass the time in prison.

There was a woman sitting on the edge of a sofa. She looked like she'd been sleeping. In front of her the top of a cardboard box was covered with piles of loose pills and prescription bottles. There must have been forty vials. Two little kids, a boy and a girl, were on the floor in front of the dark television. They looked about ready to cry.

"I'm looking for Lizzy James," I said. The woman on the couch didn't move, but both kids looked her way. The guy didn't do anything. "We want to make sure she got her hot water bottle," I said after a while.

The guy looked toward the woman, then back to me. He shook his head and smiled, like he couldn't believe what he'd just heard. After a long moment, he started my way. He kept his right hand behind his back and his eyes on mine as he walked slowly to the door. The smile faded. "She's not here," he said, and he pushed the door closed in my face. A lock snapped into place. The television went back on, louder than before.

I shrugged in the darkness. "Well, hell," I said. "She's not here, I guess."

We went out to the car and then back over the highway to Fifth Avenue, to a well-kept two-flat. One sign said: NO PEDDLERS, another ALL DELIVERIES IN REAR The hallway light was lit. The doorbell worked.

"Hello?" a woman asked through the closed door.

"Mrs. Knox?"

"Yes. What is it?"

"We're detectives," I said. "We'd like to ask you a few questions."

We waited as a series of locks were undone, then the door opened a few inches to the end of several security chains. She was a tiny black woman. "What sort of questions?"

I held up the photocopy with her name on it. "This says you had a prescription filled at Westerfield Pharmacy on October twenty-first."

"We go every two weeks. But now the last time we didn't go to Mr. Westerfield's; the bus took us to a different store on Roosevelt Road."

"Do you know the name of the store?"

"Let me see," she said, and she seemed to think for a moment; then a little smile came into her eyes. "Would you like some tea?"

"Sure," I said. Becky shrugged.

Mrs. Knox pushed the door closed, then undid the chains and opened the door wide. She led us into an apartment that looked straight out of 1925.

"You sit right here," she said, "while I start the kettle." She directed us to a piece of upholstery that might be called a davenport or a chesterfield but never a sofa. The towering arms were covered with frilly lace linens.

Every spot in the room was filled. There was woodwork and lace doilies everywhere, paintings in gilded frames, ottomans, smoking tables, a sideboard with a marble inlay, tiny lamps, pitchers, plates, candlestick holders, and miscellaneous doodads whose names or purposes I couldn't even begin to guess.

"It's like a museum," Becky whispered.

I nodded.

"You know what's funny? It sort of reminds me of my dad's office."

I nodded again.

Mrs. Knox was back in a minute with a tray filled with saucers and teacups, and then a minute later with another tray holding a colorful ceramic teapot.

We sipped tea and talked about the nice weather we'd been having, and after a while I brought the conversation back to Westerfield's.

"I don't really remember anything special about our last visit. The bus dropped us at the medical center and then we got back on and drove around the corner to Mr. Westerfield's."

"Did you see a doctor?"

"No. I just told the girl what I needed."

"So this medication you take . . ." I tried to read from the abstract. "Ateno . . ."

Becky leaned over to take a look. "Atenolol," she said. "It's for high blood pressure."

"Oh, no," Mrs. Knox said. "My blood pressure's just fine. I don't take any medicine, just one big vitamin every morning."

"How about a hot water bottle?" I asked. "Did you get a hot water bottle?"

"Here, let me show you," she said, and she led us down a hallway to a small closet and opened the door. The closet was loaded. There were boxes of bath oils and rows of soaps. There was a vaporizer, still in its box, a heating pad, not one but two hot water bottles, bandages, gauze pads, adhesive tape, petroleum jelly, bottles of peroxide and rubbing alcohol, and several pairs of nylon stockings.

"Every time I go, I come home with a bag," Mrs. Knox said. "I hope I didn't do anything wrong?"

"You didn't notice anything unusual at Westerfield's last time?" I asked.

"Let me think a moment," she said. "No. The radio was on and Mr. Westerfield seemed happy as ever. Oh, and then some symphony came on that he seemed to like, so he went in the back and turned up the music and when he came back he was leading the band." She waved her arms around like an orchestra conductor. "The new store on Roosevelt, they don't play music like that. And they're not as nice as Mr. Westerfield. Did something happen to him?"

"Why do you ask?"

"Nothing good happens out here, young man." She shook her head sadly. "When I was a little girl you could walk anywhere and never be afraid. But not no more."

We finished our tea and said our good-byes. Mrs. Knox closed the door behind us and I heard the locks being snapped back into place. It was a few minutes after five, but the sun was already gone. Lovely November.

The next stop was on Monroe near Cicero Avenue. It was another two-flat, which sat next to an abandoned courtyard building.

Mrs. Johnson didn't have time to make anyone tea. Her hands were more than full watching a batch of kids. "My grandchildren," she explained. "I've got seventeen grandchildren and three great-grandchildren."

She didn't remember anything unusual about her last visit to Westerfield's. I asked her about the hot water bottle and she shook her head no. "But let me show you something." She went away and returned with a package in her hand.

"Support hose for my varicose veins. Used to be better. Nobody makes nothing like they used to." She unwrapped the package and pulled out the stockings. They were nothing but standard nylons; the package didn't say a word about support. According to the photocopy, the state of Illinois had paid twenty-eight dollars a pair.

"So what's this prove?" Becky said when we were back in the car heading north.

"I'm not trying to prove anything," I said. "I'm just trying to find out what happened to Irv and Jimmy."

"And my dad."

"Right."

The next stop was near Chicago and Pulaski. Mr. Foreman was tall and thin, his wife short and plump. Neither one of them had ever heard of Westerfield's. "We go to Kaplan's, right down the street," Mr. Foreman said, and pointed east.

We got a similar answer at our next stop. Mrs. Wooten went to Avenue Drugs. "I wish I had a hot water bottle."

"Is there a drugstore around here?" Becky asked when we were back in the car. "A big one that takes credit cards."

"There's an Osco on Grand Avenue," I remembered.

"Can we stop there?"

I waited in the parking lot while she went inside. It was one of those huge places, open twenty-four hours, where you could buy anything from a barbecue grill, to a bottle of Old Grand-Dad, to a tin of aspirin.

I opened the glove box and took a sip of my special pain medication, then dozed for a while. I woke with the passenger door opening. Becky had a plastic bag in her hand. "Could we go back to Mrs. Johnson's for a minute?"

"Sure," I said, and we drove back to Monroe Street in silence. Becky carried the plastic bag up the stairs and into the apartment, then returned without it.

"I'm sorry I'm so grumpy," she said.

I grunted.

"It's just so hard to believe."

"You don't know the pressures he might be under," I said.

"No. There's no excuse. You didn't see her legs. The poor

woman hasn't been out of the house in weeks because she's too embarrassed to be seen."

"Who's next?" I asked.

"I really should be getting back."

"One more?"

"Just one. But no tea, OK?"

It was a small frame building that had settled long ago and now leaned on the three-flat next door. The front door led into a short hallway where the smell of decomposing flesh hit me. As we walked down the hall, the smell got stronger. I lit two cigarettes and handed one to Becky.

She shook her head. "I don't smoke."

"Take a couple of drags," I said. "Inhale through your nose." She gave me an odd look but took the cigarette.

A door to one apartment had towels stuffed in the opening at the bottom; another had newspapers. I stopped in front of the last door. There was nothing at the bottom. Becky had a strange look on her face. I knocked.

"Hello," a soft voice answered almost immediately.

"Hattie Walker?"

"She here."

"I want to ask her about her medicine."

"She won't be needing no more medicine," the voice said. "I've been waiting for someone to come and take her. Did you come to take her?"

"Who are you?"

"I'm Rosie."

"Is Hattie sick, Rosie?"

"Not no more. Did you come to take her?"

"You better open the door," I said.

The door opened and the smell was overpowering. Huge black-flies filled the air. I tried not to breathe. Becky backed away gagging.

Rosie was an incredibly skinny old woman with huge deep-set eyes. "Who's going to take care of me?" she asked softly. "Are you going to take care of me?"

"Sure," I said. "Now come on outside." She took my hand and I led her out of the apartment. I reached back to close the door, then led her slowly down the hallway. Becky was standing holding the outside door open. We walked out to the porch.

I went out to the car and called the police, then went back to the porch. Becky and Rosie were holding hands. Nobody said a word. Soon the street was filled with flashing lights, police cars, and fire trucks.

A couple of paramedics led Rosie to an ambulance. I told a patrol sergeant everything I knew about Hattie Walker. He asked us to wait for the detectives.

We leaned against my car. I lit a cigarette and looked at Becky. She nodded. I handed her the cigarette, then lit another.

"What time is it?" she asked.

I held out my watch. It was 6:15.

"Can I use your phone?"

I nodded. She opened the door and picked up the phone. After a while she turned my way. "How much longer do you think?"

"Not that long," I said. "A half hour or so."

"A half hour," she said into the phone. "OK. See you." She got out of the car and closed the door. "I feel like an idiot," she said softly.

"What?"

"All this. Everything. It doesn't seem real. I guess I never believed it was. I thought it was something for TV. I mean, it's almost the twenty-first century. And with all the science and all the technology why are people still living and dying like this? It doesn't make any sense."

"Hey, Nick," a guy in a lieutenant's uniform said as he passed, "good to see you back."

"Hey, Tony." I held up my hand. He had a big smile on his face. He looked relaxed. If the smell or the maggots bothered him, he didn't show it.

I'd been that way once. Coming on the scene was one of the great highs of the job. In the old days, I might have been standing in the same spot eating a hot dog and talking about the Bears.

But as much as I'd wanted it, it didn't feel good being back. Maybe I'd been away too long. Or maybe I was just seeing the show through Becky's eyes. It wasn't a pleasant sight, all the cops and firemen having a great time, smoking cigarettes and talking and laughing, virtually ignoring Hattie's death and Rosie's pain.

Becky was smoking like she'd smoked all her life. The heavy makeup had run down her face. She'd taken the headband off and let her hair down. Flashing lights painted her face ashen blue.

An unmarked car pulled up and three guys got out. They were all dressed in suits and ties, all relaxed and smiling. The uniforms made a path for them as they approached the house. I didn't recognize any of them, but I knew who they were. "Here's the guys we're waiting for," I said.

"Who are they?"

"Homicide detectives."

Two of the detectives headed into the building. A group of firemen slipped masks on and followed. Two cops in uniform brought up the rear carrying a stretcher.

The third detective pulled a notebook out and started talking to the sergeant who'd questioned me. The sergeant gestured our way.

The firemen were out a minute later. They took their masks off as they came down the stairs. The cops carried the stretcher out to a paddy wagon. The body bag was zipped up tight. From the looks of it, Hattie had been even skinnier than Rosie.

"What happens now?" Becky asked.

"They'll take her to a hospital, have her pronounced dead, then take her to the morgue."

"What about Rosie?"

"She'll go to a hospital, too. Hopefully, they'll find some relatives. If not, a social welfare agency. Something."

"Bill keeps going to the morgue."

"Bill?"

"Harris. He thinks Jimmy's dead. You'd be surprised how many unidentified black males there are. It's so sad."

I grunted.

"You probably wouldn't be surprised. But it is so sad. It just makes you think."

I grunted some more.

"Maybe you and Bill should sit down and talk," she said.

"If that's what you want," I said. "You're the client."

"That's who I'm meeting."

"Anything special?"

"He wants to show me something."

"What?"

"I don't know. Probably something I don't want to see."

The detective with the notebook walked up. "The famous Nick Acropolis," he said, and he extended his hand. "I'm Jeff Hertel."

We shook hands. "This is Becky," I said.

He nodded. "Your old partner wants me to ask you if this has anything to do with Westerfield's?"

"She got a prescription filled there October twenty-first," I said.

He looked toward the house for a second, then back to me. "Irv Kaplan day," he said.

I nodded.

"And?"

"I wanted to ask her if she'd seen anything unusual. I'm a little late, I guess."

"About a week, I'd say."

THIRTY-SIX

I STOPPED just beyond Harris's Town Car in front of the Gare du Nord. "Do you want to talk to Bill?" Becky asked.

"Let's leave it for tomorrow. Tell him I'm interested, OK?"

"OK," she said. She got out of the car, then stuck her head back in. She still seemed a bit pale. "Thanks for . . ." She shrugged.

"Whatever," I said.

"Right." She waved, then closed the door.

I got on the highway heading toward the Loop, came back off at the first exit, turned right and then right again. I did the last block with my headlights off, then doused my running lights as I slipped into an alley.

The Town Car hadn't moved. I trained my binoculars on the car. Harris was sitting back, eyes closed. Next to him was Latisa, Jimmy's girlfriend. She was talking or maybe singing along with the radio.

Becky was down in a few minutes. She was in jeans and a light jacket. Latisa slid over and Becky joined her in the front seat.

They headed south at a nice leisurely pace, then went even slower. I could have followed on roller skates. It might have been easier. As it was, I kept overrunning their position.

Harris made abrupt stops and turns, sudden U-turns. But he wasn't trying to lose me, although I'm sure he knew I was behind him. He was looking for something. A series of somethings. Every so often, the flashers would come on, the car would stop, and Harris would get out, walk to the curb, and tape a MISSING poster to a light pole or to a storefront window.

We went west on North Avenue, then south, then east, then south again. The big car seemed to stop indiscriminately, here, there, and the other place, and another poster or two would go up.

Harris turned on Chicago Avenue and stopped right in front of Kaplan's pharmacy and I remembered Mrs. Madison saying, "Now Mr. Gene, he has stores all over the city."

Harris put up two posters; then the car continued west. I began writing down names and addresses. Keeler Pharmacy. Park Medical Center. Avenue Drugs. AAA Home Care Medical Supplies. We went south again, then west on Madison Street. We were miles west of the Westerfield store.

We passed a brand-new Walgreen's, but Harris didn't stop. I'd have to call John Olmstead at the *Tribune* and let him know that the chain had returned to Madison Street. Maybe things were finally looking up for the far West Side.

But there wasn't much beyond the new store. If I didn't know better, I'd think this was the heart of the riot zone. Once-beautiful buildings sat deserted, surrounded by bleak moonscape.

It didn't make any sense. It would never make any sense. On the North Side, these same buildings would be worth millions, even in their current condition. Here, all they were worth was the price of the bricks and the copper plumbing, which had probably already been stolen by scavengers.

WET WILLIE'S.

For a guy without a license, it was an awfully big sign. I could see the name flashing in the night blocks away. When we got closer I read the rest of the neon message. WASH and DRY. Harris made a U-turn and double-parked in front of the Laundromat.

Years ago, there'd been a Walgreen's on the corner just past the Laundromat and kitty-corner a hamburger and malt shop on the

Oak Park side. They were both long gone, replaced by a liquor store and a currency exchange.

The bus turnaround was still there. A bus was waiting to go back toward the Loop. A CTA supervisor, sitting in a marked car, looked up as I pulled in, then returned to his paperwork.

In front of the Laundromat, an old-timer was washing the windows. He had a large yellow bucket on wheels and a squeegee on a long pole. The windows already looked clean by my standards.

A sign in the window said: DROP OFF SERVICE / WASH DRY FOLD / PACKED NEAT AS A SUITCASE / SAME DAY SERVICE. MISSING posters were spaced along the window.

The place was busy. The back wall had a line of oversize dryers with bright lights inside, so you could watch your clothes bounce around as they dried. It was hypnotic, all those tumbling colors. There was a small office dead center, surrounded by vending machines and video games.

Harris waved to the guy washing the windows, then unlocked a door next to the Laundromat and disappeared inside. A few moments later, a light went on in an upstairs window.

There weren't any signs in the windows or on the single door next to the Laundromat. No blinking eyes or men in trench coats flashing on and off. No knights on horseback riding to the rescue.

The light went off and then Harris came back out and we continued our tour of the city's worst neighborhoods. Some of the streets were like old familiar songs, and I had plenty of time to reminisce.

The girl who had been stuffed headfirst into a garbage can, one leg frozen in the air like a still of a Broadway dancer. The party that ended when one brother shot another for refusing to sing "Happy Birthday." The kid pulled into an alley and stabbed to death for seventeen cents. A wino beaten to pulp under the el.

As we continued east, the streets and the memories deteriorated. And then, just to make the night complete, Harris stopped on Harrison Street. Everybody got out, and they walked to the entrance usually reserved for ambulance crews and cops. Harris rang the bell and a moment later the door opened and they disappeared inside.

I dialed the number from memory. "Medical Examiners," a man answered.

"Willis around?" I asked.

"Willis?" the man said. "Willis ain't worked here in years."

"How about Doc Brown?"

"You're living in the past, my man. The last time I saw Dr. Brown, he was a patient."

"A patient?" I said, but then I got it. At the morgue, all the patients were dead. "Never mind." I hung up the phone. I'd definitely been away too long.

A few minutes later they were back in the car, and I continued adding names to my notebook as we headed south and east. In a little less than two hours, I had a list of twenty-seven drugstores, nine medical centers, two medical supply stores, and two nursing homes. I added another drugstore to the list. Halsted Pharmacy. This was where the bus had dropped off its second load of passengers the other day.

Harris turned east on Forty-seventh. The Town Car went under a long viaduct, then headed down a street between two railroad embankments. NO OUTLET, a sign read. Twin ramps ran up to a railroad yard. A tractor-trailer was sitting behind a gate, lights blazing away.

The Town Car went the other way and disappeared into the darkness beyond a no outlet sign. I made a U-turn and waited on Forty-seventh Street at the end of the viaduct.

A minute later, two trucks came out. The Town Car followed them toward the highway. There were still three people in the front seat.

I waited until they were out of sight, then backtracked. I passed the truck ramps. The road narrowed, curved to the right, and went up a hill. About halfway up, the pavement ended. There was a Y at the top; the left track led to a large Cyclone fence with barbed wire at the top. Beyond it, in the railroad yard, a huge crane was lifting a cargo container. There were enough lights for the yard at county jail.

The prison break would follow the other branch of the Y into darkness. A large sign warned: NO TRUCKS. There was another NO OUTLET sign on a light pole. Above it, the light had burned out. A standard city street sign identified the ruts as Stewart Avenue. I followed along and the street got darker and darker as I moved away from the railroad yard.

The road curved and a yellow sign loomed out of the darkness: LOW CLEARANCE. I went under another viaduct, rumbled over old-time paving bricks, and came to an open gate that led into a gravel-covered parking lot.

There was a building at the back of a clearing, with five cars sitting in a neat row under a single streetlight. To the right of the cars, a large Dumpster blocked my view of the front door. The building was a dingy-looking brick, built sometime in the sixties, I guessed. It was five floors, but the only lights were on the first two floors. Anywhere else, I would have guessed residential. But nobody could live back here. I decided it must be some kind of railroad office. But why had Harris come? There wasn't a drugstore in sight. Had he made a wrong turn? If he was planning to ambush me back here, he hadn't waited very long.

I was barely moving when a flashlight beam hit me in the face. A hand slapped the hood of my car.

I stopped and put one hand out to block the light.

The flashlight was off in the darkness on the passenger side. It held steady for a moment, then dropped down and flicked across the dashboard and around to the passenger door and flitted around the back of the Olds and came up on the driver's side.

"Visiting hours are over," a voice purred.

"Visiting hours?"

"You lost, pal?" The voice was low. The flash hit my left hand, resting on the steering wheel. My right hand was in my lap, wrapped around my police special.

"Just taking a drive," I said.

"No outlet, pal. Can't you read?"

"You the railroad dick?"

"Good guess, pal. If you're planning to hit the boxcars, tonight's a bad night."

"Well, thanks for the warning. I'll come back some other time."

"Why don't you step out of the car," the voice commanded, and he stepped back away from the door. He was my size, maybe a little bigger, a white guy in jeans and a quilted jacket. The flashlight was in his right hand; a piece of paper was crumpled in his left.

"I'll pass," I said, and the flashlight started to rise. "You shine that light in my eyes, I'm gonna run over your toes."

He started to back away. I stepped on the gas and jerked the wheel. He dropped the piece of paper and I recognized it as one of Harris's MISSING posters. He pushed his jacket back and I caught a glimpse of a holster; then he dived out of the way as the Olds swayed and bucked through a gravel-spitting U-turn. I flicked the lights off and ducked down as I headed back through the gate and under the viaduct.

Back on Forty-seventh Street, I grabbed my notebook and added the name I'd seen on the gate on the way out. Hilltop Nursing Home.

Yeah, I thought, *if you really hate the old bastards, send them to Hilltop.*

THIRTY-SEVEN

I T was close to eleven when the Town Car stopped in front of the Gare du Nord. Becky got out and headed toward the side entrance. A minute later, lights came on in the attic.

I waited about five minutes, then walked over and rang the bell. The buzzer sounded and I went up the stairs and the ladder. Becky was standing in front of the easel. She had a glass of wine in one hand, a paintbrush in the other.

"You should find out who it is before you push that buzzer," I said.

"I'm not good enough to do this reflection right," she said. I wasn't sure if she was talking to me or to herself.

I took a look at the canvas. The painting looked almost finished to my eyes. Everything was done except the reflection. The buildings that had once stood across from the drugstore were only a thin outline on the canvas. But they didn't look reflected on the glass. The looked like they were sitting just inside the window.

I watched as Becky mixed paint, and then she began painting over the reflected buildings. First in red, then yellow, then blue. Thin lines grew thicker, and the buildings soon disappeared.

I walked to the back and found a glass. I carried it up front, added wine, then sat down and watched her work.

It took a while. A bottle of wine. Most of my cigarettes. For a girl who didn't smoke, she was doing quite a job.

The red, yellow, and blue slowly became a blazing fire. You could see the entire West Side burning in that window, all those hopes and dreams, all that anger.

Becky stood with the brush in her hand, watching the paint dry, sipping wine, smoking. Out the window, the highway was nothing but packs of huge trucks. Their running lights blurred into unbroken lines. Their roar was a single note, as sad as a final kiss.

A half hour must have passed before Becky dropped the brush back to the paint. She held it like a sword. I thought she might have decided to destroy the painting. But she touched it lightly instead, first with one color, then the next.

The fire was no longer just a reflection. Now it was a weapon, too, shot out of her father's eyes.

She put the brush down, took one last swig of wine, then walked a few feet to a sofa, fell into it, and was immediately asleep.

I found a blanket and dropped it over her. I snuffed out a cigarette and turned off most of the lights. I went down the ladder, pulling the hatch closed behind me, and then down the stairs to the street.

There were a thousand stars in the sky, but they were as lifeless as cardboard. A truck passed up on the highway sounding lost and alone.

I started the Olds and put it in gear. The radio played one sad song after another, all the way home.

THIRTY-EIGHT

I HADN'T been sleeping long when the phone rang. A familiar voice spoke my name. "John?" I asked.

"You awake?"

"Jesus." The place was freezing. I stumbled into the kitchen. "What's up?" I tried to close the window. It moved an inch or so, then jammed in place.

"They found your license number on a stiff down in Area Two," Casper said. "There's a couple of dicks on the way to knock on your door. Thought I'd give you a heads up."

"My car license?"

"Yeah. It was on a piece of paper in the victim's pocket."

"Who?" I said, and a gust of cold wind came through the open window. I had a flash of Hattie Walker, all zipped away in her plastic bag. I went back to the bedroom in search of my robe.

"No ID yet. Only thing in his pocket was the paper, but it sure sounds like that Madison kid."

"Shit." I sat down on the bed. Casper said something, but I didn't hear. I was back on Madison Street. Me and Jimmy Madison on Madison Street. Jimmy was looking up from the statement I'd just written. "The truth," he'd said. And he'd looked right into my eyes, and I'd pretended not to see.

"Nick, you got anything at all?" Casper asked.

"Did you say something about the lake?"

"Lake Calumet. That's where they found him. Off the Hundred-eleventh Street exit ramp."

"In the water?"

"Yeah. Security guard for the port saw a couple of cars early Tuesday morning, way on the north end. By the time he got there, they were gone and he forgot all about it. But then yesterday he spotted tire tracks heading into the water and decided he better check them out."

"Cause of death?"

"Have to wait for the docs. But word is, he didn't drown."

Early Tuesday morning. He'd been dead before I'd known he was missing. "How about the car?"

"Westerfield's wagon. It's gonna be a heater, Nick. I'm hoping you can help us out."

"John," I said. "I don't know what to tell you." Becky Westerfield learned to drive in that car, I remembered. But I didn't think that was the kind of information he wanted. *An off-duty cop took a couple of shots at that same car, John.* But I couldn't give him that, could I?

"Nick, you don't have to tell me anything. This isn't my case. But those Area Two guys aren't going to be so easy to please."

"Anybody I know?"

"Couple of young guys. Doran and Cantore. They probably figure I'm talking to you. Doran just called. He knew you were my old partner. Said they were going out to rattle your door. I guess this is for old times' sake. I hope there isn't a wire on your phone."

"John, I appreciate it," I said. "Really."

"Well, one hand washes the other, Nick. At least that's the way it's supposed to work. I think it's your turn."

"I'm suddenly feeling restless. How long ago did you get this call?"

"You're too much, Nick. You know that?"

"Look, do I have time for a shower or not?"

"Yeah, but it better be quick. And you've got time to throw your old partner a bone. You must have something. Anything, Nick. Just so I don't look like a complete chump."

"Frank Stringfellow ever call?"

"No. What's that about?"

"He's looking for some guy shaking down doctors. And the guy fits the description of the hit man, everything except the hair. Same car, too."

"You got a name?"

"Leslie Crawford," I said, and I spelled the name. "But look, you didn't get this from me, OK?"

"You haven't given me anything yet."

"That's about all I have."

"Christ, Nick," he snorted in disgust. "I just got through telling Doran you were a top-notch dick."

"Oh, yeah, sorry, John, I forgot the important part. When me and Frank were going through Crawford's apartment the other day, there was a red wig hanging on a hook in the bathroom."

"You're not pulling my chain, are you?"

"Wish me luck," I said, and I hung up before he could ask any more probing questions.

THIRTY-NINE

THE streets were quiet. It was the one hour when the city almost sleeps. The drunks were falling into bed while the day people were dreaming of dawn. An empty taxicab cruised south.

I walked half a block to the Olds, listening to the sound of my footsteps and the muted chirping of a few early birds. I opened the trunk and dropped my suitcase in.

"Taking a trip?"

It was a perfectly timed stage whisper. I had both hands up on the lid of the trunk. I backed away and dropped my hands as a match flared on the far side of the sidewalk. Someone was standing in the darkness on the steps of an old graystone. Harris, also known as Wet Willie. He took his time lighting the cigarette, then flipped the match into some nearby bushes.

He looked about six-eight coming down the stairs. He was wearing his cowboy boots, a dark suit, and a yellow shirt. I closed the trunk as he approached. His eyes were a strange smoky color, a luminous black at the center. Maybe it was just the night, I thought. But I knew better.

"No more bullshit," he said. "Time to talk."

"Not now," I said.

"Now," he said. He slammed his palm on the trunk for emphasis.

"Not here," I said. "I'm expecting company."

"Somewhere."

"How about the pancake house?" I pointed. You could almost see the sign a half-mile down. "Where you parked?"

He turned his head and I saw the Town Car blocking the crosswalk at Bittersweet Place.

"Follow me," I said.

"And you take it nice and easy, like I did for you last night, right?"

I got in the Olds and headed south. We stopped at all three red lights. It gave me time to think. But not enough.

Jimmy was dead. Irv was dead. Westerfield was missing. And, if Jesse could be trusted, the hit man had made a visit to the medical center. Who'd he seen? Dr. Lutton? Nurse Hennessy? How about Jack Gabriel, the cop out in Austin who wouldn't give me the time of day? Had he been at St. Anthony's that day? Why had the hit man come back? To pick up the remainder of his money? That was the usual procedure. Half now. Half later. Or had he come to perform another hit only to find his target gone? Dr. Z. Was that who he'd been looking for? Why would anybody bother to shoot him? Wasn't that the same question someone had asked me about Irv Kaplan? Yeah. Nathan Rogers. What was it he'd said, "I know it's not considered polite to speak ill of the dead"? But then he had.

I had a hundred questions but no answers. And then there was Tracy Grace. The only witnesses the Police Board had against him had both made up helpful stories and then conveniently died. Shelly had laughed at the suggestion that Grace might have been involved in Purcell's death. But it was Grace himself who'd laid out the motive. "That cocksucker," he'd said after finding out about the cost of the new statement. "What kind of white man pulls something like that?"

But Jimmy Madison had last been seen in the company of two

black men. "I'm just going downstairs," he'd told his mother. And she was still waiting for him to come back. Had she heard the news?

Besides, even Tracy Grace wouldn't be dumb enough to dump a body in a car loaded with bullets from his own gun, would he?

And Harris. Who was Harris? An ex-con who could walk into the morgue through the back door. An ex-con who seemed to have better contacts within the police department than I did. How had he found out about Jimmy so soon? And I had no doubt that he'd heard the news. The look in his eyes had told me that much.

I pulled into the parking lot and slipped between a couple of cabs. Harris followed me into the restaurant and then to a booth.

The place was quiet. A couple of barflies, making the last stop before home. A group of cabdrivers talking about their night. Good luck. Bad luck. No luck at all.

I ordered toast and coffee. Harris just coffee.

"Remember the Marigold Gardens?" I asked. It had once been on this very corner, an outside pavilion. Harris wouldn't remember it any more than I did. It was one of my father's stories, from his days as an amateur boxer. Part of his standard tour of the places where he'd lost fights.

Harris shook his head. He was all business. "Let's start with what you were doing at Westerfield's Monday."

"Nothing important," I said.

"See, it seems mighty important to me that Jimmy was dead eight hours after you walked out that door. Two unusual things happened at Westerfield's that day. One of 'em was you showing up, and the other was Becky. And she's answered every question I put to her, but you keep giving me that shifty eye."

"I've got a client to protect."

"Shit," he said. "What if your client put two bullets in Jimmy's head? You gonna stand by him, just because he happens to wear blue? That your idea of Truth, Justice, and the American Way? What'd they ever do for you except kick your sorry ass off?"

"Who said anything about wearing blue?" I asked. "And anyway, my guy's white. Jimmy was last seen with two black males." Harris held my eyes. It was hard to argue with his logic. Would I really protect Tracy Grace if he had, in fact, murdered Jimmy? "I can't give you names," I said.

"Tell me why you were there," he said softly, and he opened his hands wide, then closed them around his coffee cup. "Just tell me why you were there," he said again.

So I told him about the accident and the shooting, leaving out names, and then about the statement I'd taken from Jimmy.

"So he knew you were coming?" he said when I was done.

"That's what it looked like."

"And his story was rehearsed and ready?"

"He had to keep stopping to fill in the blanks."

"But you didn't believe it?"

"No."

"So somebody got to him."

I nodded.

"You get a fix on what they threatened him with?"

"Why not just drop a few dollars?"

"No. That wasn't Jimmy's style," Harris said.

"I didn't know you knew him that well."

He nodded his head, looked down into his coffee, then back up. "I was inside with his father," he said. "Yeah. And they're not about to let him out for the funeral. No. He's gonna die inside, just like I was supposed to." He looked at his watch. "Couple hours, I'm gonna have to make that call."

"What if it was Becky instead?" I said.

"How's that?"

"Jimmy gives Becky that photograph. But it's an envelope, looks like business records, papers. Westerfield's hiding out, and Jimmy's giving his business secrets away to his daughter."

"Westerfield's dead."

"You think so?"

He nodded.

"Why?"

"He was all set to turn Rogers. Nate the Snake got wind of it and he got to Gene before Gene could get to the FBI."

"Nate the Snake?"

"One of the Mad Men of Madison Street. Gotta have a badass name. Crazy Henry. Frankenstein. Batman. The Grim Reaper. Rogers was Nate the Snake first time I met him."

"I thought the Vice Lords ran the West Side."

"For a few years that stretch by Westerfield's was all Mad Men. They didn't last long. Yeah, the dead men of Madison Street. Either that or inside. Nate, he's one of the few survivors, and he wasn't about to let Gene trade him to the feds."

"You know this or you're guessing?"

"I know Westerfield was trying to make a deal with the feds. I know you can't make a deal unless you've got somebody to turn. Logical choice is Nathan Rogers. So where's your theory?"

"So it started off with, what, a protection racket, and the next thing you know Rogers is a partner?"

"And now they're almost as big as Walgreen's. I hope you didn't miss all those stores last night."

"I lost you after Forty-seventh Street."

"I drive any slower, I would have been going backward. Went all the way down to a hundred and third. So tell me, you the big hotshot homicide detective. Who killed Jimmy Madison?"

Nothing jumped into my mind. No splendid clues, like the red wig that I hadn't really seen. No logical motives. No reasonable suspects. Nothing. "Something to do with that store," I said. "Irv's murder. Westerfield going away."

"Don't tell me what I already know."

". . . and with Becky showing up down there. Maybe the envelope. I don't know. Maybe you're right."

"You know what I think? You don't know how to operate without that tin star. You got all this information. But you're playing too tight with it. I was you, my man, I'd let someone knows how to investigate, investigate."

"I'm not your man," I said.

"No. You my little boy." He got up, dropped six quarters on the table, and walked out the door.

I sat there and let it echo in my head for a while: *"You my little boy."* The deep chuckle as he walked away. And maybe he was right. Maybe I had no business investigating homicides. Well, at least he hadn't patted me on the head.

The waitress came by and filled my coffee cup.

The cabdrivers and the barflies called it a night.

I looked up and I was the last one in the place, except for three waitresses sitting at a table near the kitchen door, a cloud of smoke rising above their heads.

FORTY

THE night's last two drunks were trying to scale the wall at Wrigley Field. They were on tiptoes on top of a trash can that was upside down on top of a bright red Dumpster. But they were still a bit short. As I approached, one guy cupped his hands together and the other guy stepped into them.

In the rearview, I spotted a car running without lights. A plainclothes Chevy Caprice. The drunks wouldn't be there long, I decided. Or had the dicks from Area Two made it north in record time?

I turned right, made a quick U-turn, then headed back north. The car was gone. The two drunks were rolling around on the sidewalk, moaning and laughing. The trash basket was out in the middle of the street. I went around it. Had I imagined that Caprice?

Lights were starting to come on here and there. The dog walkers were trickling out. Dawn was still an hour or so away.

Sheffield ended at Sheridan Road. I continued north. An elevated train screeched around a curve.

I flicked on the radio. "Police sources say that a body found in a car pulled from Lake Calumet is that of James Madison, a West Side medical student who has been missing since Monday."

I turned off the radio, picked up my phone, and dialed. An answering machine picked up. "You've reached the Westerfields'," a confident voice boomed. I assumed it was Gene Westerfield himself. "We're not able to take your call right now. Please leave a message after the beep and we'll get back to you as soon as possible."

"This is Nick Acropolis," I said. "It's very important I talk to you. Something's happened. I'm going to head—"

"Hello? Hello?" Janet Westerfield picked up the phone, a note of panic in her voice.

"Hi, it's Nick. Sorry to get you up."

"Has something happened to Becky?"

"No. No. She's fine," I said. "But there's something else. We have to talk."

"Something. What?"

"They found Jimmy."

"Jimmy?"

"From the store. Jimmy Madison."

"Mr. Acropolis, can this wait until a more respectable hour?"

"He was in the station wagon, down at the bottom of Lake Calumet. Look, this isn't going to go away."

"Call me after ten, please," she said, and the line went dead. Ten o'clock. I looked at my watch. It was a quarter after five.

An old lady was feeding the pigeons in the square at Montrose and Broadway. A CTA bus headed south, another west. A few blocks up, a hooker waved. A taxi zoomed around on the right and sped away.

The car without lights was back. Only now the lights were burning brightly.

I turned east on Lawrence Avenue and then north on Lake Shore Drive. The car followed right along. It was a route nobody would take, except to see the gray sheen on the lake, that first trace of sunrise. A mile later we were right back at Sheridan Road, where Lake Shore Drive ended.

I went west. Hollywood to Ridge to Peterson. The car stayed a block back. There was more traffic now, but most of it was going toward the Loop. They should have thrown dirt on those head-lights. I should have got a coffee to go.

I made a right turn on red at Western Avenue, then a quick right into a driveway. I pulled behind a row of parked cars and killed the lights. I waited thirty seconds or so, then pulled back out.

The Caprice was a half-block up, moving slowly. It was a shiny gray, I saw when I got closer, almost brand-new. One of the perks of the Homicide unit, only now they called it Violent Crimes.

There were three men inside. Doran and Cantore, Casper had said. Who was number three? And how had they got from Area Two to the North Side so quickly? Had Casper set me up? Maybe he'd simply waited too long to call. I should have skipped the shower.

The car got the light at Devon Avenue. I pulled behind it. The driver looked back in the mirror. The light turned green, but the car didn't move.

We sat there for a full cycle of lights. It gave me time to look around the neighborhood. Men in sarongs, women in saris. Indian and Pakistani restaurants. A video store advertised URDU. An hon-orary street sign said: "King Sarong Boulevard." A car beeped its horn, then went around.

The back door of the Caprice opened and John Casper stepped out. He shrugged, half-waved, and started back my way. He looked a bit embarrassed. But not as embarrassed as he should have looked. Where did he think I was going to lead them, I wondered, and did he really think I'd talk to him now?

I waited until his hand was reaching for the passenger door; then I dropped the gearshift into reverse and stepped on the gas. I made one of those tire-screeching U-turns and jumped back on the gas, heading south.

The Olds flew. God was on my side. My old partner had sold me out, and all the lights stayed green as I came soaring along and then turned red immediately behind me. The Caprice was two blocks back, headlights flashing. But they weren't really trying. Their wheels were actually touching the ground.

I scooted through the intersection at Foster Avenue as the light was changing. A pack of eastbound buses were waiting for the green. I looked back in the mirror. The Caprice gave up. The headlights stopped flashing. They pulled up to the light and waited for the buses to clear.

"See, Willy, there they go, a thousand buses in a row." I remembered an old rhyme. Now where was that from?

I took the side streets west, crossing the river at Argyle, then jumped up to Bryn Mawr, then Peterson. The Caprice never reappeared.

I took the highway north, then picked up the tollway heading toward Milwaukee. Before I knew it, I was at a tollbooth, handing a grandmotherly type with shiny blue-gray hair a buck. She handed me back sixty cents and a receipt. "How do I get to California from here?" I asked.

"Sonny, what you do, you pull into that oasis up ahead and buy yourself a road atlas. And then when you're all done dreaming, turn around and go back to your family."

"Best advice of the night," I said, and I handed her back the change.

I pulled into the oasis and went into the McDonald's and got a cup of coffee to go, carried it to a row of pay phones, and dialed Area Four.

"You sold me out, you son of a bitch," I said when Casper came on.

"Nick, you kill someone driving like that, you're gonna end up inside with Andy."

"I can't believe you couldn't be straight."

"What? So you can make up another idiotic story?"

"Tell me what do you want to know, John. Because this is your last chance to ask me questions without going through a lawyer."

"Nick, don't you get it? You're on the other side."

"No, I do get it, John. I just want to make sure you do. I disown you as my old partner. I never knew you. I never worked with you. We were never friends."

"You're breaking my heart."

"And I'm gonna get there first."

"Where?"

"Wherever it is this Westerfield thing is heading. I'm gonna beat you there. You're getting old, John, and fat, and that hairpiece is a joke. Don't you have any friends to tell you you look like a world-class fool?"

The phone went dead. "Yeah, fuck you, too," I said into it.

FORTY-ONE

I DOZED in the backseat for a few hours, then went back to the McDonald's for more coffee.

Jimmy Madison was on the front page of the *Sun-Times,* all decked out in his cap and gown, under the headline: MEDICAL STUDENT SLAIN. The story confirmed what Harris had said: Jimmy had been shot twice in the head. The body had also shown signs of torture.

At ten o'clock I dialed the Westerfield number. "Hi. It's Nick," I said after the beep, but nobody picked up.

I called my answering machine. John Casper was first: "Nick, OK, maybe you're right. So sorry. But it's time to get over it and get in here. You're only making everything worse." He didn't sound a bit sorry.

Tracy Grace was next: "Hey, Nick, give me a call. I got something you're gonna wanna see." Shelly followed, low-key in a sexy sort of whisper: "Nick, call me." Becky sounded close to tears: "Nick, please call me as soon as you can. If I'm not here try this number. It's Bill Harris's car phone."

The final message was from my old friend Lenny, the Austin district sergeant, who'd tried to introduce me to Jack Gabriel: "Nick, if you get a chance . . . call me. There's some-something you might be in-interested in. So . . . thanks."

I dialed Becky. "I just can't believe it," she said. "I don't know what to do."

"How about I pick you up and we'll go see your mother?"

"I've been calling all morning and there's no answer. Actually, I'm waiting for Bill. Harris. We were going to go see if she's home. Maybe you can meet us."

"Sure. What time?"

"He's picking me up in a couple of minutes. But we're going to see Jimmy's mother first."

"OK. Well, I'll look for you up there."

A TV news truck was parked in front of the Westerfield house, along with a Wilmette squad car and several private cars. A small group was milling about in front of the driveway. One guy was wearing a vest that must have had twenty pockets. He had several cameras around his neck. A woman with a notebook in hand looked my way, then moved away from the group. She scribbled in the notebook, then pulled out a cell phone. She'd probably have my name in a minute or two, I decided.

I turned and drove down the street behind the house, then headed for downtown Wilmette. I stopped at a gas station and got the name of a local mechanic, then called Hertz.

I dropped the Olds for an oil change and a brake job, then called the Westerfield house from a pay phone at the rental agency. "It's Nick," I said after the beep. "If you want to get out of that house without finding yourself on TV, I can tell you how to do it."

After a few seconds she picked up. "I think I'm perfectly capable of driving out of my own garage, Mr. Acropolis."

"As soon as you do, one of those cars is going to pull across the driveway and block you in."

"I'm sure the police will be able to deal with that."

"Yeah. But it's gonna take 'em a while to get the driver back in the car and get it moved. Not long. Thirty seconds, a minute. But you'd be surprised how many questions they can ask in such a short time. How much film they can shoot."

"And your suggestion?"

"Put on a pair of jeans and some old shoes. You have a step stool, something like that?"

"Yes."

"OK. Go out that door in your breakfast room. Walk toward the back fence, but angle toward the house with the gazebo in the yard. You know the one I mean?"

"Yes."

"The step stool should be enough to get you over the fence. When you get in your neighbor's yard, go to the right, around the side of the house. I'll be sitting in a blue Ford out front. But give me about ten minutes, OK?"

"I'll synchronize my watch," she said, and the line went dead.

Fifteen minutes later she slid in beside me. She looked right at home in jeans and hiking boots, a flannel shirt, and a windbreaker. "I haven't had that much fun in ages," she said as I pulled away from the curb.

"It won't work for long," I said. "Pretty soon, they'll start renting out your neighbors' houses, paying them to spy on you."

"No, Mr. Acropolis. This is the North Shore, after all."

"Nick," I said. "Yeah, maybe. But still. It's only going to get worse." I sounded like Casper.

"Nick, would you mind terribly dropping me at the train station?" She sounded like some distinguished North Shore matron, one who'd never been anywhere near the West Side.

"Janet, we have to talk."

"I appreciate your help, but I don't—"

"This thing is not going to blow over. You can't just go on hiding."

"I'm not hiding."

"Where's your husband?"

"I don't know."

"Come on. Don't insult me." She had to know.

"Nick, I honestly don't know."

"You must have some idea," I said, but she didn't answer.

I turned left, went over the tracks, and headed west, away from the train station. She didn't try to stop me.

"Years ago we stumbled on a lodge in Colorado," she said, a few minutes later. "BB. Before Becky. It was one of those magical places. Mountains, woods, a stream. We always meant to go back, but . . ."—she shrugged—"but we never did.

"When all the trouble started, Gene told me he might have to go away suddenly. He called out to Colorado to make sure the lodge was still there, and that was our plan. If he left, I was to give him a couple of days and then call from a pay phone. We even found the perfect phone, in a ladies' room at Old Orchard. But he never arrived. He made a reservation, but he never checked in."

"So where is he?"

"I think it's very likely he's dead," she said softly.

"How?"

"Murdered."

"By who?"

"All I can give you is guesses."

"OK."

"The Mafia or whatever you call it."

"That's clear enough. Who else?"

"Nathan Rogers."

"OK. Anybody else?"

"Several present and former employees. Various business associates."

"Which employees?"

"I wouldn't know their names. I know there were two doctors my husband mentioned. One he recently fired. Another he was having some sort of difficulties with."

"Your husband mentioned them as . . . ?"

"As people who might want to kill him."

"Why did he think someone would want to kill him?"

"Irv Kaplan."

"He took that as a warning?"

"Wouldn't you?"

"Did anyone actually threaten him?"

"Not in so many words. But after . . . after what happened to Irv, he didn't know who to trust. I think he began to see the kind of life he'd been leading and . . ."

I waited for her to go on, but she didn't. "So why would all these people want to kill him?" I asked. "What would they gain?"

"I'm sure it was the money," she said.

"What money?"

"The money," she said softly. "All the money."

"Are you hungry?" she asked a minute later.

I followed her directions and ten minutes later we were at an old roadhouse in the middle of the woods. It wasn't quite noon, but the parking lot was crowded. Inside, there was a wait for the dining room, but there was a small booth available alongside the bar.

"A Manhattan," Janet told the waitress when she came.

"Two."

"They make a wonderful hamburger," Janet said.

"Sold."

We sipped the drinks. "If your husband thought he was in danger, why didn't he go to the police?"

"How much do you know about my husband's business?"

"Not much. I know that he owns or has an interest in quite a few drugstores, medical centers, and nursing homes. I know that most of his customers are public aid recipients. I know he's got good connections in Springfield with the people who pay the bills. I also know the FBI is nosing around. I assume it's some kind of welfare fraud investigation. So the heat was already on. What would a murder investigation uncover that the FBI couldn't find?"

"But what if Becky heard about it? How would he ever explain an FBI investigation or welfare fraud or any of it?"

"How did he explain it to you?"

"He didn't have to. I knew. Not at first. But it gradually dawned on me where the money came from. The house. The cars. The jewelry. I suppose that makes me an accomplice, doesn't it?"

The hamburgers were thick. The juice leaked from mine, formed a stream on the plate, and flowed into the French fries. But Janet managed to eat her entire hamburger without spilling a single drop.

"Why didn't you report him missing?" I asked after the plates were cleared away. "After you called out to Colorado and he wasn't there. Why didn't you call the police?"

"I kept hoping he would be there. I called this morning."

The waitress brought coffee. Janet raised the cup to her lips. She looked over my shoulder. "You're on TV," she whispered.

The television was above the bar. I turned just in time to catch my old thin face staring back at me. It was quickly replaced by a shot of the Westerfield Pharmacy. The sound was down low and, besides one old-timer sitting directly under the television, nobody else seemed to be paying any attention.

"Fucking Casper," I said.

"Who's that?"

"A cop. He thinks this is going to bring me in."

"And it's not?"

"Not until I have something."

"Won't they be looking for you?"

"Not that hard," I said. "I can't go home, but I've got plenty of cash and I've got these." I put on a pair of eyeglasses. The lenses were clear, the frame thick plastic.

An amused look crept into Janet's eyes. "Usually glasses make people look more intelligent," she said.

"Thanks."

"If you can't go home where will you sleep?"

"The nearest Holiday Inn," I said. "You want to come along?"

I didn't expect anything but a smile. But she gave me another long look instead, then shrugged. "I should say no," she said, but she never did.

She couldn't go home, either.

FORTY-TWO

THE room was on the ninth floor, one from the top, with a view of a shopping center and the tollway and, beyond that, the endless rooftops of suburbia. There were two beds with a nightstand between them. A round table and two armchairs sat beneath a hanging lamp. A desk with a mirror had a straight-back chair tucked into the kneehole. On one wall a large piece of abstract motel art hung in a metal frame; on another a television set was bolted to a very secure-looking swivel bracket.

Janet Westerfield was lying on the bed by the window, the bed that was still made up. She was up on her elbows, turning the pages of a glossy motel travel magazine. Her right foot was up in the air, and every so often she'd give it a little kick.

Outside, the sun had set, but there was a delicate afterglow. If I squinted just a bit, I could make it dance along those dark and enchanting curves on the far bed.

It was hard to believe she was pushing fifty. It wasn't that she looked young. She didn't. If you tried, you'd probably come pretty close to guessing her age. I think for me, her age actually added to the allure. That she'd managed to keep that perfect tone and still appear so natural. I just couldn't imagine her at a health club or under a mud pack or having anything tucked or sucked or trimmed.

Maybe it was Austin High.

I could see her leaning against a locker in one of those wide and noisy hallways, wearing bobby socks, a pleated skirt, and the perfect sweater, her arms folded and a relaxed smile on her face.

I wouldn't have been able to get within a mile of her back then. Maybe that was another part of her beauty. That she didn't seem to mind that, thirty years later, I was still from the wrong side of the tracks.

"You're killing me with that leg," I said.

"This?" She gave the leg another little kick.

"That," I said. "The whole pose, it's very . . ."

"Enticing?" she suggested.

"That's it," I agreed. "That's exactly what I was thinking. Enticing. Nobody reads those magazines. Throw that away and get over here where it's warm."

She brought the other leg up and kicked that one, too.

"I'm trying to entice you over here. You can't have two beds in a room and only use one. What would the maid think?"

A while later, we were passing a cigarette back and forth. The television was on with the sound off. The lights from the highway were making ever-changing patterns on the ceiling.

"You know, this is the best part right here," she said. "Talking and looking at the ceiling. Smoking." She put her hand out and I slipped the cigarette into it. "This is really the only good reason left to smoke."

A few minutes later, she pointed toward the television and I looked up. A man with a microphone was standing in front of the Westerfield store. I reached for the bedside controls, but she stopped me. A picture of Jimmy flashed on the screen, and then we were looking at the Horner Homes.

Gene Westerfield's picture was next, and once again I thought how old he looked. Janet might have been reading my mind. "I don't know what happened. One day he decided to become an old man. He grew that beard, started smoking a pipe, taking himself so seriously."

"Recently?"

"Oh, no. Years and years ago."

The television switched to the front of the Westerfield house. The door opened. Janet took a deep breath and grabbed my hand as Harris and Becky stepped out to the porch. A microphone appeared and Becky's lips moved.

"I can't watch this," Janet said. I hit the button and the screen turned dark.

I watched the patterns on the ceiling, lit another cigarette, and smoked it all by myself.

"I know I should feel guilty," she said after a long while. "My husband has been either kidnapped or murdered. My daughter is running around with an ex-convict. And here I am in bed with a private detective. It sounds like some trashy novel, doesn't it?"

"Why would someone kidnap your husband?"

"We were happier when we had less."

"Why would someone kidnap your husband?"

"Do you ever stop working?"

I shut up and went back to enjoying life.

In my dreams the Hilltop Nursing Home was a dark, Gothic-looking place on top of a real hill. I was crawling through tall, wet grass when a flashlight beam found me. "Hope you brought your whiskey." The man holding the light laughed. There was a huge gap where his teeth had once been. But it was the wrong man. It wasn't the guy I'd seen in my apartment. It was Leslie Crawford instead, with shoulder-length red hair.

I sat up. Janet Westerfield was standing wrapped in the window curtain, looking out at the night. "They hit the wrong man," I said almost before I thought it. "The hit man thought Irv Kaplan was your husband." The two didn't look much alike, and Kaplan was almost twenty years older. But they were both nearly bald, both white males in a black neighborhood. And Westerfield looked older than his years. If you were in a hurry and nervous, you might make the mistake. "Your husband figured out he was the real target. That's why he was so afraid. That's why he took off. That's why he didn't know who to trust."

I lit a cigarette. She didn't turn from the window. Beyond her, the sky was drizzly gray. The rumble of trucks on the highway merged with faraway thunder.

"He asked for Mr. Westerfield," she said softly. "Gene assumed it was a salesman, so he sent Irv out to tell him they weren't interested."

"Oh, Jesus," I said softly.

"Gene was running a tape on the adding machine. That's the only reason he didn't go himself. He didn't want to lose his place. Irv just happened to be there that day. He only worked three days a week. If he hadn't been working my husband would have died instead."

"So there was no motive."

"I'm sorry?" She turned and let the curtain fall back into place, then slipped in beside me.

"Nobody could figure out a motive for the Kaplan hit. Turns out there wasn't one. It was a mistake. That'll make my old partner happy."

"I thought he was in jail."

"My other old partner. He's still in Homicide. The Kaplan case is his."

"Well, that's very convenient for you, I'm sure."

"Actually, it's a pain in the ass."

If Westerfield was the actual target, that changed everything. Suddenly there were suspects and motives everywhere.

There was the mob, of course; had they tried to muscle in? And how about the factorors, the companies who bought good debts at a discount? Why had Westerfield suddenly decided to give 10 or 20 percent of his gross away? And there was Nathan Rogers. Was he really a partner? If he was and Westerfield died, wouldn't he come out ahead? And then there was the woman next to me. What reason would she have to murder her husband? What reason did any woman have?

"We should have just let it burn," she said after a while. "Everything would have turned out. But we were too afraid."

"Of what?"

"I'm sure that's always the way. From the outside it looks like greed or vanity or lust. But from inside it's just plain and simple fear."

"Who was your devil?"

"Nate Rogers," she whispered. She was shivering. I dropped the cigarette in the ashtray, wrapped my arms around her. "We didn't know it, of course. But isn't that what everyone says?" She rolled away, plucked the cigarette from the ashtray.

"The store survived the sixties, and I think Gene took that as a sign from God. It wasn't just good luck. So much of the West Side was destroyed, but our section was untouched. We lost a lot of good customers, burned-out or moved away. But we survived. The seventies came along and all that was behind us, or so we thought, and then one Sunday afternoon there was a police chase. I'm sure you know what happened."

"I was telling a reporter just the other day."

"Two little boys on their way home from church, a speeding car, and, after a decade of peace, the rioting and looting began again. We were closed on Sunday, but one of the neighbors called and Gene went down there. He didn't come home for four days. But he saved the store. Almost every other building burned to the ground. But we survived. It wasn't until years later that I learned the truth about the deal he'd made with Nathan Rogers."

"Rogers saved the store and your husband set him up in the welfare fraud business."

"It started much simpler. It started with drugs. We could get all the drugs Rogers wanted. It's really that simple. We gave him drugs and he protected the store. And then it just snowballed and the next thing we knew we were rich beyond our wildest dreams. Isn't that funny? All Gene was trying to do was keep his father's store from being destroyed. And look what happened. I didn't have to work anymore. We bought a big house on the North Shore, a Mercedes for Gene. The best schools for Becky. Who says crime doesn't pay?

"Gene worked at the store from the time he was a little boy. I think that was the reason he was so determined to stay. His friends either got burned out or they closed up on their own. And most of them reopened in the suburbs and did just fine. But Gene wouldn't hear of moving. He thought that would be like spitting on his father's grave. His father was one of those dynamic men who came from nowhere, from nothing. He built the store and a family. I never met him. But I heard the stories. And Becky heard them, too, over and over again. A man who gave respect and demanded it in return. A man whose word was his bond. A man so full of life and so sure of his convictions. And I think she might have ended up confusing her father with her grandfather. Sometimes I think that was the point, actually."

"You don't sound like the loyal wife," I said.

"But that's exactly what I am. That's my entire life."

"Loyalty to what?"

"To Becky, to the family, to my husband. Yes, of course, I see his flaws. But he's never treated me badly. And he needs me, needed us, the family. We're all he has outside the business. It's funny. I've had my bags half-packed for years, telling myself, when Becky gets out of high school or when Becky gets out of college. And now I'm here, but her father isn't." She threw the covers back and slipped out of bed. "So I better go home and tell her the truth."

"And what's that?"

"Her father's a crook. And he's not coming home. He's either dead or he's on his way to prison."

FORTY-THREE

W HO was running the store?"

"I'm not sure I understand," she said.

"With your husband gone. Who was running the store: Jimmy?"

"I never really thought about the store until Nate Rogers called to tell me about Becky."

"He told you what?"

"That Becky had been down there asking questions. He wanted me to keep her away. He said the West Side was no place for a suburban child. It's funny, now that I think of it. He kept speaking for Gene. He said Gene wouldn't want her down there. Gene would want her back in school. I just realized what that implies."

"What?"

"He knows I'm not in touch with my husband. How would he know that?"

I got off the highway at Lake Avenue and we headed east. "Here's something else," I said. "Rogers told me your husband was on vacation, which is the same thing you told Becky."

"Yes."

"But you never talked to Rogers before he called you about Becky?"

"No."

"I don't know. My partner stops coming to work, one of the first calls I make is his home."

"One would think."

A Wilmette squad car trailed us for a mile or so, then turned south on Green Bay Road. We continued east, over the tracks, then drove the few short blocks to the Westerfield home.

Becky's Honda was parked in the driveway. The porch light was lit, but the rest of the house was dark.

"I'll come in if you want," I said.

"Oh, god, no. This is going to be difficult enough." She leaned over and gave me a hug and a quick kiss. "It was fun. Thank you. More than fun."

She opened the door and got out, then leaned back in. "You know all our secrets now."

"They're still secrets."

"No. Not anymore." She closed the door, then walked down the long driveway and up the stairs to the porch.

She turned and gave me a small wave. The door closed behind her, and a moment later a light came on upstairs.

I headed east to Sheridan Road, then south toward the city.

"How would he know that?" I heard Janet Westerfield's voice in my head.

How indeed? I wondered. *How indeed?* Maybe it was time to go ask Nathan Rogers some real questions.

FORTY-FOUR

YOU don't have to be out of the city long to notice that the place looks like a giant prison yard. I could see the eerie orange glow of sodium vapor lights blocks before I hit the Chicago line at Howard Street.

The mercury arc lamps, which had once cast the streets in muted blue, had been replaced years ago. Now the night city was painted like a flashy street tramp who used the cheapest, gaudiest makeup to magnify every fault.

But if you never left town, you never noticed. You could dance with the tramp night after night and believe you were in the arms of an angel.

Al's Grill was on Halsted Street, just a bit northwest of the Loop. It was a workingman's joint. Chris worked the grill, but just about everybody called him Al. I could never remember his wife's name. She was hostess, waitress, cashier, telephone operator, and chief bottle washer.

They were both usually smiling, but not always at each other. They opened at four in the morning and closed in the middle of the afternoon. Breakfast and lunch. Ham off the bone. Eggs, pancakes, omelets, biscuits and gravy, hash browns, hamburgers, Italian beef and sausage, gyros. I'd been stopping in for twenty years and they'd never called me by name. Until today.

"Hey, Nick, how you been?" Chris asked as I grabbed a stool.

"Long time," I said. His wife dropped a cup of coffee in front of me. She'd already added cream.

It wasn't quite five and there were only two other customers. Both looked like day laborers from the slave market down the street. NO WATER WITHOUT PURCHASE, one sign read. PLEASE PAY WHEN SERVED, another requested. IF YOU TAKE A NEWSPAPER FROM THIS STACK, the one above the newspaper rack warned, YOU JUST BOUGHT IT. IF YOU'RE GOING TO MAKE YOUR OFFICE HERE, the one above the pay phone said, PLEASE HELP OUT WITH THE RENT.

I ordered French toast and ham, my usual fare, and Chris waved that he'd heard and cracked an egg into a bowl.

"Here, take a look at the paper while you wait," the wife said, and she dropped a *Sun-Times* in front of me. It was the first time I'd been offered a free paper at Al's.

And there I was smack-dab in the middle of the front page. It was the same photo they'd used four years before, but this time they'd cut my FBI escorts out of the picture. I had my head down and my hands behind my back, but my eyes were up, like a bull about to charge. The caption underneath said: PRIVATE EYE SOUGHT IN DEATH PROBE. I could almost see Casper smiling.

Chris and his wife were doing a good job of not looking my way. Oh, well, at least they'd shown me the paper before picking up the phone. I turned to the sports page. The Bears were still hoping to win a game.

I finished my coffee and held up my cup. The wife added coffee and cream. "I've got time to eat, right?"

"Now you know better than that, Nick."

"You're right," I said. "Sorry. You know I never remember your name."

"Elsie," she said.

"That's a great name. How come I always forget?"

She smiled and went away. A wino had wandered in, just ahead of a trio of construction workers. He set some loose change on the counter. "Is that enough for toast?"

Elsie spread out the coins and took everything but a dime and a few pennies. She rang up eighty-five cents on the cash register, then dropped a couple of pieces of bread in the toaster, filled a cup with coffee, and carried it to the wino. "Thanks," he said softly. The menu on the wall above the grill said: TOAST 85 CENTS. COFFEE 50 CENTS *A CUP.*

Chris delivered my order himself. "What's this town coming to?" he said out of the side of his mouth. "A man can't do his job anymore."

"It's always something," I agreed.

The French toast was so perfect that I didn't even bother with syrup, just butter. The ham was worth a heart attack. I took my time with every bite, like a condemned man having his final meal. But then I felt the wino's eyes on me, or on my plate actually, and I suddenly remembered where I'd spent most of yesterday. No. A condemned man couldn't have it that good, could he?

The toaster popped. As Elsie was setting the plate down in front of the wino, she pulled a few pieces of ham out of an apron pocket and slipped them between the toast. She put a finger to her lips, and the wino gave her a crooked grin. She glanced my way and winked.

I finished eating, downed the remains of my coffee, paid the check, tipped, and waved good-bye. "Good luck," Chris said without turning from the grill. Elsie smiled. One of the construction workers looked up, then turned his newspaper back to the front page. I didn't look back on the way out the door. I slipped my glasses on. It was just about full daylight.

I had a pocketful of money and nowhere to go. I wanted to go pay a visit to Nathan Rogers, but it was too early. And he could get rid of me with one simple three-digit phone call. I wanted to go down to Forty-seventh Street and take another look at that nursing home, hidden away between the railway lines. Maybe I could hitch a ride on a truck going into that railroad yard.

I headed north instead. A few minutes later I decided I should have slipped the wino a couple of bucks. This didn't help the wino one bit, I realized, and I wondered if Chris knew about the ham. Probably, I decided. It was such a simple thing, giving someone a few slices of ham. *When was the last time I'd done anything as simple and unselfish as that?*

FORTY-FIVE

I PARKED alongside the lumberyard, walked up the alley, unlocked the service entrance, and climbed the stairs to my office.

The answering machine was flashing. I unplugged the phone,
dropped to the couch, and dreamed myself straight back into Janet
Westerfield's arms.

It was almost eleven when I awoke. I lit a cigarette, then pushed
the button on the answering machine: "Nick, Trace Grace, call me.
It's important." There were also messages from Shelly and Lenny.

"Sergeant McGuigan," a gruff voice answered at the POW camp.

"Tracy Grace around?" I asked.

"Yeah, he's fucking off somewhere." He dropped the phone
from the ceiling. It rattled around on the floor for a while; then
Tracy Grace walked up and said hello.

"Your sergeant doesn't like you."

"Yeah, well, fuck him. Look, we gotta talk."

"Shoot."

"In person. Something I want to show you."

"Can you give me a hint?"

"It's about that Madison kid."

"Say where."

"Somewhere down this way," he said. "I can't leave for long."

"You saw the news, right?"

"Yeah. Yeah. Look, somewhere out-of-the-way. How about under the Roosevelt Road bridge by Clark Street? I park down there sometimes. There's never anybody around."

"Good enough. What time?"

"Give me an hour. I got all this stuff to photocopy. You're gonna love it. Trust me."

I dialed Shelly next.

"Jesus, Nick, where are you?"

"Better rethink that question."

"You're right, Nick. I don't want to know. Are you OK?"

"I'm fine."

"I suppose you're proud of yourself."

"What do I have to be proud of?"

"Oh, I don't know. Back on the front page, right in the middle of the hottest murder in town."

"I could do without the front page, Shelly."

"Hey, Tracy Grace keeps bugging me."

"I just talked to him."

"Good. I'm sick of hearing him. One day he hates you; the next day he loves you. I can't figure him out, and anyway, I got a new guy."

"I'm almost afraid to ask," I said.

"No. You're gonna like this one, Nick. Get this; the charge is he gave his badge away."

"A bribe?"

"No. The actual physical badge. He took a one-day suspension for losing it back in 1976. But now they're saying that he intentionally gave it away."

"In 1976?"

"Nineteen-seventy-six. Las Vegas, Nevada."

"What's the punch line, Shelly?"

"You're supposed to ask who he gave it to," she said.

"OK." I was easy. "Who'd he give it to?"

"Elvis."

"He gave his badge to Elvis?"

"That's the accusation."

"In 1976. How the hell did they come up with this?"

"It turns out the superintendent is a big Elvis fan."

"Really?" The superintendent was black.

"Yeah. I know, it sounds weird. But it turns out he grew up in Mississippi, pretty close to Tupelo. The other week he goes to an Elvis auction and among the memorabilia there's an authentic Chicago Police Department badge for sale, along with a framed picture of my guy shaking hands with the King himself. Guess who's holding the badge? You can even read the star number."

"They're really going to charge him after all these years?"

"Bringing discredit to the department. Sound familiar? And filing a false report. Oh, I forgot one little thing. He gave him his gun, too."

"He gave Elvis his badge and his gun?"

"That's the accusation," she said.

"When do I get a look at the paperwork?"

"Call me when you get your one phone call," she said, and the line went dead.

I was on the way to the door when the phone rang. What the hell. I picked it up.

"Ni-nick. It's Len-len—."

"Lenny, what's up?"

"I didn't think you'd be there. I mean, with all the . . . all the news . . . and all. . . ."

"Yeah, pretty slick, huh? Hiding out in my own office. I meant to call you. Sorry."

"What I'm calling a-about . . . What happened, I saw Jack Gabriel with this . . . this guy. As soon as he saw me, Jack shut up. We really haven't talked, you know, since the other day. But I know I heard your name. I don't know if that means . . . anything."

"Who knows, Lenny, but thanks."

"Oh, what I forgot, I ran the plate."

"What plate?"

"I waited around, you know, in my car. And I followed the guy when he left. And I got his license number and called it in. I thought maybe the name would mean something. Trace . . . Tracy . . . Tracy Grace. He was driving a Toyota pickup truck."

"Oh, Jesus," I said. I felt like I'd been kicked in the stomach. I sat down slowly, like an old man. Yeah, let's meet under the Roosevelt Road bridge where there won't be anyone around to hear you scream. And I'd fallen for it.

"Nick, you there?"

"I'm here, Lenny. You just saved my life, you know that?"

"You're always kidding, Nick."

"He didn't see you, did he?"

"I'm not dumb, Nick."

"Sorry, Lenny. You did great. Thanks."

"You know, it was nice to see you on TV again. I mean, I know it's kinda screwy-louie this time. But it was still good to see you."

"Thanks, Len. Thanks. Look, I owe you a drink, OK?"

"Sure, Nick. I always have time for a tall cool one." Now there was the Lenny I knew and loved. He could try and try, but he would never be one of the boys.

I sat staring at the wall. Andy Kelly grinned back from the photograph with the extra arm. I glanced at the desk calendar. November 19. The day I almost died. A lovely autumn day, unseasonably warm, as the weathermen like to say. Hey, whatever happened to Nick Acropolis? Nobody knows. He just disappeared one day. And there was still time. The day was young.

How could I have been so blind? I'd worked too many cases for Shelly. I'd just assumed that Tracy Grace was another off-duty cop with a hard-on, driving around with one hand on the steering wheel and the other on his gun. But he wasn't. And the accident wasn't an accident. He'd intentionally gone after Jimmy. Why? What was Jimmy running from?

After a while, I dialed Mike Brewer's number. "Oh, boy," he said. "I don't know if I should be talking to you."

"Come on, you owe me."

"I owe you?"

"Sure. If it wasn't for me, you wouldn't have gone to Springfield, and if it wasn't for that, you wouldn't have been able to tell your boss you were already on the case when he called wanting to know what the hell was going on."

He laughed. "Not bad," he said. "But I still can't tell you anything about what I found. Not now, anyway."

"That's OK. That's not why I called. I know what you found. Volume's up all over the city. Especially on the West and South Side. How's I doin'?"

"Keep talking," he said.

"Lots of similar patterns. Easy to spot. It's almost like they're not trying to hide what they're doing."

"I don't get what you need me for."

"You know anything about the Hilltop Nursing Home?"

"Hilltop. That sounds familiar. Where is it?"

"On Stewart south of Forty-seventh Street."

"Give me a couple minutes. Where you at?"

"I'll call you," I said.

"Yes, of course. Fugitives don't have phone numbers, do they?"

I was reaching for the door when someone knocked. I froze in place. One window led to a fire escape, the other to the roof of the lumberyard, two stories down. The knock came again, louder. "Nick, it's Becky," she said in a near whisper. "You in there?"

The door didn't have a peephole. I pulled it open. There was nothing behind her but a swirl of smoke and an exit sign. "Get in here," I said. I stepped to the side.

She was all dressed up. Black slacks, a rose-colored sweater, and a big leather purse. She had oversize sunglasses tucked into the neck of the sweater. She looked like a French starlet on her way to the premiere.

"What do you know about the Hilltop Nursing Home?"

She shook her head. "I never heard of it."

"No. No. No," I said. "You were there with Harris the other night. Up the hill from that railroad-truck yard. Remember?"

"That place was creepy," she said.

"But why did you go there?"

"Latisa said that's where Jimmy dropped off . . . you know, the bills. What's the word?"

"Vouchers?"

"That's it. The vouchers. Jimmy would pick them up from the different stores and take them there. That's the billing office."

"Who did he give them to?"

"Nick, I don't know. Calm down a little, OK? You're way too hyper."

"Yeah. I guess I am. Well, look, gotta go. Was it anything special?"

"Where are we going?"

"Forget it."

"Nick, I'm coming with you."

"No. It was stupid enough dragging you around the other night." Of course, I'd loved every minute. It was like being a cop again, with a partner to talk to. It was almost like being human. "Where's Harris anyway?"

"I keep calling, but he doesn't answer. So where are we going?"

"I've got to meet a guy under a bridge downtown. A troll. Another case entirely."

"You are such a liar."

"Becky—"

"You pretend you're helping me. But all you ever do is lie."

"Don't be like that."

"Maybe I should just call the police. I'll bet they'd like to know where you're hiding." She reached into her purse and pulled out a cell phone. This was the first time I'd seen her with one. Pretty soon they'd be handing them out at birth.

"Do I look like I'm hiding from anybody?" I asked.

She shook her head. "Those glasses. I don't know. You look like yourself, only dumber."

"Dumber?" I hadn't realized I had the glasses on. "You know who you sound like? Oh, never mind."

She followed me down the stairs and out the back door and then down the alley. "Shouldn't we take my car?"

"You can take any car you want," I said as I unlocked the rental. I turned to have a final word, and Becky slipped past and dived into the front seat.

"Oh, come on," I said. "What are you, a little kid?"

"Nick, you can insult me all you want, but I'm going with you."

We headed southeast on Lincoln Avenue. There was an army-navy store a mile down. I parked in front of a fire hydrant, pulled out my roll, and peeled off a hundred. "Do me a favor. Run in and get the best pair of binoculars this will buy."

She hesitated. "Why don't we both go?"

"I'm trying to stay out of the public eye at the moment."

She grabbed the bill, opened the door, then stopped. "You're not trying to ditch me, are you?"

"Becky, you either trust me or you don't."

She gave me a long, steady look. "OK," she said. "But let me leave my purse. You wouldn't run off and leave a girl without her purse, would you?"

Women, I thought, as I watched her in the rearview. I don't know if I was planning on leaving her or not. I'm sure the thought would have crossed my mind. But now I had her purse to make sure I waited.

It was a big purse and it went nicely with the rest of her outfit. But it was the first purse I'd seen her carry.

So I opened it and peeked inside. The cell phone, some makeup, Chapstick, Tampax, a paperback book, and a package of Marlboros in a hard pack. Christ, I'd started her smoking. That'd be a couple of extra years in Purgatory for sure.

But when I shook the pack to find out how many cigarettes she'd gone through, it was heavier than I expected. I popped the lid and there weren't any cigarettes inside, just a piece of black metal. It looked like a pager, but it also looked very much like a transmitter for a tracking unit. And the back was magnetic, which would make it easy to slip to the underside of a car.

Not too far away, someone was probably listening to a steady beep. As we began to move away, the beeps would come further apart. If the distance closed, the beeps would come closer. "Harris, where are you?" I sang.

I slipped the transmitter back in the purse and pulled out the cell phone. Here was something else I'd never seen Becky carry. Was Harris listening to every word we said? I put my ear to the phone, nothing. I pushed a button and got a dial tone. What the hell, I dialed Mike Brewer.

"The Hilltop Nursing Home was closed by our office more than two years ago," he said.

"Why?"

"The usual horrible shit."

"So they're not still in business?"

"They're off our list, so we certainly wouldn't pay any bills they submitted."

"Okay. Thanks for your help."

"Anything I should know?"

"Just a hunch," I said. "Just a hunch."

A few minutes later Becky slid in beside me. She handed me a plastic bag, a pile of change, and a receipt. I pointed across the street to the Biograph Theatre. "You know about John Dillinger?"

"I'm not sure."

"He was a bank robber back in the thirties. The FBI was after him. Anyway, he was hanging out with a woman who was in the country illegally. Hiding out. So she made a deal with the feds. She turned Dillinger in and they agreed to let her stay in the U.S."

"Oh."

"So she brought him here for a movie. They called her the lady in red because she wore a red dress. That's how the FBI knew it was Dillinger. They killed him right there in the mouth of that alley. I guess he went for a gun. Anyway, Dillinger was so famous that they say the ladies dipped the hems of their dresses in his blood so they would have souvenirs."

"That's pretty gross," Becky said.

"Yeah. But that's not the worst part of the story."

"I'm not sure I want to hear this."

"The worst part was they deported her anyway. The lady in red. She turned her lover in, and they killed him right in front of her, and then they reneged on the deal and sent her back to Romania or wherever the hell she was from."

"Why?"

"Because they could," I said. "Because they could. The moral of the story: if you're gonna rat somebody out, make sure you rat them out to somebody you can trust. Which always rules out the FBI, by the way."

"You're talking about my dad, right?"

"Someone in the family," I said.

We sat watching traffic pass. "Did you talk to my mother yesterday?" she asked after a while.

"Briefly."

"Did she tell you how my dad saved the store from the riots?"

I nodded.

"She was afraid to tell me."

"She knows you love your father."

"I do. And I don't care what he did. No. I do care, and I'll probably never forgive him. But I still love him. And there's one thing I'm sure of."

"What's that?"

"He didn't have anything to do with what happened to Jimmy."

"I think you're right," I said. "More and more, I think you're right."

FORTY-SIX

WHERE are we going?" Becky asked as we headed toward the lake.

"I'm not sure."

"Harris thinks you're a fool."

"Maybe he's right."

"I don't think so," she said as I turned south on Lake Shore Drive. "I think you just like to play the part."

The lake was pretending to be an ocean that day. The waves were crashing into the seawall, sending huge sprouts of water directly into the air.

Gliding around the curve at Oak Street, I remembered the photograph of Irv Kaplan in his army uniform. The Drake Hotel looked the same today, more than fifty years later. And East Lake Shore was probably richer than ever. But the look on Irv's face as he gazed at his bride was really the best part of the picture. I wondered if she was still sleeping her life away. "I keep thinking it must have been a mistake," she'd said, and now it turned out she'd been right. Would that make her feel any better?

"Can I use your phone?" I asked.

Becky handed it over. I dialed Area Four. "The Kaplan hit was a mistake," I said when Casper came on.

"And you got this where?" he asked.

"I can't give you that. But I can tell you the real target."

"I'm listening."

"Westerfield."

"I'm still listening."

"What happened, he was running a tape on the adding machine. The guy came in and asked for him. Westerfield thought it was a salesman. So he sent Irv out to tell him no. He didn't want to lose his spot on the tape."

"You're sure?"

"It's from a very reliable source."

"So why the cover-up?"

"I can't tell you that right now."

"That implies that you'll tell me later."

"If you're still talking to me."

"Just keep it flowing. So far you're batting a thousand, by the way."

"How's that?"

"Leslie Crawford. I've got my best team working on him right now. This ought to push him over the edge. The poor sap hit the wrong guy. No wonder he won't give it up."

"Oh, Jesus, John. You can't do this."

"I can't do what?"

"You can't go beating confessions out of people. You'll end up out here with me."

"Nick, you're the one told us to check him out."

"Yeah, but—"

"Anyway, we've got the briefcase with the bullet holes in it. We've got the wig."

"Really?"

"We don't have the gun and we don't know who paid the bill, but I'll bet money we get both. This guy's a mope. I don't know where Stringfellow came up with that computer hacker theory. His sheet's nothing but burglary, blackmail, and drugs."

"You got the briefcase?"

"Yeah. It was in the trunk of his car. Unbelievable, huh? I don't know if he was keeping it as a souvenir or what. Maybe he's just one of those guys never throws anything out. The wig was under the front seat.

"Jesus, John, that's great."

"Yeah. I apologize for giving you a hard time. I thought you were just pulling my chain."

"Come on, John. You know better than that."

"One curious thing: Stringfellow doesn't remember seeing any wig in that apartment. But I think I'll trust your eyes over his."

"So all is forgiven?"

"Well, Area Two wants to talk to you about a certain Jimmy Madison and there's still the matter of that warrant with your name on it."

"For what?"

"Oh, I don't know. Eluding police. Obstructing justice. Making fun of your old partner's hair. We threw in everything we could think of."

"You'll never take me alive." I disconnected the phone and handed it back to Becky. "Wow. That's too much," I said. Leslie Crawford was really the guy. Or was it now Casper's turn to pull my chain? Crawford couldn't really be the guy, could he?

"You OK?" I asked.

"I was thinking about my dad," she said. "Every time I start to cry, I remember Irv Kaplan and I stop."

I took Roosevelt west, passing just south of police headquarters. It was an old building that had been remodeled into repulsiveness. It had to be one of the uglier buildings in town, even without Tracy Grace working there. Even without the room where they took your badge for good.

But there were worse things than losing your job. In the lobby, there was a wall of badges on a background of blue. Shiny badges that no one would ever again wear.

I went up the gleaming new bridge. Down below in the darkness, Tracy Grace and whatever trolls he'd rounded up were waiting. I wondered how many of them had badges of their own. If you're going to give yours away, isn't Elvis really the better choice?

I headed south in the Dan Ryan local lanes, plodding along with half the trucks in America. Coming up to Thirty-fifth Street, I pointed off to the right, to that shopping mall masquerading as a ballpark. "Remember old Comiskey?" I asked. But Becky wasn't listening.

As I came up the ramp at Forty-seventh Street, the scent of butterscotch reached me. Artificial butterscotch for artificial food, for people whose taste buds had been desensitized by life in an artificial world. It was Raymond Purcell's favorite artificial flavor, I remembered, and I wondered where that beautiful bicycle had gone.

A truck turned between the viaducts. I continued past, went under the second viaduct, then turned down a street that ran parallel to the railroad embankment.

There were a few scattered houses on the far side of the street. A siding salesman must have made a killing on the block back about 1952, but very little had been remodeled since, except by fire and neglect. A pack of stray dogs wandered past, one skinnier than the last. A large black dog in the safety of a fenced-in yard began to bark. A couple of growls from the pack silenced him.

A pair of burned-out cars sat at the curb. Another had been stripped. It sat waiting for the fire to come.

A block down there was a gap in the embankment. An old pedestrian walkway had been closed off with a Cyclone fence that ran clear to the top. The fence was rusty and bent in at the bottom. There was a pile of junk inside, rags, I thought, and a shopping cart loaded with more junk in the corner. There was another fence on the far side of the walkway. This one was overgrown with vines. But through one of the gaps I could see a brick wall. The Hilltop Nursing Home.

"There's somebody in there," Becky said softly.

"Huh?"

"A homeless guy. He's lying along the wall. See?"

Oh, Christ, I found his eyes, which were looking straight back. Those weren't rags. And the guy wasn't homeless. We were staring right into his living room. How rude. I released the brake and continued south.

"Why don't we just go in the front way?" Becky asked.

"I tried that once. There's a guard."

"I don't understand what you're looking for."

"I don't know exactly. I know Jimmy's accident happened just around the corner. And I know it wasn't really an accident. The guy was chasing Jimmy, trying to stop him."

"Why?"

"That's the part I don't know. My bet is Jimmy saw something he wasn't supposed to see when he dropped the vouchers off that day."

We continued south, but there was only the one opening. It was either over the top or through the bum's home.

I made a U-turn. The bum stood up as I made another U-turn and pulled to a stop on the far side of the street. I opened a door and dropped a foot to the pavement.

"I'm going in," I said. "You wait for Harris. Keep the doors locked. Anybody bothers you, lay on the horn. I'll be back in a flash."

"I'm coming with you."

"Look, I don't even know if I can get in there. I don't know what I'm going to find. But I know these are dangerous people."

"I'm not afraid."

"Well, you should be. Anyway, I need you to tell Harris where I'm at. I've got the funny feeling he's gonna show up any minute."

"I'm coming with you," she said again. "Harris will probably find us wherever we are, right? Isn't that how those things work?"

Well, what did I expect? If I didn't want her to come along, I should have left her at the army-navy store.

"OK, you're an adult," I said, and I got out of the car. Becky followed me toward the bum's home. "You get killed, I'll feel bad, but I'm not gonna feel guilty."

"Nobody's getting killed," she said.

"Tell that to Jimmy and Irv."

FORTY-SEVEN

THE bum moved toward the fence as we approached, a short length of pipe in his hand. I held a twenty out. He eyed the bill but didn't relax his grip on the pipe.

He was wearing a blue quilted jacket over a black trench coat, over a leather vest, over a collection of dress shirts. And god only knows what was under those. He was of medium height, five-ten or so, and on the skinny side even with the layers. But he looked strong and fairly fit for a man who lived where he did. He had a big bushy beard as black as his face, which was nearly as black as coal. The whites of his eyes were bright and clear. If he took the twenty, he probably wouldn't spend it on drugs or alcohol. But he gave little indication that he intended to take it.

"We just want to get through to the other side." I moved the bill closer.

He shook his head, then switched the pipe to his left hand. He opened two fingers of his right hand then closed them, then brought them back to a V, then closed them again.

"A scissors," Becky said.

"Cut what?" I said, but then I got it. I pulled out my roll and found seventeen dollars in singles and fives. The bum smiled. His teeth were bright and as white as the whites of his eyes. "You got three bucks?" I asked Becky. The bum shook his head, held a palm out, and flashed a few hand signals.

"It's OK," Becky deciphered the code. "That's enough."

I slipped the money through the fence. The bum tucked it away in his vest, then pulled a section of fence away from the embankment. I bent down a bit and slipped through. Becky followed.

The bum led the way to the opposite fence. When he got there he held up his hand, like a squad leader stopping his troops.

"Wait," Becky said. We waited.

We were facing the side of the nursing home, toward the rear. There was a single door in the back, with a small window near the top. There were seven large sliding windows on the first floor and nine on the other four. I didn't see any signs of life.

Time passed, a minute, two, five. A train rumbled by overhead. I looked at the bum. He shrugged. "Relax," Becky said. A rat scurried along the far wall and the bum went after it with the heel of his boot. He missed, but he came back smiling. His teeth were perfect. Becky and I exchanged a look. What would he have done with the rat if he had caught it?

The door at the back of the nursing home opened and a woman stepped out, dressed in medical whites. She placed something in the jamb of the door, shook a cigarette out of a pack, flicked a Bic, took a deep drag, then started walking our way.

The bum drew a circle in the air and took a drag on an invisible cigarette. The woman turned the side of the building and headed for the front.

"She walks around the building and smokes the cigarette," Becky whispered.

The bum nodded and held up his hand. When the woman disappeared, he dropped the hand and pulled the fence open. We slipped through.

I headed for the corner of the building, then crouched low as I scooted to the door. A paperback book was propped in the jamb. There was a small security window at eye level. I peeked in. A hallway with a stairway leading to a closed door, and then a turn as the stairway continued up. Cinder block walls, iron railings.

I pulled the door open and held it for Becky, then followed her in. I let the door close gently on the book, then unholstered my gun and tiptoed up to the first floor. There was the hum of activity beyond the door, the murmur of voices.

We went up another flight of stairs to a door with 2 stenciled on it. I put my ear to it and heard nothing but a gentle buzz. A sound came from down below, a rustle of wind, a door closing, then footsteps coming up the stairs.

I peeked over the railing. The woman in white. She opened the door on the first floor. Unintelligible voices were cut off as the door closed.

We went up. The higher we got, the quieter the building became. I listened at the top door, which was stenciled with the number 5, and all I heard was my own heavy breathing.

I opened the door and stepped into a dim and dusty hallway. Off to the left sat a glassed-in nurses' station. Elevators were dead ahead. Indicator lights showed both cars on the first floor. I let the door close behind me. Light came from an EXIT sign above our head and others at either end of the hallway. To the east, a few doors stood open and gray daylight splashed into the hallway.

"What happened to the patients?" Becky whispered.

"The state shut the place down."

"Why?"

"I'm not sure."

I headed east along the hallway and Becky followed. Our shoes left prints in the dust.

"Why is there a nurse downstairs?"

"How do you know she's not a doctor?"

"Doctors don't read romance novels."

I peeked into an open room. There was a bathroom off a short hallway and single beds with a pair of nightstands between them. Hospital-style curtains ran on tracks around each bed. The bed by the window was covered in plastic, but the second bed was unmade, just a bare mattress.

We stopped a few feet shy of the windows. We had a beautiful view of the railroad-truck yard.

"Why would anybody put a nursing home here?" Becky asked.

I crept forward. Down below, a thirty-yard Dumpster was sitting half-full. "Can you make out what's in that Dumpster?"

Becky looked down. "Paper," she said after a moment.

"What kind of paper?"

"It looks like files, stuff like that. Records."

Two guys walked up and dumped armloads of paper. A while later they were back with another load. A single piece tried to escape. Both guys went after it. The white guy caught it. He crumpled it into a ball and threw it to the black guy, who passed it behind his back into the Dumpster. I was pretty sure I'd seen the white guy the other night in the same front yard.

The two continued to fill the Dumpster. They took a smoke break and then a third man joined the team, another black guy. The paper started coming faster and faster. Every few trips the entire crew would take a smoke break around the Dumpster.

"Are we just going to stand here?" Becky asked.

"I'm counting the trips between smoke breaks."

"Seven," she said.

"You sure?"

"So far."

"Let's get closer."

We went back down the same stairway. The fourth floor was as empty as the one above it. The third-floor hallway was lined with mattresses and nightstands and large metal laundry carts. There were plenty of footprints in the dust.

The second floor wasn't covered with dust. There were a few loose pieces of paper on the floor. I picked one up. It was an Illinois Department of Public Aid form listing twelve prescriptions filled October 29 at Sawyer Pharmacy. According to the sheet, it was page 1 of a ten-page document.

Multiple sheets of paper were taped to all the doors. I recog-

nized many of the names from our tour the other night. Westerfield's and St. Anthony's shared a door with Albany Drugs and
Southtown Pharmacy.

I opened the door. The beds had been replaced by folding tables
and chairs. The tables were crowded with cardboard file boxes, but
the boxes themselves were empty. I opened a few more doors with
the same result, then walked toward the window.

Two more trips and then a smoke break. I timed the break.
Three minutes. They flicked their cigarettes away or ground them
into the gravel, then went back to carrying paper.

A pickup truck pulled in and Tracy Grace stepped out. A skinny
black guy followed. He took off a white smock and tossed it into
the truck. He had a revolver tucked in his waistband.

"How's that guy's teeth?"

"Which guy?"

"The black guy," I said.

"Pretty bad," Becky said. "He's got a huge hole right in the
middle."

"Thanks."

"Why didn't you bring your binoculars?"

Grace and the guy with the gap in his teeth joined the brigade.
We waited one full cycle to make sure the pattern stayed the same.
Once again, they took a break after the seventh trip.

On their sixth trip of the next cycle, we headed down the west
stairway to the first floor. I could hear movement and talking on
the other side of the door. Somewhere not too far away, a radio
was playing. There was a security window. I crouched down and
waited until the talking stopped; then I stood up, took a look
through the window, and slowly opened the door.

The hallway lights were on down here. But it was virtually the
same layout as upstairs. The biggest difference was a waiting room
next to the nurses' station and the double doors leading out the
front of the building.

The floor was littered with papers. There were more names on the doors. Once again, the beds had been replaced by tables and chairs. The file boxes were stuffed with papers.

As we moved along the hallway, the radio got louder. It sounded like it was coming from a room on the far side of the nurses' station. There was no paper on the door, just the number, 109. Two chairs sat on either side of an overflowing ashtray.

Outside, I could hear Grace telling a joke. He was the only one laughing. I peered around the corner. The Dumpster was twenty feet away. One guy was much closer, leaning against the door, his back to me. A small automatic was tucked in a holster. Grace started another joke. By my count, the break still had more than a minute to run.

I wanted to see what was in room 109, but there was no way we'd get past the outside doorway without being spotted. We'd come down the wrong stairway. We'd have to go back up and come down the stairway at the opposite end of the hall.

I had turned to start back when a phone rang. "Shit," Becky whispered, and she reached into her purse, pulled out the phone, and shut it off. I heard footsteps approaching. I pulled Becky into the nearest room, then into the bathroom.

"I'm sorry," she whispered.

I put a finger to my lips and looked around. There was no window. I opened a narrow door. It led into a tiny linen closet. We were in a box with only one way out.

Outside in the hallway, I heard shouting. I slipped off my jacket, unhooked my shoulder holster, tucked my gun into it, opened the door to the closet, and slipped the rig onto the highest shelf. I put the jacket back on.

The bathroom door opened, and there was Tracy Grace with a Glock .9 in his hand. The shock on his face soon turned to a smile. "Nick, why didn't you tell me you were coming? You could have saved me all that time I spent waiting for you. And who's this, your little sister?"

"Something like that," I said.

"Hey, Amigo!" Grace shouted, over his shoulder. "In here."

Amigo was the guy with the gap in his teeth. He smiled when he saw me and nodded his head, like we were long-lost friends. Maybe he was just thanking me for sharing my whiskey and beer.

"OK, sweetie, come on out of there." Grace beckoned Becky with one finger. "Nick, you stay right where you are. Turn around. Hands on the wall."

"You don't want to do this," I said, with much more confidence than I felt. "Better cover your ass, Trace. Cover your ass."

"Oh, Nick, you can't believe how much I want to do this," he said as Amigo touched my shoulder. I turned around, put my hands on the wall.

"OK, cutie-pie," Grace said. "Let's see what we've got here. That's right. My, what a nice purse. Now just sit down. That's right, right there on the floor. That's fine. Now hands on your head. Good. OK, Amigo, search him and make it good. He's sneakier than I gave him credit for."

But it wasn't much of a search. If I'd brought my Derringer along, I'd probably still have it. Unfortunately, it was sitting at home. "Nothing," Amigo said when he was done. He put a hand on my shoulder and turned me around.

"Still too good to carry a gun, Nick?" Grace said. "Don't you ever learn?" He had Becky's purse in his hands. She was sitting on the floor with her hands on her head.

Grace pulled the phone out first, then a wallet. "Rebecca," he read, and then he stopped and got a big smile on his face. "Lovely Rebecca," he said. "I do believe you've just earned me a bonus." He reached down and grabbed one of Becky's hands and pulled her up.

"Amigo, let's put 'em on ice."

"Upstairs," Amigo said.

We were led out into the hallway where the rest of the paper-carrying crew was waiting.

"This is Nick Acropolis, everybody," Grace said. "He's supposed to be working for me, but he's really been working against me. What do you think of that?"

I took a little bow, but before I could complete it, Grace slapped me on the side of the head with his gun. I staggered sideways. Amigo caught me, held me steady.

"That's what happens to people who pretend to work for me, comprehend?" Grace said. I felt Amigo flinch. "And this is Rebecca Westerfield. I think some of you might know her father."

"Where is he?" Becky shouted.

"Oh, you're gonna find out soon enough, Rebecca," Grace said. "Just be patient."

"Where is he?" she shouted again.

"Don't you worry, Rebecca," Grace said. "You're gonna be together for a good long time. Trust me."

"Fuck you!" she spit.

"Wrong answer," he said, then slapped her lightly.

I moved toward Grace, but Amigo pulled me back.

"Just remember to say your prayers," Grace said, and he pulled Becky past the front door and into a darkened elevator. Amigo pushed me in the same direction.

Grace hit a switch and the elevator lights came on. "Come on, Amigo," he said, and Amigo stepped into the car. "Everybody else, back to work. We'll handle this." He pushed the button for the third floor. The door closed and we started to ascend.

The doors opened and Amigo pushed me out into the third-floor hallway. Becky and Grace brought up the rear.

"Right this way, boys and girls, right this way," Grace said as we passed mattresses and nightstands and then a row of large hospital-style laundry carts.

We were almost to the end when Amigo jogged around in front and opened a narrow door at the very end of the corridor.

"Step right in, folks. Step right in," Grace said. "Welcome to your new home. Wait, not so quick. One last frisk, Amigo. OK, Nick, assume the position."

It was an even more lackadaisical frisk. The guy without teeth did not like being called Amigo. I had the feeling he didn't like Grace at all.

After the frisk I was pushed through the door. It was a small, windowless closet, maybe four feet by three. There were narrow shelves on the back wall. Nothing on them but a layer of dust. Becky came in behind me.

"Make a racket and I'll shoot right through the door," Grace said, and the door closed and a lock snapped into place.

We were in darkness.

FORTY-EIGHT

SOMETHING rolled down the corridor and bumped into the door.

"Laundry cart," I said, and then another cart was rolled down, and another and another. They clanged when they met and clicked and banged as the wheels were locked in place.

I could hear Becky breathing a foot away. I reached out and found her hand. We stood that way a long while.

I could almost see the laundry carts with their locked wheels wedged clear across the hallway. We were never getting out of here. We could scream forever and no one would hear. We would rot and no one would even smell us. The maggots would come and go and what was left of us would disintegrate and drift out the narrow opening at the bottom of the door. But we'd be here forever. We'd be the ghosts in the closet, joining all the other ghosts in the building.

For some reason, that cheered me up. We wouldn't be the first to die here. The building had been designed with dying in mind.

I should have swallowed my pride and asked Casper for help, I decided. I should have kept my gun and fired the moment Grace opened the door. I probably would have got us both killed. But that would have been better than dying slowly in this closet. I should have called 911 on Becky's phone. We'd had thirty seconds, maybe more, before that door opened. What street were we on?

Stewart, I remembered, south of Forty-seventh. Good to know, just in case I got another chance. Stewart south of Forty-seventh. The Hilltop Nursing Home.

Even if the police came, would they search the building? I couldn't see the typical beat ever finding us. They wouldn't bother to roll the carts out of the way. They were beat men. It wasn't their job to investigate, to look in closets.

I should have called Casper instead, I decided. But there wasn't time. What if he wasn't in? What if he was on another line?

Would we really be ghosts? Becky had unfinished business with her father, dead or alive, and wasn't that the hallmark of a ghost? But what was my unfinished business? Beating Casper to a murderer? Was that really so important? Or was I there to pin the whole thing on Gene Westerfield so I could steal his wife away?

"I can't believe I did that," Becky said after a while.

"What?"

"The phone. God, I'm so sorry."

"I was the last one to use it," I said. "Anyway, it happens to everybody once. That's how you learn to turn them off."

"I feel like such an idiot," she said.

"I should never have brought you in here."

"I made you."

"Yeah, but I knew better. Oh, well, here we are."

"So what do we do now?"

"We're not getting out the door; that's pretty clear. I'm hoping for a false ceiling, but that's probably asking too much. Here, let me boost you. See what we find."

"I think I can climb up the shelves," she said.

"OK, good." I reached out. The shelves were about eighteen inches apart, a bit high for a ladder, but Becky was young.

"You had me worried there for a while," she said.

"What?"

"When you started talking about ghosts." Christ, had I said that out loud?

The shelves barely took her weight. I reached back and felt along the bottom of the board. They were held in place by metal corner brackets.

"See if you can push it. Maybe it's a false ceiling."

"It doesn't move. It's real hard."

"OK. Hey, feel around on the shelves on the way down. You never know what you might find. Wait. Don't come down yet. Let's try to get one of these shelves loose."

It didn't take long. We picked one about three feet off the floor. Becky stood on the edge of the shelf and I pushed and it began to bend downward. Becky climbed up to the next shelf while I pulled the bent shelf level again; then we did it again.

After five or six tries, I felt one of the brackets slip. "OK, hold on." I twisted the shelf and finally got my fingers in the narrow gap between the board and the wall. I pulled and the bracket popped loose from the wall.

"You get it?" Becky asked.

"Just about," I said. "You might as well come down."

I guided her down to the floor, then went to work on the bracket, which was still attached to the shelf. "Metal fatigue," I explained as I worked. "You just keep bending it back and forth, eventually it'll break."

"I can almost see you," Becky said.

"You've got better eyes than me," I said as I continued to bend the bracket back and forth. There was just the slightest patch of gray light at the bottom of the door. I could see Becky's feet, nothing more. They moved back and forth, covering the same ground over and over, like a car that would never make it up the hill.

"Remember that song about the guy in prison?" I asked.

"Which one?"

" 'I see my light come shining.' "

"That's Dylan."

"Any day now, I shall be released," I sang, and just like that the metal snapped. All it needed was a song. "Got it," I said.

"Great. Now what?"

"We go through the wall."

"Really?" Becky found my hand in the dark. I guided her fingers to the sharp edge where the bracket had broken. "With this?" She didn't sound very confident.

"It's just drywall," I said. And I started to thump the side wall. "When you hear that hollow sound, there's nothing behind it but air." I found a stud. "Hear how it's solid? That's the stud."

I used the sharp edge of the bracket to scratch a rectangle between the studs. "When I got thrown off the force I worked with my brother-in-law for a while. Construction. Remodeling. I hung a lot of drywall, but I never had the patience to tape it. That's an art. But I never quite got the feel for it."

Now I started digging a groove, going back and forth over the lines of the rectangle, deeper and deeper, digging out the chalk.

"The best part about the job was when you finished. You could really see what you'd accomplished. Garages. Those were the best. There'd be nothing but dirt and a couple of days later there'd be this beautiful garage sitting there. Concrete floor, windows, roof, an automatic door. I used to get a big kick out of that. You know what I mean?"

"Yeah. That sounds cool," she said. "You want me to do that for a while?"

"No. No. I'm fine." It was a mindless sort of work. A nice groove to get lost in. Anything was better than the reality of being locked in a closet waiting to die.

"My brother-in-law was a good guy. It's too bad. You get divorced and everybody chooses up sides and you end up losing a lot of good people. Yeah, we used to go driving some nights. We'd get a six-pack and a pint and we'd get in his pickup and drive around town. He'd always end up driving by places he'd built. And he got such a kick out of it. He'd tell me about this job, that job. What they did. Who he worked with. Everything. He'd been working construction since he was a kid, and every once in a while we'd stumble on some place he'd forgotten all about. Some house he'd built or remodeled. Or a garage. Those were always my favorite. Yeah. We had a lot of fun.

"One night I decided to show him some of my places. Places where people had died. Street corners, buildings, back alleys. He enjoyed it. Nothing like hanging out with an old homicide dick if you want to see the seedy side of town. But it really depressed me. Most of the places looked as horrible as ever or even worse. So what did we do? Nothing. Even the blood stains on the sidewalk, you couldn't always tell if they were old or new. Was that from your murder or was that somebody else's murder? What am I talking about? Where was I going with this?"

"I don't know," Becky said. "But keep going, OK?"

"You build a good garage, you come back in twenty years, odds are it's still there. Homicide. There's nothing except some old files buried at Eleventh and State.

"It's funny. Once we had this victim, this old man, who'd done time for murder when he was a kid. Now he was on the other end. Somebody shot him in the head. So we dug out the old file, on the off chance that it was a revenge killing. You know, somebody with a very long memory. Anyway, we thought it'd be a real laugh, seeing a file from the old cowboy-and-Indian days. The thing was covered in dust, I mean, literally covered in dust. But you know what? It could have been written yesterday. 'Isn't this one of ours?' my partner says. And, swear to god, we'd had a murder on the same block maybe a year before. And it was just so typical. Robbery murder. The guy's stumbling home from the tavern and a couple of kids try to roll him. He fights and they hit him with a pipe and on the way down, just to rub it in, he cracks his head on the curb. Murder one. And the dicks, we thought they'd be real stone age guys. But they sounded just like us. They even misspelled the same words. *Occasion*. I can never remember how many *c*'s."

"Two *c*'s, one *s*," Becky said.

"OK, show me up, college girl. But the point I was trying to make. Oh, who cares? I think I've got enough here. Should be able to punch it out. Here, hold this." I handed her the bracket.

"This is how burglars use a glass cutter. They just score it, stick a little flypaper on, and punch."

I punched and the drywall gave in the middle but didn't fall through. I hit it again and the middle broke. "OK," I said. "Now let me just clean this out." I started pulling out wedges of drywall and dropping them inside the wall.

I could feel Becky's hand moving around the hole. "There's another wall on the other side," I said. "We've got to get through that one, too."

"What's that?" Becky grabbed my arm.

"What?"

"Shhhh," she whispered. "Listen." Footsteps were coming our way.

I found her hand and the bracket. "I might be using this as a weapon," I said. "So keep on your toes. If you see a chance to get out, take it."

"Maybe it's Harris. Maybe he found us."

"Keep your fingers crossed."

I tucked the bracket in a back pocket, then brushed my suit and my face. I stood with my back against the hole and pulled Becky in front of me to hide any plaster dust.

Laundry carts were unlocked and rolled away; then the door opened. It was Harris all right, with a sheepish look on his face. Amigo was right behind him. Grace stood back with a huge Colt Python in his hand, a .357 with a six-inch barrel.

"Is everybody comfy?" he asked, and he looked from Becky to me. "Oh, naughty, naughty, naughty." He wagged the gun at us. "Somebody's been having fun, haven't they? Well, too bad, Willie. Looks like you'll have to settle for seconds. One more frisk, Amigo. Hands on the wall, Mr. Wet."

Harris put his hands up on the wall and Amigo did a quick frisk while Grace twirled the Colt, like a kid with a brand-new toy. "Always frisk 'em twice, Amigo. Especially the brothers. They love to keep a shiv in the boot." Amigo bent down again, then straightened up. "OK, join the closet club, Willie. That's right; get in there with your friends." Amigo gave Harris a little push and he didn't resist.

"Sorry," I heard Amigo say under his breath; then the door closed, and the lock clicked shut. We were in darkness again.

Nobody said a word as the laundry carts were rolled back into place. It was suddenly tight in the closet. Harris was huge. He seemed to take up the whole place. The temperature began to rise. I could taste plaster dust with every breath.

"Who's the cracker?" Harris said. "I know Andre. He's one of Rogers' old asshole buddies. Probably just got out of prison. But who's the white boy?"

"Tracy Grace."

"He on the job?"

"Yeah."

"So how come he ain't serving and protecting us, like it says on the sides of the cars?"

"He's the guy who was in the accident with Jimmy," I said. "Only it wasn't an accident."

"Keep going."

"Rogers and Westerfield hire off-duty cops to work security. I think Grace is one of 'em. Jimmy was here one day dropping off vouchers and he saw something he shouldn't have and Grace went after him, but Jimmy managed to get away."

"What'd he see?"

"I don't know. There's a room downstairs with two chairs outside like a guard post. I think whatever he saw was in that room. It's just the other side of the nurses' station. Room one-o-nine. Somehow they must have convinced him it was OK or they bought him off. Because after trying to kill him in broad daylight right out here on Forty-seventh Street, they let him keep working at the store for almost a week. Until the day me and Becky showed up."

"OK, how we getting out of here?"

"Through the wall," I said. "I got one side open. But I'm gonna need room to work. Can you squeeze back in the corner a bit?"

"I can go up the shelves," Becky said. "Bill, give me a boost."

I went back to work with the broken shelf bracket. It was harder now. I had to lean into the hole. It was impossible to avoid the dust.

"What are you cutting with?" Harris asked.

"I broke a bracket off a shelf."

"You know, your friend was right."

"Which friend was that?"

"That cracker said we always keep a knife in the boot."

"You're kidding," I whispered.

But he wasn't. He slipped a knife into my hand, handle first. It was just a flat piece of steel, really, the handle barely thicker than the blade, which was double-edged. One side was serrated like a saw.

"This is perfect," I said. "What's in your other boot?"

"See, Becky. There's a lesson for you. It's never enough. No matter what you do, it's never enough for some people."

FORTY-NINE

THE knife made for quick going. When I punched, the drywall fell in one piece. But no light came from the far side of the hole. I stuck my arm into the opening and used the knife as a probe. "I think it's another closet," I said, and then I went in head-first.

Almost immediately I bumped my head. I reached up, found a knob, and turned. Light flooded the closet as I fell into the room.

It was a smaller version of the other rooms we'd seen, with only one bed. The mattress was covered in plastic. An empty beer bottle was sitting on the window ledge. I moved it aside and slid the window open. The pedestrian walkway was down to the right.

Becky came through next and joined me at the window. Artificial butterscotch was the smell of freedom.

Harris cracked the hallway door, then opened it wide. I walked over and stuck my head out. The hallway was dark and empty. The laundry carts were a solid wall at the end.

Everybody was covered with drywall dust. Harris was brushing it off his suit, but his face was streaked, like war paint on an Indian. Becky was running fingers through her hair. She'd picked the wrong day not to wear jeans.

I flipped the mattress off the bed, then went to work on the bed frame. "What are you doing?" Becky asked.

"I need a weapon," I said. "You, too." I'd already given the knife back to Harris. There were shiny springs on each corner of the frame, about a foot long, better than an inch in diameter.

"We need a plan," Harris said.

"I've got a gun downstairs," I said.

"Yeah, me, too," he said sadly, and I realized the big Colt was his. "But that don't do us any good."

"No," I explained. "I know where mine is." And I told him about the hidden gun. I got one spring loose, handed it to Becky, then worked another free. Becky hefted the spring in her hand.

"If you can," Harris said, "hit 'em on the back of the head."

"Right." She attempted a smile, but it didn't quite work.

"Get me one, too," Harris said. I pulled out another spring. "Like the old days," he said. "Baseball bats, bottles, whatever we could find. Now these little punks got Uzis." He slipped the spring into a pocket.

We walked softly down the hallway. I described the layout of the first floor. Harris hadn't had much time to see it. He'd pulled into the driveway and there'd been guns on him before he could get out of the car.

"Should be room one-twenty downstairs," I said as I walked into 320. I opened the bathroom door and then the closet and pointed to the top shelf, to where my gun would be.

Becky was standing just back from the outside windows. "The thing's almost full," she said.

I looked down in time to see Tracy Grace throw a load into the Dumpster. "Count the trips," I said.

"We should split up," Harris said. "You go for your gun. I'll go see what's in one-o-nine."

"What if there's a guard in there?"

"If your friend's carrying paper, everybody else is, too. I think I can handle a nurse."

"Aren't we better off together?" Becky asked.

"No, he's right," I decided. "This way we can get to both places on one break. Who knows how many more chances we'll get? And we'll be coming from opposite directions. That'll spread us out a bit. And remember we've got an escape route down the middle stairway and out the back door."

Becky continued to count the trips. Harris and I walked across the hall, and I pointed out the pedestrian walkway. "The fence is loose on the right side. But he's got a pipe. So if you've got time, give him some money. He prefers small bills."

"I'll try to remember that."

"An ambulance just pulled in," Becky said when we came back across the hallway.

I looked out. A private ambulance was sitting behind the Dumpster. The driver was smoking a cigarette. If he raised his head he'd be looking right at us.

"Don't stand so close," I whispered. Becky backed up. "How many trips?"

"Fourth."

"We're running out of time," Harris said. "Let's just assume they're still doing seven trips. Becky, count the time between trips. From the time they go inside until the time they all come out. Count one thousand one, one thousand two. And then keep counting until they go back in again. You follow me?"

"Yes."

"We want to come out those doors at the same time."

Was the ambulance for us, I wondered as we waited.

"Fifty-three seconds," Becky said. "And then they were all back inside by seventy-seven."

"How many trips?"

"They're on the fifth."

"How long were the breaks before?"

"Three minutes."

"OK," Harris said. "We leave after the next trip. We'll give 'em eighty seconds, one thousand one, one thousand two, then open the door."

290 ⇗ JACK CLARK

"If you've got everything under control in that room," I said, "stick a piece of paper or something under the door. Anything. Otherwise, I'll assume you're in trouble."

"Good enough," Harris said.

"Who am I going with?" Becky asked.

"Take your pick," I said.

"I better go with Bill," she said. "I want to see what's in that room."

"OK," I said.

"They just came out," Becky said.

"Say when," Harris said.

A few seconds later, Becky said the magic word.

"Eighty seconds," Harris said. Becky followed him out the door and toward the east stairway.

The west stairway was blocked by the laundry carts. I used the middle stairway and went up to the fourth floor, then headed west, making footprints in the dust.

I made the first floor in just under a minute. It was quiet. The radio was off. I waited another twenty seconds. Still quiet. I opened the door. Harris and Becky were already out. They were moving slowly and steadily toward 109. I headed their way, the spring in my hand.

The door to 120 was standing open. Across the hall, the door to 109 was closing. They were in. I peeked around the corner, then walked into the room. I started for the bathroom, then stopped. Becky's cell phone was sitting on the floor. I grabbed it and carried it into the bathroom.

I opened the closet and reached up. "Thank you," I said softly. I pulled the rig down, then slipped the gun from the holster. I let the holster fall to the floor, then sat down on the closed toilet, turned on the phone, and dialed 911.

"Chicago Police Department, Gash speaking."

"There's been a shooting at the Hilltop Nursing Home. It's on Stewart Avenue just south of Forty-seventh."

"Hilltop?"

"That's right," I said, and I repeated the location; then I pushed the END button and disconnected him. Next I dialed Area Four and asked for Casper.

"OK, I'm there," I said when he came on.

"Where?"

"Hilltop Nursing Home. It's on Stewart, south of Forty-seventh."

"OK. I got that. What's going on?"

"I don't know, John, but it's going to be a heater. So I'd appreciate if you'd get your ass out here." I pushed the POWER button, stood up, and slipped the phone into my pocket.

Across the hall, a piece of paper was sitting under the door to 109. Everything was under control, whatever everything was.

I heard a roar outside and went to the window. A car sped in, trailing a cloud of dust. I thought it might be a squad car trying to set a new response-time record. But when the dust cleared I saw a blue Jaguar instead. Nathan Rogers got out and suddenly everybody was back on their feet, moving around in the rising dust.

Rogers started toward the front door and everybody followed. I slipped back into the bathroom but left the door cracked.

Rogers shouted orders, most of which I couldn't understand. But I heard: "Bring 'em down," loud and clear.

Grace said something I didn't understand. But his meek tone told me who the boss was. I heard the elevator start up. I slipped out of the bathroom and moved toward the door, the gun at my side. Rogers had two large books in his hands. Ledger books. He crossed to 109, opened the door, and stepped inside. I didn't notice any unnatural movements as the door closed behind him. The piece of paper was still under the door, but now it didn't mean a thing.

I moved back toward the window. There were only three guys carrying paper now. Grace and Amigo must have both gone upstairs. I waited until the paper carriers went inside, then headed back for the door. The elevator had stopped moving. I counted to ten and stuck my head out the doorway. The hallway was clear. There were now two pieces of paper under the door across the hall. I walked across the wide open space, opened the door quickly, and went in with my gun leading the way.

Rogers was sitting on a chair in the middle of the room, holding the back of his head. Blood was trickling down and pooling on the floor. Harris had a small automatic in one hand and the knife in the other. The knife was to Rogers's neck. "The police are on the way," I said, and I pulled out Becky's phone. Harris nodded.

"Acropolis, you don't—" Rogers said.

"Shut up," Harris said, and he poked the knife into the flesh, then turned my way. "We need an ambulance, too." He turned his head again. "A real ambulance."

Becky was standing by the only bed in the room. There was an old man on the bed. He was thin and very gray, obviously near death. Becky was holding the old man's wrist. I assumed she was taking his pulse. There was no nurse to be seen.

I dialed 911 and told the dispatcher we needed an ambulance, then hung up as he started to ask questions.

The ledger books were sitting on a second chair; one of them was open. But it wasn't a ledger. It was a large business checkbook. The kind that keeps a carbon of every check written. I started flipping through the pages.

The checks were for various amounts but always for thousands of dollars. The dates covered the last few weeks. The most recent checks had been written the day before. They'd all been signed by Eugene Westerfield.

I looked up. Harris used the knife to point toward the bed. "You're looking at a human check-signing machine."

Becky was still holding the old man's hands. Tears were streaming down her face. Her father had aged twenty years from the pictures I'd seen.

The door opened. I swung the gun around.

Amigo was standing there, his hands on his head. Tracy Grace was right behind him, a gun in each hand. They were both aimed at Amigo's back. Outside, I could hear sirens in the distance.

"Nick, thank god you're all right," Grace said. "I called it in. The cavalry should be here any minute. OK, Amigo, down on the floor. Keep your hands right where they are."

"You kill him or do I?" Harris asked. His gun was pointed straight at Grace.

Grace swung his guns up as Amigo knelt down. "Now, now, now," Grace said. The big Colt turned toward Harris, the Glock towards me. "We're all on the same side here. Let's not do anything we're gonna regret."

We were still standing that way a minute or so later when the first beat men came running in.

FIFTY

IT was four in the morning when I finally got out of Area One, at Fifty-first and the Dan Ryan. Casper offered me a ride back to my car, then lingered, saying good-bye to a couple of local dicks. I waited out front, watching the middle-of-the-night trucks speeding through town.

Casper drove west, over the highway, then started taking side streets north. He was an old South Side kid.

"Thanks," I said.

"For what?"

"For everything, John. Thanks for everything."

"That bad, huh?"

"You don't know what it's like being on the other side."

"Yeah. How'd you like to have your old partner on the other side and have to straighten it out?"

"Thanks," I said again. And I wasn't sick of saying it.

"Nothing more about the weave, OK?"

"What weave?"

"My hair, you idiot. It's not a hairpiece. It's a weave."

"John, it's pathetic is what it is. But that's the last time you'll hear it from me."

"Asshole," he said.

"And look, thanks for getting Harris his gun back."

"That never happened, Nick. The Chicago Police Department

does not give unregistered guns back to unlicensed private detectives."

"That's why I was thanking you."

But I knew it was a mixed blessing. Harris got his big Colt back, and Tracy Grace walked without being charged. It seemed to me we'd come up on the short end of the deal. "If it was me, I would have flushed him," I said.

"Nick, there isn't a judge in town who'd convict and you know it. There's no proof he knew what was going on. You were trespassing. He put you in a closet, then called nine-one-one. The time element would not stand up."

"You know how long it takes to dig through a wall, John?"

"That was very impressive, Nick. Now where's your car?"

"Jesus, where are we?" But then I saw. "Keep going. It's on the left just across from that. . . ." The old pedestrian walkway was still there, the burned-out cars hadn't gone anywhere, but the rent-a-car, with my brand-new binoculars inside, was gone.

"Let me call it in," Casper said, and reached for his microphone.

"Oh, who cares? I'll call Hertz in the morning."

"Hertz? What happened to the Olds?"

"You think I'd drive around in a car you're looking for?"

"I didn't put your car out."

"You didn't? Really?"

"Come on, Nick. You're my old partner."

"Let's call Teddy, see if he's still open."

"Forget it. I'm not going to Teddy's. I may never go to Teddy's, ever again."

"Oh, Jesus. What's she done to you?"

"How about Al's?" Casper asked. "I'll buy you breakfast."

"I'm starving, now that I think of it." I started to laugh.

"What's so funny?"

"That was my last meal, breakfast at Al's. It seems like a month ago."

When we got there, the same wino was sitting on the same stool, a bit of ham peeking out from his toast.

Elsie caught my glance. She shrugged and set two coffees in front of us. "Hardly cost anything," she said softly.

"Buy him a real breakfast on us," I said.

She smiled. "Really?"

"Sure. But don't tell him where it's from."

"OK. How about you fellows, the usual?"

We both nodded. Casper probably hadn't been in the joint in years. He got up. "Let me see if they got anywhere."

I sipped coffee. Casper was back in a minute or so. He dropped a *Sun-Times* in front of me.

CO-ED TRACKS DOWN KIDNAPPED DAD, a huge headline read. There was a photograph of Westerfield being wheeled into the emergency room at the University of Chicago Hospital. Becky was running with the ambulance crew, holding the IV line. The photo caption said: PHARMACIST SUFFERED STROKE IN CAPTIVITY.

I suddenly remembered the promise I'd made to John Olmstead at the *Tribune*. He was supposed to get an exclusive and I hadn't even called. Oh, well, he'd get over it.

"Anything?" I asked.

"He just won't give it up," Casper said. Leslie Crawford had been sitting in an interrogation room at Area Four all day and all night. The cops had enough evidence to charge him. They had the briefcase with the bullet holes. They had the red wig. They had Clyde's and Jesse's and the bus driver's identification. But they wanted the guy who hired him, too. You always want the guy who paid, more than you want the actual shooter. They'd offered Crawford great deals to name names, but so far he'd refused.

"So what's your next move?"

"Well, we figure that medical center's the key. Why would he take the chance of being spotted right behind the scene unless it was something important?"

"Or someone," I said.

"Yeah, like the guy who hired him," Casper said. "My guess is we're looking for a doc."

"Why?"

"Crawford was shaking down doctors. You've been there. You meet any docs look like they graduated last in their class?"

"Dr. Z.," I said.

Casper pulled out a notebook and a pen. "Zailradenik," I said, and I spelled the name. "But I think he's just senile. The only other doctor I talked to was Lutton and he's pretty sharp." But then I remembered our conversation at Mitchell's bar. "Oh, Jesus," I said softly.

"What?"

"Dr. Lutton."

"What about him?"

"Couple things. One, he told me he left medical school early, which is how he got to be part of the D-day invasion."

"What am I missing?"

"Well, maybe by leaving early he lowered his grades enough to graduate last."

"Boy, that's a stretch."

"Another thing: Lutton said something strange. I'm trying to remember the wording. Oh, yeah. 'I wish the son of a bitch had gotten Westerfield instead.' "

"Ohhh," Casper said softly. "I like that."

"It gets better," I said. "Irv was his best friend."

"Oh, now I really like him," Casper said, and we began to chuckle, and we had a hard time stopping. We'd both seen plenty of stupid murders in our time. Accidentally getting your best friend killed would fit the mold. "Let me make another call. Maybe they can make a play."

He went to the phone and came back just as the food arrived. "You know this is the only place I eat anymore," I said, and I went to work on the French toast.

Elsie had remembered Casper's order perfectly: a bacon-and-tomato omelet. I looked down the counter. The bum was inhaling a plate of ham and eggs.

We were just pushing the plates away when the pay phone rang. Elsie answered it. "Lieutenant Casper?" She held the phone our way.

"Well, la-di-da," Chris sang as Casper got up.

Elsie pointed to the sign above the phone—IF YOU'RE GOING TO MAKE YOUR OFFICE HERE, PLEASE HELP OUT WITH THE RENT—and held out a plastic donation box for the March of Dimes. Casper reached into his pocket, pulled out a bill, and slipped it into the box.

He was back in a few minutes. "He gave it up."

"Really? That's great."

"They told him Lutton confessed. 'Is he in jail?' he asks, and that was all it took. You don't know where Lutton lives, by any chance?"

"I've got his plate number," I said. I opened my notebook to the right page. Casper carried it to the phone.

He was back in a minute. "What happened, the doc refused to pay the second installment unless Crawford went back and got Westerfield. Crawford said he'd done exactly what Lutton told him; it wasn't his fault the wrong guy came out. He threatened to call the police and the doc told him if he did, he'd cut his heart out while he was still alive."

"Lutton's a tough old guy," I said. "I wouldn't put it past him."

"My guys are really going to hate you now."

"Why would they hate me? I don't even know 'em."

"I'm always talking about you and Andy. They're sick of hearing what great dicks you were. And now you just cleared a contract hit in the middle of breakfast."

"*We* cleared it, John," I corrected him. "And they would have got it eventually."

"Yeah, probably," he conceded. "But hell, you gave us Crawford, too. I'd still like to know where that came from. I mean, you couldn't have seen the wig in that apartment, because it was under the front seat of his car."

"I can't explain it, John."

"That's what I keep telling my guys. A good dick doesn't need much. You get a glimmer, you follow it."

"You know, this is what I miss, John. Right here. Right now. This."

"Breakfast at Al's Grill?"

"Everything," I said. "You know what I did a few weeks back? I spent four days locked in a courtroom watching them pick a jury. I got paid top dollar, but it was like watching grass grow except there was no sunshine, no fresh air, and no grass to lie down on."

"Nick, if you were still on, all you'd do is sit in an office. The only reason I got out on this was because you were involved."

"I know, John. Thanks."

"It's time for the kids to take over. We're old men. Our time is past."

"You guys don't know a thing about old," Elsie said as she refilled our coffees.

"No?" Casper said.

She pointed to Chris. "Now that's old." He stuck out his tongue, winked, and flipped a pancake.

"Why don't you come by the house Thursday?" Casper said.

"What's up?"

"Thursday. It's Thanksgiving, Nick. You got plans or what?"

"This Thursday is Thanksgiving?"

"Come by about noon. We can watch the Bears lose."

We finished our coffee, paid the bill and waved good-bye, then walked into the sunshine.

A gust of wind came up. It unwove Casper's weave.

"What are you looking at?"

"Nothing, John. Nothing at all."

FIFTY-ONE

Two days before Christmas, the sun peeked out in the middle of the afternoon. A moment later there was a knock on my office door. "It's open!" I called.

Becky walked in with a large, flat package in hand. She stood in the doorway, bundled up in a red down jacket, bouncing awkwardly from one insulated boot to another. "I thought I'd stop by and say thanks," she said, and she took off a stocking cap and straightened her hair.

The last time I'd seen her, she'd been climbing into a fire department ambulance in front of the Hilltop Nursing Home. We'd talked on the phone a couple of times and, after she'd got back to school, she'd sent a thank-you note along with a check.

"You look like you're ready for February," I said.

"It's cold in Wisconsin." She smiled and shivered.

"How's school?"

"I'm still catching up. I probably should have stayed, but I had to come down. I mean, it's Christmas. We already missed Thanksgiving with my dad in the hospital. So we're gonna celebrate both. And we have so much to be thankful for."

I'd been following the story in the newspapers. Eugene Westerfield had given up an even dozen past and present Public Aid employees, plus Nathan Rogers and his whole crew. There'd been a flurry of federal indictments in Springfield and Chicago. And now some of the indicted were talking and rumor had it that the investigation was heading straight to the governor's mansion.

The feds, going through that Dumpster load of evidence, had tied more than sixty stores to the Westerfield-Rogers chain. In the weeks following Irv Kaplan's murder, Rogers had taken his name off every single one. They'd all been transferred to Westerfield, even Prospect Drugs.

According to one report, you could follow Westerfield's rapidly declining health, as he was hit by a series of strokes, by the deteriorating condition of his handwriting. But he'd signed everything they put in front of him.

I caught Mike Brewer on television one night and he called the indictments the tip of the iceberg. He estimated that in its final weeks the Westerfield-Rogers operation had taken in more than $6 million. The state and the federal government were both trying to track the money. But Brewer predicted that much of it would never be found.

I remembered his prediction that Westerfield would do little prison time. Now it looked like he would avoid even that. The kidnapping and his subsequent strokes had turned Eugene Westerfield into a victim. In the indictment he had been named as a coconspirator, but he hadn't been indicted himself.

Dr. Zailradenik had been charged with conspiracy plus multiple counts of welfare and mail fraud. But he would never stand trial. The day after the indictments he checked into a downtown hotel. First he tried to slit his wrists with a safety razor; when he couldn't make the cut deep enough, he jumped out the twenty-first-floor window instead. He'd landed on the elevated tracks in the middle of rush hour, causing massive delays.

In his statement to police, Dr. Lutton said he'd paid to have Westerfield killed after Gene reneged on a promise to help finance his mobile field hospital plan. According to Lutton, Leslie Crawford had tried to shake him down later that same day. Lutton had laughed at the idea of blackmail, then made Crawford a counter-offer at twice the price.

Lutton's bond was set at $1 million. His sister came up from Florida and posted 10 percent, $100,000, then flew back. That night Dr. Lutton checked into a suburban motel.

A maid found him late the next morning, dead of an overdose of sleeping pills. The local coroner, an old family friend, ruled the death accidental. The sister flew back to bury Lutton.

Neither doctor left a note.

"How's your dad?" I asked.

"He's weak," Becky said. "And his side is still pretty much paralyzed. But he's getting better. His speech is coming back, but I don't think he'll ever be the same. It's so weird. I feel like the parent sometimes. He's always apologizing to me. He's always thanking me. He never laughs anymore or tells stories. He's . . ." She stopped, shrugged, then held up the package she'd brought.

"Remember that painting? I thought you might like to have it."

"Sure," I said. "Thanks."

"If you don't want it, it's OK."

"I'd like to have it. Really. Thank you very much."

"Oh, good," she said. She leaned it against the wall. "But don't open it now, OK? I get a little too weird sometimes."

"I'll put it under the Christmas tree," I said. "Come on. Let's take a walk. I'll buy you a cup of coffee."

"Oh, here. My mother asked me to give you this."

It was a plain white envelope. I put it on the desk and slid a paperweight on top.

We took the elevator to the lobby and walked out to Lincoln Avenue. The sun was gone again. The clouds were low and gray. But there were huge candy canes on the light poles and Christmas music and lights in most of the stores. The smell of snow was in the air.

We walked to the S & G, a Greek joint two corners down. We

both ordered coffee and then had another cup and a piece of pie.

"Why did they have to kill Jimmy?" she asked. "That's the part I'll never understand."

"Sometimes there are no answers," I said. But I was still betting on Nathan Rogers. He'd heard that Jimmy had been seen talking to Becky. And Rogers didn't trust him to keep his mouth shut about where he'd last seen her father.

If I was right, someone was almost certain to turn Rogers in. There were too many people trying to avoid long prison terms. And Rogers was an easy card to deal. He was already going down for kidnapping and welfare fraud.

"What happened to that cop?"

"Which cop?"

"The creep who locked us in that closet."

"Tracy Grace," I said. "He's back on the job."

"That's scary," Becky said. She shook her head.

"It's something to remember, you ever get stopped for speeding."

I'd testified at the Police Board hearing. I'd sworn that the statements I'd taken from Raymond Purcell and Jimmy Madison were uncoerced and true, to the best of my knowledge. I didn't have much choice. If I'd told the truth, I'd have ended up indicted myself.

I didn't tell Becky that, of course. But I think her father had already taught her that very lesson. There were few saints around.

"Have you talked to Harris?" I asked.

"Yeah." She smiled. "He got the Madisons out of that place. He found them an apartment in Evanston."

"That's great," I said.

"My mom and dad helped out."

"Good."

"Harris says all the white people will get off and all the black people will go to jail."

"It wouldn't be the first time."

She played with her pie for a moment, then looked up. "I know you don't like my father," she said.

"Becky, I don't know your father. I was in the same room with him for a couple of very long minutes, but other than that—"

"It's OK. Harris doesn't like him, either. I'm not sure I do. But I love him. I can't help that."

"Sure," I said.

She went back to playing with the pie. "We're going to have to keep in touch," she said.

"Of course."

"No. Really. I'm going to want to visit that painting."

"Anytime."

"I know sooner or later, I'll need to remind myself."

"OK."

"He didn't start out that way, you know."

"I know." None of us had started out that way.

She reached over and grabbed my hand. We sat that way for a while, neither one of us talking. She had a nice, firm grip. Her eyes were shining brightly. I nodded my head and she nodded back.

"So what kind of doctor are you going to be?"

"I don't know yet. Something down here."

"The city."

She nodded. "The West Side. They really need doctors."

"Good."

She shrugged her shoulders. "It's where we're from, you know. My mom, too."

"I know," I said.

We finished the coffee and then walked back up Lincoln Avenue.

"Do you ever see Patrice?" she asked.

"We take a ride now and then."

"Oh, good."

Her Honda was parked across from my office. Becky gave me

a big hug and a small kiss on the cheek; then she got in the car, waved, and drove away.

I went upstairs and opened the envelope. Tucked inside was a check for $5,000.

"Nick," Janet Westerfield had written in a small, tight script, "it looks like we're not going to the poorhouse, at least not right now. Please accept this bonus as a token of our appreciation. I don't know what our family would have done if you had not come along at the exact right moment. Thanks again. And thanks for the memories of Austin High." There were three Xs behind her signature, each a bit fainter than the one before.

I walked across Ashland to the bank and deposited the check. On the way out, I dropped a twenty in the Salvation Army kettle.

Back at my office, I wrote checks to every creditor I could think of and, when I was done, I still had a hefty balance. I put the checkbook away, turned off the lights, and opened the blinds. Snow flurries were dancing in the wind.

Down in the lumberyard, a couple of guys were stacking rolls of insulation in a truck. They tossed a tarp over the load, tied it down, then drove away. The wind picked up. I got the office bottle out, pulled a chair to the window, and watched as the flurries blossomed into winter's first true snow.

The city disappeared slowly, a snowflake at a time. Before too long, all that was left was snow and a howling wind.

But through it, I could see the same snow falling on Westerfield's Pharmacy, now just another ruin, a Madison Street bus creeping carefully west, and Jesse and Clyde keeping warm around an old woodstove.

The snow swirled around the Horner Homes. There were Christmas lights in a few of the windows. But they would never be bright enough to bring much in the way of holiday cheer. They were just enough to break your heart once again. The West Side would always break hearts, again and again and again.

The snow fell on the ghostly Hilltop Nursing Home as the bum with the perfect teeth snuggled in his railroad cave. The snow drifted over Jimmy's grave and over Irv Kaplan's, too. I remembered that wonderful picture, Irv and the girl he was so proud of. Was she taking another nap? Would she wake to this winter wonderland and make an angel in the snow, or would she finally sleep herself back to Irv?

I couldn't find Harris in the snow, but I knew he was out there. "Somebody's going down for Jimmy," he'd said, the last time I'd seen him. "And if it doesn't happen in a courtroom, it'll happen in an alley."

"You can't kill a cop," I'd warned him.

"No," he'd agreed softly. "But I can make one disappear."

So Tracy Grace might want to watch his back. But it wasn't my job to warn him. And if something happened, I wouldn't shed any tears. If I was lucky, I wouldn't even hear.

And there was Becky. I could see the Honda, slipping and sliding around the curves of Sheridan Road, the wipers so packed with snow that they barely moved, visibility close to zero. But she'd make it through. She was a good kid. She was tough. She'd make one hell of a doctor someday. And, if nothing else, she knew how to dress for the weather.

I could see Janet Westerfield looking out the window of that big blue house, watching for Becky's car, waiting, worrying. She'd probably already unpacked that suitcase she'd been keeping ready all those years. She wasn't going anywhere right now. She wouldn't walk out on an invalid.

And somewhere behind her, the invalid would be waiting, too. Waiting for death. That was all he had to look forward to now.

His survival had been a cruel kind of luck. He'd managed to hold onto the house and the money and he was free. Freer than Nathan Rogers, watching the snow fall from his high-rise cell at the Metropolitan Correction Center. Freer than Andre "Amigo" Robinson, locked deep inside the Cook County Jail, where the snowstorm was only a vague rumor.

But Westerfield had lost, no matter what the bottom line said. Besides his health, he'd lost two exceptional women. They were just waiting for the funeral now.

And, as much as I tried, I couldn't hold myself above Eugene Westerfield. I'd had that fleeting chance to save Jimmy—when he'd hesitated before signing the statement—and I'd winked and let it slip away. But I'd learned a lesson. The truth exists no matter how hard you work against it. You can't mold it to fit your needs. The more you twist it, the harder it fights back.

So Becky's gift would probably come in handy. She wasn't the only one who'd need a reminder now and then.

It wasn't a painting to match your decor, and it would probably never see the inside of a museum or a gallery. But you might pull it out on a night like this, with the city masquerading as a winter wonderland. One look into those blazing eyes would be enough to remind you of the real city—that relentless hustler's town—that lay buried under that lovely blanket of freshly fallen snow.